Soulguard
Soullord
Bloodlord
Rash'Tor'Ri (forthcoming)

This Fallen World Novellas
This Fallen World
Broken City
Power Play (forthcoming)

Christopher Ward

Soulguard | Christopher Woods

All rights reserved
Copyright © 2014 by Christopher Woods
Cover art by Derrick Gallagher

Soulguard
By Christopher Woods

Section 1
GUARD

Prologue

Two vans raced down the private drive toward the Soulguard outpost. Kharl Jaegher winced as Kelvin Rourke gripped the arms of the seat with enough strength to crush the frames. It was likely he didn't even notice the mangled seat arms as he practically vibrated.

His huge hand landed lightly on Kelvin's right shoulder and his deep voice rumbled from the back seat.

"Almost there, Kel," Kharl said, "I'm sure it's just a problem with the com syst..."

The van rounded the last bend and a horrible sound escaped Kelvin's throat. The door exploded outward with a screech of tearing metal and Kelvin Rourke burst from his seat. He surged forward with inhuman speed, not toward the ruins of headquarters, but toward the housing located in the rear.

Kharl was out the side door of the van nearly as quick and was closely followed by Kyra Nightwing. These two Soulguards were Kelvin's closest friends and had served under the Mage for twenty years.

He felt dread growing inside him as he followed his friend toward the home Kelvin shared with his wife, Rhayne. There was no way the two Guards could keep up with the Mage. They were fast, but a Mage operates on an entirely different level. And Kelvin was one of the best.

Once again, he winced as he heard the wail from the house that Kelvin had just entered. Only one thing would have drawn such despair from Kelvin Rourke.

He burst into the building to find the inside of the house gutted with Demon bodies and parts lying everywhere. In the midst of that carnage, Kelvin knelt with his love pulled tightly to his chest. She still lived, but Kharl could see the wounds. Not even a Soulguard lives with wounds so grievous. She screamed once in agony and gave birth to the child that had been in the process of being born as the Demons attacked. Rhayne Rourke had killed all of the Demons in the house while in labor.

Her dying scream was followed by the first scream of her child.

"Oh God, no," Kyra gasped. She was at the side of Kelvin in a split second.

Kelvin gently eased his wife's body to the ground and reached down to raise his blood-soaked son from the carnage where he lay. With a flick of a finger and a small gout of flame, he severed the umbilical cord and stood. He looked down once more in utter despair.

Kharl remembered the Demon they had cornered in Denver. It had laughed at them and said in barely understandable English, "You are too late, man-thing, the bloodline ends with your mate."

If it was a blood line they were trying to end, they had failed. Kelvin's son would survive. Kharl's shoulders slumped as Kel turned to Kyra and placed his son in her arms.

"You know what I have to do now," he said. "You both heard what it said. No one can know he survived, and I mean no one."

Kel looked at Kharl, "I need you two to keep him safe."

He looked once more at his dead wife, "She wanted to name him after my father, I wanted to name him after hers. He'll just have to carry both now. Colin Artemus Rourke."

Kelvin leaned down and kissed his son's tiny head and turned away with tears in his eyes.

"You can feel the power in him already. He'll be a strong Mage. Train him well," he said as he walked by his friends toward the gaping hole in the side of the house, "He'll need it if they ever find out he lives."

"We'll keep him safe, Kel," Kharl said. He watched sadly as his friend of twenty years walked out of the house, flames beginning to roll across his body. He was glowing with Soulfire as he launched himself northward toward what could only be described as a feeling of wrongness. This is the feeling a Soulguard has learned means the presence of Demons. The feeling was weak because of the distance as the Demons were returning to their nest.

On this day, Kelvin Rourke's last, a path of death and destruction that shook the Soulguard to its core left him known as The Demonkiller.

Chapter 1

"Colin Smith!"

I jerked in my seat at the annoying voice of the bane of my existence, Miss Haynes, the Geometry teacher.

"Am I boring you?" the nasal, squeaky voice continued, "Perhaps you should come to the board and show the class how to write this formula correctly."

How someone manages to have a nasal and squeaky voice at the same time is something I've wondered for some time but she had managed it. I wondered if she had actually trained herself to talk in the most annoying way imaginable on purpose.

"It's a *sad* day when a student can graduate with no mathematical skill whatsoever. Is there anything that you excel at, Mr. Smith?" she was tapping her pointer in her other hand as she spoke, "Because it certainly isn't geometry. A student who does so poorly at this subject should pay a bit more attention in class."

This was a typical day in Miss Haynes' classroom. Of course, it wasn't always me she would single out and torment, but I guess this was just my day. Hell of a way to treat a Soulguard, defender of humanity. Even if I wasn't an official Soulguard yet, that training couldn't even start until I was eighteen. My adoptive parents Kharl and Kyra had, unofficially, been training me since the day I learned to walk.

Soulguard | Christopher Woods

Miss Haynes was a short, precise woman whose clothes were always perfect and her hair pulled back in a bun. She was the sister of the Headmaster of Morndel Academy which gave her license to treat people as she pleased. She loved to make anyone seem small to the rest of the classroom. I think she was just a small-minded person with a mean streak due to her lack of success in her own life. But that was just my opinion. I'd never actually looked into her aura to see if this was true because I really didn't care to know any more about her.

That's one of my gifts, the ability to look into another person's Soul, or aura, whichever a person chooses to call it. And I can see their Soulstream, the link from every living thing on the planet and the massive well of life force just below the surface of the world.

Her tirade went on for a few more minutes and I looked embarrassed enough for her to move on to another victim. I actually felt that I might have gotten off easy this time. She'd not even said a word about my low breeding or being the son of a construction worker. That's what she called Kharl. If she had known my real lineage, she probably would have keeled over on the spot.

As her attention swept on away from me, I looked around a bit to see everyone looking straight ahead trying not to give the crazy woman an excuse to start on any of them. The new girl, Mattie, sat there shaking her head slowly with a confused look on her face.

"Is there a problem, Matilda Riordan?"

I could see Mattie's teeth grinding as she returned, "That's Mattie, and there's no problem."

"I'm sorry, Matilda, but we don't use informal names in this school. We are a prestigious institution and we are always proper and formal. Perhaps you are from a low-bred family like Colin. His father is a construction worker."

The last two words were spat out in distaste. I winced as her attention was once again on me. God, this woman is bitter, I thought. Could be why she's a Miss instead of Mrs. Luckily the bell went off and everyone bolted for the door.

"Walk like ladies and gentlemen! You are not a herd of cattle! Although some of you have less breeding." The last sentence was muttered but it was still loud enough for most of us to hear.

As I said, bane of my existence.

***

As it turned out, there was something I excelled at, PE was my favorite course. Although I couldn't actually show anyone, due to the circumstances I lived with.

Kharl taught me from the moment he had revealed the truth to me as a young child that I needed to fit somewhere in the middle of the crowd. I couldn't draw any attention to myself if it could be helped. The mysteries of the Soulguard were a tightly kept secret. I didn't care for it, but it was the sensible thing to do.

"Try to keep up, Colon!" yelled my friend, Trent, as he ran past me on the track.

Trent was one of the football players. He was big and fast and all the girls loved him. He was over six feet tall and all muscle with blond hair and blue eyes. Girls turned to Jell-O when he was near and it pissed me off to no end.

If it weren't for my need to be discrete, I could have left him in the dust in the blink of an eye. There were days when it was hard not to do just that.

"That's Colin, not Colon, you ass," I returned, "Piss off."

Trent always messed with me, and I actually enjoyed it. He was a harmless, good natured guy, even though he was pretty and made the girls turn to goo.

I had a right to be a bit jealous. I'm about five feet and eight inches tall with muddy brown hair and green eyes. I'm really not that much to look at and since no one actually knew what I could do, no one really noticed me.

I looked to the left to find Mattie Riordan jogging along beside me. I huffed as I noticed what part of Trent she was looking at and her face turned red.

"Hi there, Mattie, or is it Matilda?"

She looked at me, evilly, "Call me Matilda again and I'll stab you."

"I give up," I chuckled and raised my hands in surrender, "Peace?"

"I suppose," she returned, "but only cause that psycho really gave you a hard time earlier."

"I'm used to it, the woman is a nut."

"So, what's with the construction worker comments?" she asked.

"Dad's a general contractor," I answered, "He built several of the skyscrapers in Detroit and

makes a lot of money from it and I think she's probably jealous."

"Or she could just be an ass."

"True," I agreed.

Coach Newman blew the whistle and we all
slowed to a walk returning to the locker rooms.
Mattie waved and joined the girls heading in.

Mattie was a tiny girl, maybe five feet tall,
slim, but very shapely as well. She had black curly
hair and the best word I could use to describe her
would be cute.

"Good luck with that, Colon," Trent walked
up beside me and chuckled.

"How long is that name gonna stick
around," I sighed, "I mean, really, can't you come up
with something better?"

"I don't think there is a better one, Col," he
said with a short laugh, "I think I'd shoot my parents
if they named me something like that."

Sometimes I agreed with Trent on that subject, but I couldn't even ask why they would saddle a
kid with a name like Colin. I knew who my real parents were.

I've actually witnessed the whole incident
through Kharl's memories, another of my unique
gifts. I can see into someone's memories as they remember them. Emotion and memory both flow
across the aura while they are happening, I don't
think I can actually read minds or anything. Sometimes I wish I hadn't looked at that one.

Reading emotion and memories from the
Soul is not as easy as it sounds. The emotions are
easy enough to see by the color and patterns flowing

through a person's Soul. But it took quite a few years to actually interpret the various combinations.

Memories, on the other hand flicker through a person's Soul so quickly, it takes a great deal of focus to actually read them. The more a person is focused on said memory, the clearer and slower it flows through. They always seem to flow right across the front of the face. It's somewhat disconcerting to a person to have someone looking them in the eye with the amount of focus it takes to read those memories.

Kyra says it's rude and that I shouldn't invade another's privacy without permission. I avoid it under most circumstances.

"At least it's better than my middle name," I said, "Artemus. Jeez, what were they thinking?"

Trent laughed, "Really, it's Artemus?"

"Shhh, don't tell anyone."

He laughed again and changed the subject, "I saw your painting in Miss Conley's class. What's up with that?"

This year, in art class, we were expressing ourselves with oil paint. That's how Miss Conley had described it. She always talked about expression and showing the world our true selves through art.

I think the woman took too many hallucinogens in her younger years. She was pretty flaky. No one was supposed to have seen the other students work yet. But, apparently, Trent even has a way with flaky, hippie girls.

"What about it?"

"Dude, its morbid," he continued, "that thing you painted is just plain scary. Sometimes I worry about you, man."

13

I had seen a Demon while witnessing some of Kharl's memories, and it had stayed in my head ever since. These creatures are the reason the Soulguard exist. They are evil creatures that enter our dimension from another to capture or slaughter and eat people.

I painted one of them in art class, although I probably shouldn't have. It was a humanoid with long legs and long arms. The beast was extremely muscular and its head had elongated jaws with huge, razor sharp teeth. Its hands had talons on the ends of the fingers that looked wicked sharp. The skin was scaled and almost black, shining with reflected light in places. All in all, it was a scary beast. I'm not sure what possessed me to paint it, though.

"It's nothing, man, I just saw something like it on a book cover," I answered, "Pretty freaky, huh?"

"Sometimes you're just weird, dude," He said, as he walked toward his locker shaking his head.

The rest of the morning was pretty normal for me, although I did watch for Mattie. We apparently didn't have any more classes together before lunch, maybe I'd get to talk to her then. I enjoyed the small bit of conversation we had shared, and it wasn't like I got to speak with pretty girls very often anyway.

I'd tried to talk to Haley Scott once and she looked at me like I was a bug or something. Really, what was I doing here? Privacy is important to my circumstance but most of the kids and teachers were snobs and very hard to get close to. Maybe, that was the reason. It left me less of an excuse to slip up with the truth about my family. But it does make for a lonely time.

The only person who would actually talk to me was Trent. He had no qualms about it, he just didn't give a damn what everyone thought and went his own way. He could fit in with any crowd here and no one would think different of him.

Maybe I was a little jealous of the big guy. But I just couldn't help but like him. He was the Golden Boy.

Chapter 2

I had already eaten my lunch and headed to my normal perch on the wall in front of the cafeteria. I liked to sit there and watch people. Most would see a young man girl watching. They would only be half right. I opened my Inner eye, turning on my ability to see the Souls around me.

As a child, I couldn't turn my ability off and on. It was very disconcerting to people to be studied so deeply by a three year old. I learned to, sort of, push the ability aside and see like an ordinary person. Or fairly close to that anyway. But I still like to just watch people with my Sight. It's soothing.

The Soul is truly a beautiful thing. I look past the body to the energy flows inside, every color imaginable swirling around inside of each and every one of them.

Occasionally I would see an ugly Soul and these would be truly evil people. I'd rarely seen one of these Souls at the school though. I'd seen a few in some of my few trips into Detroit with Kharl.

I was focused on a really beautiful one when someone coughed next to me to get my attention. I turned and my mouth dropped open. Mattie stood beside me and I saw her Soulstream.

When I see a Soulstream, they all lead from the ground, up and around the person a few times, and then into them at the solar plexus. It's not a lie when some people say that you find your center there, it literally is the center of your life-force.

A Soulguard's Soulstream enters the solar plexus and exits his back then loops back into him,

16

enhancing him well past a normal human. Then it loops back out again to enter at a different point and loops again, and so on. A Soulguard's aura looks like a huge knot wrapped around him. Mine was woven a bit different than a Soulguard's knot but I could be much more precise since I could actually see it.

I was looking at the knotted Soulstream of a Soulguard when I looked at Mattie.

"Now that's how a girl likes to be looked at," she remarked.

"You're..."

"Beautiful, awesome, dead sexy," she laughed.

"Soulguard."

It just fell out. I knew I shouldn't have said it but I could see the knot of her Soulstream. I could see the shimmer of her privacy shield and...And I'm just a big dumbass sometimes. Her privacy shield flamed as she tried to strengthen it, thinking I had felt her power. Anyone can feel the enhanced Soul of a Soulguard without this shield that every one of us is taught to form. I read fear, worry and a good bit of anger in her aura. All building up to fight or flight.

"Wait, me too."

I reached inside myself with my mind and turned my shield off so she could feel my Soulstream, then I turned it back on. She was backing away from me. I read even more fear in her aura. I caught flashes of a memory of a man telling her to avoid any contact with the Guard till she was eighteen, especially the Mages.

"Soulmage," she stammered, and then fear was replaced with anger. Anger at me and especially anger at herself for being afraid. Her hand was twitching and I felt that she was going for a weapon soon.

"Just wait, I'm not a Mage yet. I've only had Soulguard training. I'm not your enemy, I think we're actually in the same boat. Early training isn't supposed to happen. Kharl and Kyra warned me...I wish sometimes I'd listen...Don't tell anyone, ever, they say..." I was babbling and I knew it, so I shut up.

I could see a budding astonishment in her aura as I said those two names. God I'm stupid.

"Kharl? Kyra? Would that be Kharl Jaegher and Kyra Nightwing?" she asked.

I nodded as I was deciding not to say anything else and realized that I had already said it with the nod. Idiot. That's me. I wasn't sure how she knew them, but it meant a great deal to her, because she calmed down almost immediately.

"My dad talks about them all the time, they disappeared years ago, back when the Demonkiller died," She was interrupted by the bell to end lunch.

"Meet me in the gym after classes so we can continue this conversation," I said with excitement coursing through me.

She nodded and headed to class.

"Kharl's gonna kill me."

Chapter 3

The rest of the day flew by. I was excited that I would actually get to talk to someone else like me. The only Guards I had ever met, aside from witnessing memories in their auras, were Kharl and Kyra.

Classes finally ended and I made my way to the gym. A lot of students used the gym after school, mostly the students who stayed on campus. Students came from all over the US to go to school here.

I made my way up to the track on the second floor and met Mattie at the far end from where Coach Newman was working with some of the basketball team.

"So..." that was the only word she got out before all hell broke loose at the far end of the gym. A twisted darkness formed right in front of the doors and something burst from it with a bestial roar. It was straight out of my painting in art class.

"Oh Hell," I muttered.

The Demon shot straight for the closest group of people and tore into Coach Newman and five teens like a buzz saw, as another Demon burst from the portal and another. Right in their path was the tiny slip of a girl I had noticed earlier with the prettiest Soul I had ever seen. She couldn't have been more than twelve.

I had never actually faced Demons before and usually, I would have eased into my enhanced speed. At the sight of those two beasts charging that girl, I remembered my mother lying in a pool of blood surrounded by Demon corpses. I felt a rage like nothing I had ever felt before explode within me and I went ballistic. The rail in front of me exploded as I went through it and sailed across the gym, my fists glowing with pure Soulfire and I struck the first Demon in the throat before my feet had even touched the ground. Its head exploded from its body and I turned to the other one.

Its back was to me and it was inches from the little girl when I grasped the ridges of its back and threw it bodily across the room where it impacted one of the steel posts. Demon blood exploded from the body and on the other side of it I saw Trent Deacons looking at me in astonishment.

I looked to the left and there was Mattie, a gleaming silver knife in each hand. Just where the hell was she hiding those? She'd just carved a Demon to shreds with them and was going for another. The portal was spewing Demons in a steady stream. I grabbed the girl with the pretty Soul who gasped as I jumped across the space between me and Trent.

"Get these people back while we hold them off!" I yelled as I handed the girl to him and sprinted back toward the portal.

You have to give Trent his due, he was yelling and motioning toward the kids in the gym almost immediately. He wasn't the type to lose his mind like some, for instance, Haley Scott, and her cheerleader squad.

I paused near them and yelled for them to head toward the not-demon-infested side of the room. Most of them listened, but Haley looked at me in terror, and ran right into the waiting hands of a Demon. It tore her in half with a bestial roar and an explosion of blood. I was dumbfounded. She was more scared of me than a monster from Hell.

Somewhere Trent had found a whistle and was blowing for all he was worth. Everyone looked and finally started moving. Unfortunately the Demons also were attracted to the sound.

I met them halfway and used the lessons Kharl had taught me. Hit hard, hit fast, and leave no survivors. Mattie was cutting Demons to shreds beside me, when I glanced back to see Trent with a baseball bat standing between a Demon and the people he'd gathered.

"Mattie!" she looked at me and we both turned and shot toward them.

Just as the Demon started to swing its huge arm toward Trent something caused it to stop. I felt an awful presence behind us as we ripped the Demon away from our path. I was facing Trent and his bat.

"We got to get these people outta here, big guy," I yelled and he nodded.

I looked back at the Demons still pouring out of the twisted portal and noticed the ugly threads that linked them to it. I was seeing their Soul streams and they looked vile to my Inner eye. Ugly, twisted strands of black and purple led back through the portal.

Two bigger Demons had come through and their Soul streams were a great deal larger as well.

"Oh shit, Soldiers," Mattie muttered.

When Demons enter our realm they slaughter anything in sight. When Wrathguards, commonly referred to as soldiers, come across, they control the lesser Demons. When this occurs, they herd people together to take back across to their world. God only knows what happens to them there.

"All right, Mattie, take point I'll keep them from our tails and let's get the hell outta here."

She nodded and Trent turned to the fifteen people huddled behind him, "OK people, we're following her and running like hell! I'll signal when we're out!"

I nodded and Mattie hit the door with Trent herding the crowd behind her. The Demons charged and I hit anything that came within reach. Trent blew his whistle to alert me that everyone was clear of the gym and I leaped backward through the door.

More people were in the hallway beyond and Trent was herding them along as well so I parked at the door, where only a few could come at me at once. There, I ripped off anything that came through. I had beaten that initial rage down and now my training was what fueled my actions.

The whistle blew again and I turned to sprint down the hallway but the two Soldiers crashed through the doors where I had just been. I turned to face them as they charged me and I parried with my arms and lashed out with my foot. The kick shattered the first one's chest and it flew backwards.

For a split second I saw my mother lying in that bloody floor surrounded by dead Soldier Demons and rage ripped through me again. With a roar, I seized the throat of the other one and ripped its head from its shoulders. It fell and I sprinted through the outside doors to almost run over Trent, who'd watched the short battle with the Wrathguards.

22

The Demons stopped coming after us and surged through the school, I'd just killed their controllers. Stepping outside, I noticed a black dome of energy with my Inner eye and felt that we'd be safe if we got outside of it.

"Trent," I grabbed him before he headed back to the crowd, "We need to move out to the other side of the parking lot and I need a cell phone. Can you do that?"

"Sure thing," He started again on the crowd and we moved quickly to the parking lot. One of the girls stumbled and fell, so I reached to help her up. She cringed and scuttled back from me. It was like a pit opened up in my chest. I'd gone from outcast to monster, and it hurt, God it hurt.

Trent stepped up and pulled the girl to her feet. He looked at me and I didn't need to read his aura to see the pity. He put his hand on my shoulder and squeezed, then handed me a cell phone.

Chapter 4

I looked back at the school as I felt more soldiers come through the gate. And I watched as human Souls began moving back toward the gym.

"Damnit! They're taking prisoners," I muttered.

Mattie was back over by me by then, "I felt more soldiers cross, Colin."

"Me too, they're gathering people in the gym."

"They're gonna take em back across aren't they?"

I nodded and made the call.

"Hello," Kharl answered.

"Dad, code Zulu at the school"

"Zulu?!"

"Yeah, Soldiers," I said, "and lesser Demons, a lot of em."

"You're out or you couldn't call. Wait where you are, we'll be less than a half hour."

"Dad they're herding people up for a grab they don't have a half hour."

"You're going back in," He said it as a statement, because he already knew the answer.

"They're gonna eat those people, or worse. I can't let that happen."

"I know," he paused a second, "OK, Here's what you do. You get to those people and you put up one of those crazy shields of yours. Don't fight 'em, put everything into the shield. Hold for thirty minutes, that's all I need."

"Yes sir," I heard the phone hit the floor and something crashed in the background. I don't think he even used the door.

Shields are something I learned early on. A Soulguard is taught how to form the privacy shields to conceal their Soul streams at the beginning of training. You have to project a small amount of your life-force out past your body. It takes a little effort to hold it up but not much. Since I can actually see what I am doing, I constructed a privacy shield that radiates from the Soul stream itself, and surrounds me. I really respect the Guard, who can't see what I see. They accomplish so much while working in the dark.

I call it a passive shield. It doesn't require any effort because it's from the stream, not me. Actually, it takes an effort to keep it turned off when I need to. Using this as a pattern I'd experimented with making defensive shields as well. It takes a couple of moments to construct one but they are tough.

Tough enough to hold out a bunch of soldiers? I didn't know.

"I gotta go back in," I said.

I told Mattie and Trent the plan, and Trent interrupted.

"No, it won't work, dude. I hate to say it but everyone is as scared of you guys as the monsters," he was shaking his head, "I've got to go in, too."

"You're probably right," I answered, remembering the cringing girl who wouldn't even let me help her to her feet, "but it's crazy to go back in there."

"Doesn't matter, I'm going," he squared his shoulders, "It'll save more lives."

25

"All right," I nodded, "jump on my back, we're going' in fast. Mattie can you call your dad, too, and try to get these people moving' out of the area?"

"No, dad's in California and I'm going in with you, someone has to hold them off while you do this shield thing. Don't argue, it's a done deal. But you're carrying the ox, not me."

"I am not an ox, and I'll just walk in on my own, thank you."

I gave him my best Kharl look.

"They're taking folks to the gym, they'll just take me to the gym. Give me a few minutes before you blow the doors down and I'll get folks packed together for the shield thing."

"Actually, that'll probably work, Colin," Mattie said.

"You don't have to do this, big guy," I said.

"You know, I've never been more terrified in my whole life, but you *need* me. I can't just stand here and watch."

I nodded, "How much time do you need after you reach the others?"

"Just a couple of minutes and you get your ass in there. Don't you let them eat me," He took a deep breath and started back inside at a jog.

I watched the light of his Soul as the Demons converged, then he was on his way to the gym.

I looked to Mattie, "You ready for this?"

She spun her daggers in her hands, "Let's do it," she said softly

I'll not lie, I was scared, but this is what we're born to do. When I think of leaving those people in the hands of the Demons, I see my mother bleeding on the floor and I know that it just isn't in me to allow that to continue.

I looked to the school, Trent was in the gym and now was the time.

"Go."

We plunged across the space toward the buildings plowing through walls and anything in our path. The last wall exploded inward as we hit it. We launched ourselves across the gym to land within feet of Trent as he kept people calm.

I slammed my fist into the ground to anchor the shield in the earth. It wasn't really necessary because the shield actually was formed from my stream but what can I say? I was seventeen and it looked very, very cool. I began weaving the pattern from my Soul stream. I made it visible to the naked eye so that no one would get too close.

As it started to form the Demons must have realized what was happening because there was an awful roar and they charged.

Mattie stepped in front of me and guarded the hole as it grew smaller, her knives a blur as Demon blood sprayed from cut limbs, torsos, and anything else that poked through. Finally my shield snapped closed and a Demon's arm and head splatted on the floor at Mattie's feet.

She looked down, "That's never gonna come off my shoes," She said sadly.

I looked back where we'd come in and another Demon came in dragging Miss Haynes. I started to open the shield when the Demon suddenly stopped and with a roar and a shake of the head it ripped her completely in half and threw her back through the door he'd come in through. I heard someone throw up and another behind me coughed nervously.

"I don't know if she was *that* annoying," Trent said, "It didn't even eat her."

I felt the portal come alive again and Wrathguards flooded out of it, the regular Demons pulled back and the soldiers sprang forward to pound on my shield. It held.

After a short time, the Chemistry teacher, I couldn't remember his name, stepped forward facing Trent.

"Now what do we do?"

"We wait. Cavalry's on the way," he answered.

"Did you call 911?"

"Nah, we called his dad," Trent returned, pointing at me. The teacher looked at me and I could see the fear in his aura but he didn't look away.

"And who is your father? What can he do?"

I could see their auras at a mile away, closing fast. I smiled, "You're about to see."

Chapter 5

The whole end of the building exploded as Kharl and Kyra hit it at seventy miles per hour. I've sparred with both of them but what I saw that day was amazing. Kharl was glowing with Soulfire and where he walked Demon parts flew in all directions. He waded into the ranks of Soldier demons without slowing down and ripped them apart.

Kharl and Kyra are like forces of nature. Kyra is five feet and six inches tall with a slim but firm build. She is of Native American descent with dark skin and black hair and she is a tornado, a maelstrom of death with a sword in each hand. She is so fast, it's hard to even see her in action. Mostly you just see Demon parts falling to the floor as she flashes by.

Kharl is the avalanche, the juggernaut. He is six feet and five inches tall and, I kid you not, four feet across at the shoulders. His fighting style is to wade in and destroy anything that gets in his path. Never go around, when you can go through it. It doesn't matter what *it* is. No deception, no fear, and no stopping him.

This is why they're legends in the Soulguard. This is why their names are even known to people like Mattie, who aren't even old enough to have met them.

The portal was pouring Soldiers into the gym but they were dying faster than the others were arriving.

Suddenly something huge stepped through and with one sweep of its enormous arm, both Soulguards flew backwards through the air. They slammed against the shield and I opened a portal for them. Before I could close it, the Demon had crossed the room, one long arm reaching through the portal, to swipe at me. I felt fire run down my face and I pushed the shield out, pushing the Demon away. It backed up and I finished closing the portal.

The Demon pounded at the shield and I felt every blow. Blood ran freely down the left side of my face.

"Damn Wraith!" Kharl exclaimed, "What the hell is a Wraith doing here?"

A Wraith is a much more powerful Demon than the soldier. Soldiers are sent to take people back across but a Wraith only comes across the dimensions with an agenda. They have a specific goal and they control the soldiers and lesser Demons under them.

A Wraith can stand up to Soulguards without fear. It usually takes multiple Mages to kill one of them.

"Oh hell, they know he's here," Kyra said.

I knew what they were saying. All this for me, they wanted me dead. All these people had died because of me.

"Four Soulguards can't take a Wraith, even us." Kyra said softly, "but we two can slow it down enough for him to get away."

"When I say to, Boy, you drop the shield and let us out. Then you get these people outta here and run like hell," Kharl rumbled. He snapped his wrists and two huge swords of pure Soulfire were in his hands.

He rolled his massive shoulders and said, "Drop"

"No."

He turned to me, "We can't win this one, Son, the best we can do is give you some time."

"A Mage can do it," I returned

"You've been in here," he motioned toward his head with one of those massive swords, "You know what happens to Mages who try to use it without training."

He had made me witness a memory a long time ago to make sure I was convinced not to try to mess with the Source. A man had tried to pull from the Source and it burned him alive. He was ashes in minutes, the power in the Source is that strong. It was horrible and I've never been tempted to try to use that burning mass of power, always at the edge of my awareness.

"No one else dies for me."

Kharl looked at me for a minute and nodded. I saw the resignation, in his aura and a great sadness. He turned to face the Wraith.

"We'll keep it off you long enough for you to do what you got to, Son."

Up until this very moment I had never understood my real father, how he had gone off, knowing it was to his death. Now I did. After seeing how badly the Demons wanted me dead, I realized that he had died, not for revenge, but to give me a life, to have time to grow up, possibly defend myself. But they got here too soon. At least I could keep anyone else from dying for me.

I looked at the massive back in front of me and looked to the left, at Kyra. She had tears running down her face. I'd seen her sad, mad, happy, even depressed, but I'd never seen her cry. I knew that *this* was my family, my father and mother in all ways except blood. I looked to my right to see Mattie, knives dripping with Soulfire, loyal because that is what Soulguards are supposed to be. I turned and looked at possibly the bravest man I have ever known, who not only escaped Hell, but ran right back in to save others, my friend.

Kelvin Rourke had found the same thing I had, something worth dying for.

"What are you talking about? What are you gonna do?" Trent asked, worried.

I turned back toward the Demon pounding on my shields.

"Burn," I said softly

Then I reached deep down into that writhing mass just below the surface of the Earth and Pulled.

Burning agony surged up from the Earth and engulfed me, my shield exploded outward destroying everything in its path. The Wraith, carried backward, screaming, burst into flame. It still clawed at the shield until, it too, exploded. All the Demons were incinerated along with the portal, the gymnasium and about half the school.

I was one with a roaring mass of life and death, twisted together to create a great pyre of destruction. From a great distance I kept hearing a voice.

"Shut it down! Shut it down!"

I felt something on my arms and looked down to see two huge hands holding my arms and shaking me. Blisters were already forming on them. I fought to close off the Source but it was massive and I was so full of that awesome power. It was like a high you might get from some drug. I wanted to keep it forever but I couldn't hold this much power and it was killing me.

I formed a shield in the shape of a tube just around me and Kharl was flung back, his arms blistered and smoking. Then I looked up and released it all with a scream. As the flow moved through me I finally forced myself to close the connection to the Source. Power flooded out of me for minutes after the link was severed, straight up into the sky. Finally it was over, all that remained was pain and the memory of Power.

As darkness closed in on me I heard Kyra's voice.

"Soulmage, my ass," She said as she caught me, before I could slam into the floor.

Chapter 6

I heard voices in the dark.

"...not a Soulmage...something else...Mage can't channel that much power."

"What else would you call him?" I heard Kharl's voice.

"I think I'll call him Sir," I heard Trent say and I tried to laugh.

It came out more like a rasping cough and I felt coldness against my face. Then I was gone again.

The next time I came to, I was in my bed at home. When I opened my eyes I found that it was dark but I could see perfectly well without the light.

I'd always had better night vision than regular folks, but this was much more. My hearing was sharper as well and there was a horrible noise in the corner where my recliner was.

I looked over to see Trent sleeping there, snoring loudly. Mattie was sitting on my sofa in the dark glaring daggers at Trent until she noticed me moving around.

"Wake up!" she threw a pillow at him.

"Wha..." He snorted as he jerked awake

"You're not an ox, no, you sound like a moose. I can't believe your family didn't strangle you in your sleep!"

"What, what'd I do?"

"I think you woke the dead," she answered as she turned on the lamp on the end table.

Turning toward me he said, "Well, unless he died with that goofy smile on his face, I'd say he's

34

awake. So how you feeling Col? After, uh, blowing up the school."

"I feel like I was hit by a train. Or Kharl."

"That guy is awesome, Col. I saw the trail of destruction he and that crazy woman left behind on their way to the school. Looked like a tornado had come through and demolished everything in a straight line from the road to the school. And what they did to those things in the gym," he shook his head, "I saw you fight those two in the hall, but they killed forty or fifty before that other thing showed up."

I could detect a little hero worship going on here and I figured Kharl had definitely gotten a new fan.

"I now know why you guys are so tough, though," he said, "I think your mom's been putting carburetor cleaner in your food."

"Oh God, don't say anything to her about it," I said with a snort. I would never dream of telling her, but Kyra's cooking is truly wretched.

"Too late," Mattie chuckled, "You should have seen it. Everyone was sitting in the living room and your mom said she would fix some dinner. The moose over there jumped up and offered to fix it. He actually said something about gasoline and rat poison."

"You could have heard a pin drop. Three *mighty* Soulguards cringed in fear and looked at your mom. She just looked at Trent for a minute, and then just busted out laughing," She giggled, "I do have to admit, moose boy can cook."

"Why I gotta be a moose? I think you're just jealous, since you're about the size of a squirrel."

I laughed aloud and made myself sit up. I started to stand up and realized I was naked. I snatched the covers back around me, my face burning. Mattie smiled and winked at me then turned and ran upstairs. My face got even redder.

Trent laughed loudly, "That one's all yours, buddy, she's way too mean for my taste. The way she plays with those knives all the time is scary."

"I have to ask, is there some way I can get what you have? I always planned to join the Marines but this is much bigger. The way Kharl and Jack talk, there's a huge organization here. I want to be a part of that."

"Yeah, they recruit from everywhere and I'd say Kharl already has ideas on the subject, but I'll put in a good word for you if you want me to," I answered, "and who's Jack?"

"That's Mattie's dad. He got back from the west coast earlier today."

"How long have I been out of it?"

"It's been two days and we're waiting for my dad to get here. The group upstairs is trying to do damage control, but some very important people's kids were killed and a lot of their kids are telling some very scary stories. I convinced them that they really could use a Senator as an ally and that my dad is one of the few with scruples."

He got up and headed for the stairs, "And Kyra told us to tell you when you wake up to get your shield back up."

I opened my Inner eye and gasped, my Soul stream was the size of a tree trunk and every tendril of the weave I'd spent so much time creating was swollen almost as big as a Soulguards Soul stream. I guess my body had adapted to the power output I was subjecting it to.

My passive privacy shield was in tatters. I began weaving a new one, slowly building around my soul stream and much bigger aura.

When I finished, I stood up shakily and began getting dressed. As I walked by the mirror I stopped, I hadn't come out of this unscathed. There was a livid scar on my face running from my hairline, down across my eye, and along my left cheek.

On my chest was a patch of scar tissue from a severe burn. I turned around and there were two more of these scars on my back.

A Soulguard heals fast. If it doesn't outright kill him or her, they can generally heal from it. As severe as the scars were, I think I healed much faster than I should have. The enlarged soul stream probably caused that.

Why did so many people have to die? Was it because I had dropped my shields to let Mattie see I was Guard? I still had the metallic smell of blood in my nostrils, or maybe I was just remembering it. Was it really all my fault? Did they want me dead so badly that they monitor that closely for me, or was it a huge coincidence? I don't believe it was a coincidence, they attacked a place with not just one but two Soulguard trained kids. I just don't know.

I could sense Kyra on her way down as well as hear her. I never used to be able to hear her coming. My hearing was affected just as my sight was, it seemed.

She stopped at the foot of the stairs and looked at me. I could see all the emotions flash across her aura, relief, joy, and love. I almost broke down right there. I walked to her and hugged her tightly.

Most people take for granted so many things in life. When you come so close to losing all of those things, you really learn how to cherish them.

She stepped back and looked me in the eyes for a moment, then smiled and shot back up the stairs without saying a word.

I finished dressing and made my way up-stairs. I had to concentrate to keep from going too fast. It had taken a few days to get used to the extra strength and speed a Soulguard gains when he twists his Soulstream to enhance himself. And it looked like I was about to have to do it again. The enlarged stream amplified me to a much greater ex-tent.

With some concentration I kept myself to a normal pace. With my Sight I could detect six auras in the dining room, sitting around the table and two of them were strangers. I checked my privacy shield once more and walked through the door.

Kharl smiled and I could see the relief flash through his aura.

"Welcome back to the living," he rumbled. He stood up and met me with a hug, "We thought we lost you, Boy."

He turned to the two men sitting at the ta-ble. "This is Jack Riordan, Mattie's dad." He mo-tioned toward a Medium sized man with black hair. He was, in appearance, just an average man. Average height, average build, but his aura was almost as in-timidating as Kharl's. "He's an Elite, like me and Ky."

The Elites were the best of the best. They are at the top of the heap in the Soulguard hierarchy, outranked only by the Mages, and judging by his stream and aura he was probably as old as either Kharl or Kyra.

I'd never really nailed down how old the two of them were yet but I was making progress. It's hard to use my Sight as a lie detector if they won't even answer the question. Both of them were older than one hundred years and less than two hundred, I was sure.

"Good to meet you, youngster, and I'm glad to see the shield back up. It was hard to concentrate with all that racket," Jack Riordan said with a smile.

Kharl motioned to the other man, an Asian, but I couldn't tell from where in Asia he'd come from. His aura was also huge and very tightly knotted.

"This is Tien Yueh, also an Elite and the Weapon Master of the Academy."

The small man nodded at me and I saw no emotion pass across his aura. It had a shiny sort of film around it and I realized that it was a complex shield that even shielded his aura from my Sight. But judging from what I *could* see, his aura was possibly even bigger and older than Kharl's.

I nodded back to Yueh and turned to the others, Kyra, Mattie and Trent. Trent jumped up and started toward the kitchen.

"I'll get us something started for dinner."

"There's some carburetor cleaner under the sink," Kyra smiled, "It makes a great base for a soup."

Kharl snorted and Mattie laughed aloud. Trent's stride picked up and he almost ran into the other room.

"Crazy women...hear everything...bionic ears..." mutters came from the kitchen.

"Son, where'd you find him? I really like that boy."

"He's the only person at that school I liked, at least till Mattie showed up. And I'm not really sure about her yet. She may still want to stab me."

"Nah, I think I got most of that outta my system, now," She grinned, "But things may change, so don't rush to any judgments yet."

"I've been around him all his life, and I'm still not sure whether to stab him or not," Kyra shook her head, then looked at me, "Speaking of stabbing, I think a little sparring, to see how well you have recovered, would be in order. Don't worry, I'll be gentle"

"In all seriousness, Boy, the Mages will be here soon. We need to see if you can defend yourself if you need to," Kharl said.

"Defend myself?"

Kharl nodded, "Protocol is to block any one who channels early from the Source, if they survive it. This is not acceptable, not with Demons actively searching for you. So you may need to defend yourself, depending on who they send."

"What the hell," I returned, "I thought we were all on the same side here."

"It's complicated," Tien Yueh said softly.

Chapter 7

Our house is located in the middle of a five hundred acre plot of land, mostly timber. The clearing in the center couldn't be viewed from outside the property. Kharl had done this for the sake of privacy. We didn't have to hide what we were at home. The inside of the tree line was my running track and I'd worn a path from use over the last ten years or so.

I spent several hours running laps around the tree line to get used to my new speed. I'd never been able to run that fast before and it took some time to adjust.

Luckily, I was on the far side of the clearing and out of sight when the car with Senator Samuel Deacons pulled up the driveway.

It could be quite a shock, to see a boy run across in front of your car at ninety miles per hour.

Two hours straight, and I hadn't even broken a sweat. That was definitely different from my norm. I guess I needed to push harder, but that could wait till later. I felt ok with the higher speeds by then and probably needed to get the tests over with.

I was worried about the Mages. I had no idea there was so much friction between the Soulmages and the Soulguards. I mean, really? We're here to fight Demons and protect humanity, this is what the Guard was formed for.

I guess you can't get more than ten people into something without stupid politics getting in the way. Nothing ruins any organization faster than organizers. I hate politics, but we were right in the middle of a huge pile of it. Between the problems with the Mages and having an actual Senator at the house, I was a little distraught.

Then pile on the fact that I'd just seen so many people viciously slaughtered by the Demons. And I'm pretty sure it was my fault. I really didn't understand why everyone wasn't told the dangers and made aware of us. The people in Morndel were so scared of me, after seeing what I did, that I couldn't help some of them.

That's just plain ridiculous, if people knew we were there they wouldn't fear us and maybe, just maybe we could save some lives. It's just my opinion but who am I? No one will listen to a seventeen year old boy, anyway.

I really should have been paying attention, because I turned the corner in my track to find Trent and the Senator walking along it toward me. At ninety miles per hour, there's really no way to stop so I just veered into the trees. A couple of oak trees slowed me down sufficiently, although the trees didn't fare too well.

I picked myself back up and turned back toward the path. Trent was smiling from ear to ear and his dad was looking at me with wide eyes and a pale face.

He recovered his composure a lot quicker than most people would though and stepped forward with his hand stretched out to me.

I opened my Inner eye and felt relief as I saw no deception in the man's aura, only a slight fear and a lot of gratitude. I shook his hand and he had a firm grip.

"I understand you're the reason my son is still alive and for that you have my eternal gratitude, Young Man."

"I don't know if you know it, Sir, but Trent is the reason a lot of those people are still here. He is the bravest man I have ever seen and he saved more lives than any of us."

Trent's face was red, and I guess he hadn't said one word about what he'd done because his dad turned to him, not really in surprise, but with a questioning look on his face. I could see pride flash across his aura as he looked at his son and I smiled.

The Senator turned back to me, "I wouldn't talk to anyone in the house until I was allowed to thank you for what you've done for me and my family."

Trent had given him an, apparently, much shortened version of what happened.

"But I've also interviewed several people who were there, including a chemistry teacher named Thomas Warren."

"All the versions point to the fact that you and a young lady were their saviors. That you attacked these," He paused a second, "Demons, as they appeared. And that the young lady led them out of the school while you held off the Demons. They also made me aware of my son's actions and I am quite proud of him."

"I wondered at first why they were saying that the three of you went back in, and then I talked to Mr. Warren. But this is where it got shaky. He was quite lucid, but he was talking about magical force fields and flaming swords."

"And so I'm here. And Trent has started explaining some of it but most of what I have learned from him is that the Marines are going to lose a good man to this Soulguard of yours."

I looked deeply at his aura and there was, surprising in a politician, no deception in this man. So I told him the truth.

Twice in one week, I thought, Kharl is gonna strangle me.

I told none of the details about the Soulguard. Officially, I'm not Soulguard yet, so that isn't my tale to tell.

But all that had happened at the school, I told him. As I was telling him about Trent's decision to walk right back into the fire, Deacons was looking at his son as if he was seeing him for the first time and was greatly impressed. I could read the pride flowing through his aura and I could see the embarrassment in Trent's aura.

Real heroes are like that, they are modest and they will do what is right without looking for reward or praise. And they deserve it much more than most. Trent Deacons was more a hero in this than I could ever be.

Yes, I had risked my life, but for my family. Up until the Wraith had shown up, I wasn't at risk. Killing Demons is what the Guard does. He'd risked his life for strangers. He was at risk throughout the ordeal and had shown me what true heroism was really about.

His father had a right to by proud of a son like him and the Guard would be lucky, indeed, if he chose to join their ranks.

Chapter 8

Trent, Mattie, and I sat with our backs against the wall at the barn where most of the martial training I'd had over the years had been done. None of us knew what was happening in the house. The Senator had gone in to meet with the Soulguards over an hour ago and we had gone outside to leave them to it.

"I've never seen so much blood in my life," Trent said softly.

"I know. It was awful," Mattie returned, "I've trained for this most of my life, but it doesn't really prepare you for that."

I was silent, remembering a bloodbath I had witnessed through Kharl's memories. Seeing my mother's death had probably prepared me much more than the other two. The blood hadn't bothered me as much as the needless death of several people who had run from Mattie and me straight into the hands of Demons.

"Do you think they'll let me join the Soulguard?" He asked.

"I'm sure they will," she answered and looked at me, "You're being awful quiet, what's wrong?"

"Mages are gonna try and block me from the Source," I said, "The Demons are searching for me and if I'm blocked, I'm dead meat. I'll have to fight them and I'm not trained to be a Mage. And the worst part is, I shouldn't have to fight people, we're meant to fight Demons."

"So how tough are these Mages?" Trent asked.

"You saw what I did. I'm a Mage, just not trained. They'll be trained and probably stronger than me."

"Is there any way you can raise a shield faster than the one you did in the gym?" Mattie asked.

"Maybe," I answered thoughtfully, "Let me concentrate a minute."

I looked at my privacy shield. What if I make it with much thicker tendrils and put some sort of power adjustment? I thought. My on/off switch is a small sliding surface that will cut off the power to the shield, so what if I make it more like a portal that dilates open and closed so I can regulate the power?

Once I established the portal I enlarged the tendrils to the privacy shield. I set the portal to a trickle to keep the privacy screen active.

"I think I might have it, Mattie, try to hit me," I said as I stood up.

She swung so fast I almost didn't catch it, but managed to open the portal and her fist hit about a foot from my body. I still flew backwards into the barn wall.

"I forgot to anchor it," I said as I picked myself up, "but I think it'll work. Thanks, Mattie, I hadn't even thought about it before."

"She just knocked you into a wall and you call it a success? I swear it just gets weirder and weirder around you."

I gave him the Kharl look again and he said, "Stop looking at me like that, man, it's disturbing."

Mattie laughed and shook her head, "So what else can you do already? I heard it takes Mages months to create shields like you do in minutes."

"I can see the Soul streams and the Souls as well. Kharl says I'm the only person he's ever heard of that can do that. That's not common knowledge and I would appreciate it if it stayed between us."

They both nodded and I saw, in their auras, that neither lied about it.

"And I can read the emotions in other people's auras. Also I can always tell if someone is lying or not." I didn't tell of several of my other skills like the ability to see memories.

"The reason I can create shields so well, is that I can see them. The Guard gets so much done while working in the dark, it's impressive."

Our conversation was interrupted when the house door opened and everyone made their way outside. They all headed our direction and I knew I was about to get my butt kicked again. Sparring sessions were always painful, but I usually didn't make the same mistake twice. It just seemed that Kharl and Kyra always had some new trick to use on me.

"You ready?" Kyra asked as she walked past me.

I winced and she chuckled. I followed her and Kharl into the barn. Everyone else followed us inside and found places to sit, well back from the center area we had marked off in the floor.

"Practice wands," Kyra stated. I walked across the open area and picked up four practice swords. They were made of bamboo wood and were roughly the size of Kyra's short swords. One of the tests with wooden swords is to keep from breaking them with our enhanced strength. This is true when wielding real blades as well. If you break your blade, you're in a fist fight with a demon.

Not all Soulguards can make the blades from pure Soulfire like Kharl had done at the school. Most of them needed a weapon to pour the Soulfire into. Of course, when the blade is imbued with Soulfire, it is much stronger than a regular blade.

I handed Kyra two of the wands and kept two for myself. We faced off about twenty feet apart.

"3...2..." Kharl's voice rumbled, "...1..."

The world slowed down as Kharl's voice continued, "Go."

We met in the middle of the practice area, swords ready. Then the Dance began.

Kyra calls it the Dance of Blades and she is a master of it. As our blades met, she was surprised.

"You're faster," She smiled and sped up. "Let's see how fast."

I felt the hit on my left and sped up as well. She was moving faster than I'd ever seen her go, except when battling the Demons at Morndel. I was amazed, I was moving just as fast as she was. I still couldn't seem to connect, though.

We continued until Kharl's voice boomed, "Halt!"

I was sore in a dozen places and sweating profusely. Kyra had worked up a sweat as well.

"A lot faster," she commented. I hadn't even got in one hit. Of course, I never get in a hit on Ky.

"That's where experience tells the tale, son." she said, as if reading my mind, "You are as fast as I am but I've learned a few tricks over the years.

You'll be better than me when you've got the experience to match your power."

I doubt that, I thought. I looked around at the other Guards and both of them were smiling.

"I'm going to have so much fun with him," the weapon master said happily.

"My turn," Kharl said.

Sometimes I think the two of them enjoy this kind of abuse too much. I looked toward Trent and his dad. They both looked a bit dazed.

"Just wait till you start training," I said and nodded at Trent.

We faced off just as Ky and I had, twenty feet apart, facing each other. There were no swords now. Kharl is my unarmed combat trainer.

"3...2...1...Go!"

We charged one another and I figured I would use my extra speed to my advantage. I jumped over his head and felt a vice close on my left leg.

Oh crap, this is gonna hurt, I thought as he threw me across the room to slam into "The Mat".

"The Mat" is the place I end up every time I try something stupid while fighting Kharl. I think there is a permanent face print in the two feet thick padding on the reinforced back wall of the barn. Maybe several.

"I told you, Quit jumping around like a damn grasshopper! Your power is in the earth, stay connected to it."

I picked myself up from the floor in front of "The Mat", with a stupid grin on my face. Kharl was waiting, so I planted my feet and charged. There isn't a lot of finesse in Kharl's style of fighting, but there isn't a lot of finesse in a train either. When he hits you, it feels like you were hit by a *big* train.

I found that my strength and durability was also affected by the larger Soulstream, I was holding my own with Kharl. But like Ky, he had worlds of experience and he used some of it to put me on the floor several times.

"Halt!" Ky shouted.

I was sore in places I didn't even know I had. It never fails, if I start to think too highly of myself, a spar with either of them can set me straight right quick.

Tien stood up and approached. "You're good enough at fighting to face any Mage I know, but the shield is the most important thing when facing Mages. How are your shields?"

I opened the portal and anchored to the ground.

"Try it," I stated and stood still as Kharl swung at me. His fist hit a foot from me but I didn't fly into a wall this time. I didn't budge.

Kharl smiled and began to pound on my shield with a vengeance. Jack stood up and joined him, as well as Ky and Tien. Four Elite Soulguards couldn't pierce my shields.

"That will do," Tien stated.

Chapter 9

It was a couple of days later before the Mages arrived. Trent and his dad had gone back home after it was agreed that the Senator would tell the right people about what really happened and start the right rumors to keep as much of it a secret as he could.

Trent would start Soulguard training in several months, when he turned eighteen.

Jack Riordan and Mattie had gone home as well. She would start her official training in a few months as well. Jack offered to stay and help if the Mages became difficult.

"If things go bad, this doesn't need to fall on the Guard," was Kharl's answer.

Tien had gone back to the Academy for much the same reason.

I was nervous as I watched a stretch limo pull up the drive. I watched Kharl's aura as two men and a woman exited the car. Relief flowed across his aura as he saw the second man, and he smiled.

"Don't worry, Son, the second guy is Gregor Kherkov," Kharl said, "He's one of the good guys."

Gregor was a dark haired man of medium height. He was stocky and seemed quite fit. The other man was tall and skinny with dirty blonde hair. He had one of those huge noses that brought visions of Ichabod Crane from the headless horseman cartoon to mind.

The woman was tall and gorgeous. She was blonde and very well built. Her looks would generally have me stuttering and making a fool of myself except I saw her Soul and it wasn't pretty at all.

I looked at their Soulstreams. A typical Guard has a stream about three inches in diameter. Kharl and Kyra had streams of about five inches. I think they must grow with age and use.

The first two Mages' streams were a bit bigger than Kharl's, maybe eight or ten inches. They didn't have the intricate knot of a guard but it still looped in and out of their bodies several times.

The third Mage, Gregor, had a stream of at least sixteen or eighteen inches, larger than my own, and I could see the power rolling in his aura. He looked at me as he entered the room and his eyes widened in surprise. Then he saw Kharl.

"Kharl," He smiled and offered his hand. Kharl shook it with a smile

"Hi Greg."

"Be still my beating heart, is that Kyra?" Gregor laughed, "As beautiful as ever, I see."

He looked at me with a penetrating gaze. His eyes widened and I saw realization flash across his aura, along with a flash of memory about a man who looked a great deal like me.

He chuckled, "This explains a great deal."

He turned to his companions, "Let me introduce you to Regina Worthington and Allen Denton. Regina, Allen, these are the infamous Kharl Jaegher and Kyra Nightwing, former Soulguard Elites."

I saw recognition in both Mages at the names.

"So this must be the boy we are here to block," Regina Worthington said as she turned to me.

Gregor snorted, "You *are* aware of my particular gifts?"

"Yes," she answered, her eyes narrowing in anger.

I could see the anger and hate in her aura, arrogance rolled across it as well.

"He's an untrained child, and you're the second most powerful Mage in the United States, so what's the problem?"

Gregor turned to me, "I would like for you to do me a favor, Young Man. We don't ask Mages to do this but would you be kind enough to lower your privacy shield for a moment?"

"The last time I did, I was attacked by a bunch of Demons and close to a hundred people died," I answered.

"Hold on a second, I'll put up a shield around us," Gregor returned. I watched as he pushed a shield out from his body. It was much faster than how I weaved one from my stream, "I think that should do it."

I looked to Kharl and caught his small nod. So I closed the portal switch.

Both Mages stepped back and Regina actually gasped her face pale as a sheet.

I opened the portal to a trickle again, raising my shield.

"That will never be asked of you again, Young Man. We set a lot of store in our privacy, but that just cut through about an hour of argument," He turned to the other two mages, "If you want to try to block that, you can. I think the solution is obvious, someone with this much power needs training. We need to enter him into the Academy, now."

"It seems, we have no choice," Allen Denton agreed.

Regina nodded. I could see the emotions rolling within her. Jealousy, arrogance, hate, and underlying it all, fear.

Why would they fear me? I'm just a kid. Somehow I knew I would never get to be a kid again. When I left this place I would have to leave a man, or I wouldn't survive where I was going.

"Bring him to the Academy," Regina ordered Kharl with an imperious tone, "He starts in one week."

She turned and exited the house without even a glance in my direction. Allen followed, but I saw a fearful glance at me from the man.

As Gregor walked toward the door, he stopped in front of me. "Come see me when you are enrolled..." He looked at me questioningly.

"Colin."

"Colin Rourke," he finished. "I have a feeling things are going to be interesting around the Academy now. Your father upset things greatly when he attended. And he wasn't 'corrupted' by the infamous Kharl Jaegher and Kyra Nightwing."

He nodded to me and turned to Kharl and Kyra. "It'll be nice to get you two back in action as well."

I saw genuine happiness and excitement in his aura.

He laughed loudly, "We're living in interesting times, my friends. Interesting times, indeed."

Section 2
Mage

Chapter 10

The Mage Academy is located on the top of a mountain range in Montana. It's very close to Glacier National Park and completely hidden from view. When the plane landed at the small airstrip, near a ramshackle hanger, I was skeptical. But I was to find that most of the complex is underground, cut into the mountain range itself.

Kharl had needed to stay behind until later. He needed to turn his contracting company over to Giles Meldon, one of his head foremen. He had been planning this for some time because my eighteenth birthday was approaching. He really hadn't expected to do it quite this soon though and there was a bunch of paperwork involved.

Kyra had been able to quit her job much easier and she had come with me.

"Are you ready for this?" she asked.

"As ready as I'll ever be, I guess," I felt like I was infiltrating an enemy stronghold.

"There are some good Mages, son, like Gregor," she said in a soft voice, "Most of them are just scared of the Archmage. I'm sure you'll see why soon enough. Just try not to make waves and you'll do fine."

"I just want to learn how to control this power in me. I'm not here to make enemies," I chuckled, "I should be pretty good at blending in by now anyway."

She smiled, "Just remember, never drop your privacy shield. There are few Mages with the power you have and it would cause more trouble than good, I think. There aren't many Mages and they are a jealous lot."

"Hopefully I can come to the Guard barracks some. If for no other reason than to have you and dad kick my butt around a sparring ring."

"I think we could oblige you. Although, if you're feeling like getting a good lesson in humble, you should try to spar with Tien. He puts all the Guards in their place, even the Elites."

We entered the hangar and walked across a large space for the plane to be parked. On the other side sat a Soulguard, reading a book.

I saw the title and laughed, it was my favorite author. The sci fi series was about an alien invasion, and with the help of good aliens humans got to choose some of the weapons to fight them. They'd approached Sci fi writers to decide what to use and my favorite was the guys in the powered armor. It was a great series.

The Guard put his book down and looked questioningly at us.

"New arrival for Mage training," Kyra informed.

He looked at me, "You must be Colin Jaegher. I know Kharl and if you're half the man he is, you'll be the best of that lot."

The name was a bit of a surprise, but as we entered the door behind the guard, Kyra whispered, "We thought it best, with all the tension, not to bring up Kel right now."

"It's fine with me, you and Kharl are my parents," I answered, "I'm proud to carry either of your names."

"There'll be some tension from being a Soulguard's son, but I think it will be easier than being Kelvin Demonkiller's son. They almost deify that name in the Academy."

She looked at me seriously, "Don't take me wrong. He was my friend and we all loved him, but what he did is still remembered to this day and it's made the Mages much more cautious than they should be. He proved that they're mortal and it scared some of them."

I understood why it scared them. My father had killed nearly five thousand demons in that nest, working his way to the top of the clan. He'd finished with a group of Wraiths and all of their Soldier protectors at one time.

I actually understand what he did, now that I had fought Demons myself and it amazes me what he must have been capable of. According to Kharl and Kyra both, they feel more power from me than they'd ever felt from him. It scares the crap out of me.

The hallway we entered led to an elevator, where Kyra punched the button for the first floor below us.

"That's where you get off and go in for orientation. I go to the bottom, where the exits to the outside, lower down the mountain, lead to the Guard barracks," she said, "I love you son, and be careful."

We hugged and I stepped off the elevator when the door opened.

Chapter 11

I stepped into a waiting room with a desk at the far end. A woman sat behind the desk typing something on a computer keyboard in front of her. As I walked over, she stopped typing.

"May I help you?"

"Yes, Ma'am, I'm Colin Jaegher." I answered, "I'm supposed to report here for Mage training."

"You're the kid from Michigan," She nodded as she realized who I was, "We've been expecting you."

She motioned to a hallway that curved around to the left of her desk, "Head that way and take the fourth door on the left. You'll meet a Senior Mage there who will interview you then take you to the Dome for testing."

I nodded, "Thanks."

"Good luck."

The woman wasn't a Soulguard or Mage so the Guard must actually employ regular folks for some tasks. There weren't enough Mages to do stuff like this, anyway. According to Jack Riordan, there aren't over one hundred or so Mages in the whole United States. Maybe as much as seven hundred in the world.

And I couldn't see Kharl sitting behind a desk greeting newcomers as they came in the door either.

I turned left and walked down the slightly curving hallway. The compound must be round, because the hallway stretched in the other direction as well. Instead of curving right, it curved to the left.

At the fourth door I took a deep breath and turned the knob.

To my surprise, behind a large mahogany desk sat a smiling Gregor Kherkov.

"Welcome," Gregor's cheerful voice erased the sense of dread that had been building up, "I know, I could have told you I would be meeting you, but where's the fun in that?"

He laughed and motioned to a seat across from him, "Have a seat, Colin. The first thing I want to talk about is how in the hell you killed a Wraith and left a smoking crater where your school used to be."

I had been thinking about this for some time now, "I think the way I make shields is what killed the Wraith, Sir. I didn't even know what to expect when I Pulled. A lot of that power went straight into the shield instead of me."

He looked perplexed, "Exactly, how do you make shields?"

"Kharl told me that I can trust you," I opened my Inner Eye to see his aura, "Is this true?"

He looked at me for a few seconds, "Up to a point. I will not betray the Soulguard to keep a secret."

He spoke in total honesty. I didn't think keeping my secret would cause any problems there.

"The first thing, then, is I have a special talent that Kharl says no other Mage he's ever heard of can do. I can actually see the Soul and the Soulstream. Because of this, I can see shields and power flows."

"You can literally see them?"
"Yes."

He nodded, "And how does this affect your shield making?"

"No one told my how to make a shield. Kharl taught me to make a privacy screen. Over the years I figured out how to make a screen I don't have to concentrate to keep active. I weave the screen from my stream before it actually gets to me."

I saw amazement flash across his aura and even a bit of jealousy. He squashed that quickly and I could see his shame at feeling it in the first place. That, alone, would have convinced me that Gregor was a good man.

"I can see where that would be much easier to keep active," He nodded. "I take it, that your shield was also built this way?"

I nodded, "When I Pulled from the Source, a lot of the power went straight into my shield and probably saved my life."

"I can see the logic there. Next, when you Pulled, how much did you Pull? Did you just nudge it? Describe how you would call what you did."

"I Pulled with everything I had," I answered. "My Soulstream is a third bigger now than it was before then."

He looked at me in amazement again, "How big is it now?"

I held my fingers in a circle about twelve to fourteen inches in diameter, "Yours is about two or three inches bigger than mine."

"And you Pulled as hard as you could?"

"Yes Sir."

"Hmmm," he scratched his head as he thought about it. "This definitely gives me a lot to think about. And Kharl was right, there are no Mages who can actually see the Soulstreams. I can see where that would give someone an amazing advantage over the typical Mage. If I were you I would definitely keep that between us."

"I will."

"There are a few details we need to go over before going to the Dome. Your pay starts when you sign your papers. You receive $2,000 per month, payable at the end of training, until you are assigned your first post. There is a $2,000 sign on bonus, you receive that immediately after swearing the Oath. Kharl tells me that you swore the Oath years ago. The Oath is binding and the most important part of Soulguard training."

I had sworn to use my Soulguard training to fight Demons long ago. We use our power to fight Demons, not Humans. It is the foundation that the whole Soulguard is built upon. With the knowledge and power that we gain when we knot our Soulstreams, we could seize control of the world altogether. The Oath is what prevents that from occurring. The Soulguard enforces the Oath. Not even the most powerful Mage could stand up to the whole Soulguard in a circumstance like that.

"Everything is provided for you until your release from the Academy. This is standard for any Mage in training. Once you reach your first post, you receive $3,500 per month. Depending on where you are assigned, there may be some other things you'll be paid for such as housing and food. If you are in one of the larger stations there is housing already provided. I also need a next of kin to contact in case of emergencies. Kharl and Kyra, I assume?"

"Yeah," that sounded ominous, but I'll be fighting Demons so I expect I won't be dying of old age. Having some money might be nice, though.

"Let's get down to the Dome, then and you can show me some of this shield work. And we can test your weapon skills as well. Although, considering who trained you, you're probably better than our weapon trainer. I'll probably set your weapon training up with Tien Yueh, the Soulguard Weaponmaster."

Chapter 12

The Dome is a huge cavern located on the bottom level of the underground compound. It stretches at least five hundred yards across the bottom and is shaped like a dome. There are hallways leading off in three different directions from the Dome.

Two of them lead to locker rooms and showers, one for the men and one for the women. The other leads outside to where the Soulguard barracks is located.

The whole inside of the Dome is a giant shield with portals at the three hallways. As I looked around, I could see several massive tendrils leading down into the ground. The shield was fed by the Source with no one Pulling the power to do so.

"This is the Dome," Gregor motioned to the area in front of us, "It took twenty five mages to build the shield that covers the whole area. It's there so that Mages can use power inside without damaging their surroundings. Any power that hits the shield is absorbed and feeds its strength."

As I looked around I could see a few Soulguards sparring and at the far end there were several Mages. They looked like they were shooting balls of fire at shielded target dummies.

Gregor noticed where I was looking and chuckled, "You'll learn about fireballs soon enough. Today we're going to check this shield of yours and our weapon trainer will assess your weapon skills."

I followed Gregor across the open area toward an empty section, noticing several more guards coming inside.

"Jaegher's kid...new mage...a Wraith, don't believe..." I could hear voices in the distance. They were unaware I could hear them.

"First, I need to see a personal shield," Gregor began, "Raise one and I will inspect it."

I opened the portal on my privacy shield and it shimmered with power.

Gregor looked closely at it and looked puzzled, "If you look very closely, you can just see the shield around a person. It takes a bit of concentration but I can see it. Why does it not cover your palms?"

"To hold my swords and still use Soulfire in them," I answered.

He smiled, "If you were a Guard that would be a good idea, but a Mage can channel power without touching the sword. You can fill the shield in across the hand and still use Soulfire."

I nodded.

"Can you shield something while you stay outside of your shield?"

"I can try."

We approached an unshielded Target dummy. "Put a shield around the dummy and step as far back as you can and still hold it."

I built a shield from my stream about two feet around the dummy and anchored it into the earth. When it was done I backed up to where Gregor stood, about twenty feet from the dummy.

"You can hold it this far away?" Gregor asked.

"I think so, maybe farther. I haven't ever really tried to shield something with me on the outside."

"Back up until it falters and we'll see how far away you can get," He motioned back the way we came.

We walked fifty feet from the dummy before the shield began to dim a little.

"It dimmed a little, just now."

"Ok, I'm going to shoot a fireball at it and see how strong it is from this distance."

I watched as he formed a shield between his hands and Pulled from the Source. The power glowed as it flowed up his stream, but before it reached his body it formed a tendril to the shield and Soulfire began rolling within it. When the power level reached a certain point the far end of the shield ruptured and the fireball shot forward to slam into my shield.

All of this took place in just a few seconds, and when the fireball hit my shields, I jerked. I felt like someone had punched me in the gut. But my shield held.

"Sorry about that, I can see you felt that one," he put his hand on my shoulder, "It hurts less the closer you are to the shield."

"Most Masters can't make a shield like that, so I would say your shields are quite impressive. Shields are stronger as well when you are inside so that all the power radiates the same amount outward on all sides." He laughed, "But I really didn't want to shoot fireballs at you on your first day here."

"The biggest thing I can see that will need work is speed. And it won't hurt to learn how to make a conventional shield as well. I can see uses for both when dealing with Demons."

I actually agreed on that subject. I'd seen him make a shield around us at home, and it had been almost instant. Much faster than weaving one from my stream.

"You can drop the shield now, one fireball is enough for the first day," He laughed softly.

"Ah, here comes Justin. He's our weapon trainer for the Mages."

I watched as a tall, muscular man with blonde hair and large mustache made his way toward us.

We all turned as a small commotion took place at the other end of the Dome. I recognized Tien Yueh as he walked toward us. Justin nodded to the small Asian and Tien smiled.

"If you don't mind, Justin, I'll do this assessment," Tien spoke softly.

Justin smiled at Tien, then looked at me in pity, "Sure, Master Yueh, go ahead."

A Guard with a smirk on his face came forward carrying four practice wands, much like the ones I had used at home while sparring with Kyra. I read the anticipation in his aura. There seemed to be much of that in the Guards around the Dome as they gathered to watch.

There was another small commotion as Kyra also entered the dome and headed our way. She joined the group to watch. I could read humor and pride in her aura.

I accepted the two wands offered to me and made my way to an area that was painted just like the sparring ring at home. I stepped to one of the marked spaces for the contestants and nodded to Tien as he watched from the other contestant's space. He nodded in return and I heard the countdown begin.

"3...2..." The world slowed to a crawl, "1...Go!"

We met in the middle and began the Dance of Blades. At the beginning, we started slower than Kyra and I do, but this gave me time to work out some of his moves.

"Faster," he said softly and I sped up. He met my speed and we danced faster and faster. Our wands were striking faster and faster. He hit me several times to show me he could, and I strove harder.

"Halt!"

I hadn't hit Tien even once, and he'd hit me at least ten times. About what I'm used to anyway, they say spar, I say a Colin butt-kicking fest.

"I'm glad Tien took that one," Justin laughed, "That would have been embarrassing. Who trained you, Young Man?"

I looked toward Kyra and she gave me a small nod, "Kyra Nightwing is my mother and Kharl Jaegher my father. She trained me with weapons, Kharl trained me in unarmed combat," I answered.

He laughed loudly, "That explains a lot. Thanks Tien, you just got a new student."

The same Guard came and retrieved the practice wands. The smirk was gone and I read that he was impressed in his aura.

"About time we got a fighting Mage," He said with an approving smile.

Gregor approached and smiled, "I'm going to drop you with an instructor who is already having a session. But I think you'll probably benefit from the discussion."

Chapter 13

"Focus is the most important weapon of a Soulmage. If a Mage loses their focus, the Source is an unforgiving teacher. If a Mage loses their focus while Pulling strongly, the Source will turn them to ash. Always, remember that focus will save your life and lack of focus will kill you."

This was the beginning statement from the Senior Mage teaching the newest Mages. Her name was Nora Kestril and her Soul stream was nearly as big as Gregor's.

I could see the raw power rolling around inside of her aura as she stood in front of us.

"The larger the Pull a Mage attempts, the more danger to the Mage and those around them," she said, "Some of you know, personally, how dangerous Pulling can be."

She looked straight at me when she said that. "Some of you may think that a Mage has limitless power, but you'd be wrong. The more a Mage Pulls, the more bleed over flows into their body. Each Mage has a different tolerance level in their body. After you reach the limit, you burn."

I nodded in understanding. I can see how focus would be much harder if you can't see the streams and the power around you.

My focus doesn't have to be as great as most Mages because of my abilities. But it sounded like it needed to be as great as possible while using the Source and I needed to learn as much as I could about it. It might play a much larger part of my skills later, and nothing could be worse than needing something you just didn't bother to learn. If it helps me kill Demons more efficiently then I'm all for it.

"When we start with shield training, we will ascertain how much focus each of you possesses. From there, we can ascertain what skills in Mage craft to specialize in your training. Some Mages just aren't able to cope with some of the things needed to be a Battle Mage. There are a great many things a Mage can do whether or not he can master shield work or fireballs."

"Soon we will break for the day, and Colin, Someone will come to show you to your new quarters in the dorm," she motioned toward me, "Tomorrow at nine o'clock sharp, everyone is to meet in the Dome. Uniforms are required. This is a formal dispensation of the sentence passed on Warren Grimes for abuse of power. He will be permanently blocked from the Source. You are dismissed. Colin, follow me, we will go get your uniforms and meet someone to take you to your quarters."

***

I followed a woman through the hallway with my arms loaded down with four uniforms and a pair of boots. We had gone up three floors to the dorm ring.

"All of the student Mages are quartered in the dorm ring," she said, "The newest always gets the smallest room and we move up as others graduate. Gavin Price is the current Top, which is what we call the student with the most seniority."

The short red-headed woman really liked to talk. She was cute and her voice was easy to listen to, "He probably would be Top even if others were higher. He's the Archmage's son and he is the strongest of us in the dorm. He's always dropping his privacy shield so we all know it, too."

"He's actually a colossal prick but he has a group of followers who hang around swelling his ego even larger than it already is."

"Is it true, you killed a Wraith?"

It took me a minute to notice she'd actually stopped talking and was looking at me.

"Yeah," I answered, "It was pure luck though. I was almost burned alive."

"Everyone is talking about it. They say that you are as strong as Gregor Kherkov and he's the second strongest Mage in the US. The Archmage is the strongest in the whole world. If you are that strong, Gavin will probably die. He's been the strongest Mage in the dorm for two years now. It would kill him to find someone stronger just coming into the Guard. I know I'm not supposed to ask but are you? As powerful as Gregor Kherkov?"

"No," I said more sharply than I had intended, "I'm nowhere near that strong. I'm not here to replace this Gavin guy. I'm here to learn how to kill Demons."

I'd seen over a hundred people die at Morndel, and if I had been trained, they might have been saved. It still eats at me that all those people died because the Demons wanted me dead.

"I'm sorry," she said, her face red, and I didn't need to see her aura to tell she was embarrassed. "Sometimes I don't know when to stop talking."

"It's ok, I shouldn't have snapped at you," I returned, "I'm just a little nervous, this is my first day here."

"Oh, it's ok, sometimes people just get tired of hearing me talk all the time. My parents used to yell at me a lot when I got on their nerves. I catch myself just rambling on and on sometimes."

We stopped at a door, "Here are your quarters, there's a room, a closet, and a bathroom in each one. It's been nice meeting you, Colin, maybe I'll see you again tomorrow."

As she walked away, I realized that I hadn't even got her name. She talked nonstop all the way here and never said it. Being around her all the time would be exhausting, I thought and chuckled as I opened my door and stepped inside.

Chapter 14

I woke up early Tuesday morning and took a shower. I put on sweats and left the dorm to find a place to run. As I left I passed another Mage student who would barely even look at me. I opened my Inner eye and saw a Soulstream of about ten inches flowing into him.

"Good morning," I said in passing.

He just looked at me, arrogance and dislike flowing across his aura. His soul wasn't exactly ugly, but it wasn't very pretty, either. There were splotches of darkness throughout it.

I snorted and continued on. The more things change, the more they stayed the same. I'd seen people like him for years at Morndel Academy. The type who think that because they're rich or powerful, they're better than you.

I met another Mage, his stream somewhat smaller than the first, about seven or eight inches, and he smiled.

"You're the new guy aren't you?" he asked.

"Yeah, I'm Colin Jaegher," I answered with my hand outstretched.

He shook my hand, "I'm Darrel Barnes. I see you've met Gavin already."

He nodded toward the first Mage I'd passed, "He's the Top around here. Top of the heap, you might say."

"Not very friendly, is he?"

He snorted, "Not with the rumors going round about you. He'll see you as a challenge to his position, no matter how friendly you are. But, don't sweat it, he'll be out of here after this year. You'll only have to put up with it for ten more months."

I nodded, "Where can I go to get a good run in?"

"The Guards have a trail outside that covers about five miles. It's good for a run, or hike, those guys like to run straight up mountains and stuff. A couple of Mages use it but it's mostly Guards."

"Or you can run laps around the inside of the dome. There's a track laid out there but you gotta watch out for fireballs on the end with the targets. There usually isn't anyone there in the mornings though. Of course, there'll be people there today, cause of Grimes."

"I keep hearing about this Grimes guy, what did he do?"

"Abuse of power. He went to Vegas and used his power to cheat at a lot of casinos. Won over a million bucks. But he got caught and now he gets to pay for it. Permanent block from the Source."

"I see."

"Heh, at least he gets to keep the money. He's getting off easy, he wasn't a very good Mage anyway. Now he won't have to fight Demons and he gets a million bucks. He might actually be the smart one."

It was nearly seven thirty already so I gave up on my run for the day and decided to go get some breakfast. I'd seen a cafeteria the day before, so I headed there. It was on the second floor from the bottom.

When I got there I found about twenty Guards already there, "New Mage..."

"..sparred with Yueh ..."

Soulguard | Christopher Woods

"..fighting mage...Jaegher's boy..."

I heard several mutters as I made my way across the room. I smiled and waved to several who were looking in my direction. Some of them nodded or waved back. I opened my Inner eye to find quite a few of the Guards were angry.

"Mages have a Mess hall on the fourth floor, Youngster," An older guy standing behind the food with a plate in hand, whispered. "Not saying you can't eat here. Mages don't come here much."

At least I knew what the hostility was about, "This looks good," I said while eying the spread, "Bacon, eggs, biscuits and gravy."

He nodded and began filling a plate, I saw a little approval in his aura. Maybe I'd passed a test or something. I don't know, I was really hungry and hadn't eaten since yesterday morning.

As I sat down Kyra walked into the Mess hall. When she saw me I could see the question in her aura but I could also see that she was glad I was there. She got her tray of food from the same guy I did and sat down across from me.

"How's the Mage training, son?"

"It's ok I guess," I answered, "I haven't really learned much yet. It's only been a day. I did see Gregor shoot a fireball yesterday. I think I could probably shoot one except I'm not sure how I'm supposed to gauge how much I Pull from the Source."

"I'd think they'll cover that soon enough," she returned, "Don't get too impatient with the Mages, they don't have the same advantage you do. Lord knows, you learn skills faster than anyone I've ever seen. You manipulated your Soulstream about as fast as we could tell you it was possible."

"You even did something to it later that made it feel different. Stronger than before, but different. Just keep in mind, all that the Mages know have been passed down from the original Mages. I'm not sure innovation is what they appreciate. Not that you'd ever do things the way you want instead of how you're told to," She laughed.

My face turned a little red, "I don't know what you're talking about," I returned innocently.

She just gave me the look that both she and Kharl had cultivated over the years.

"Oh, and Kharl should be here by the end of the week. We expect some sparring time, so make sure you allow some time for it in your busy schedule," she winked, "we won't be too hard on you. I think Tien will take care of that."

"Oh, joy."

She laughed again. I'm not sure why my mom takes so much pleasure in beating me up. According to Kharl, it's because she is a woman and all women are crazy. In my very limited experience, I'm beginning to see his point.

Chapter 15

There were about thirty Mages at the Academy, including the trainers and every one of them was in the Dome. There weren't many Soulguards present, but this was a Mage thing.

Nora Kestril had positioned us all in a circle around a single mage. He was a slightly overweight man with a Soulstream not much bigger than a Guard's. His aura didn't show any evil in it but I could tell he actually wanted this. Some people don't have the right mindset to be Guard.

Mages don't have a choice. If you have the power you almost have to be trained or you'll flame yourself. People who don't know about us call it spontaneous combustion, but we know it's a Mage who Pulls. There aren't many of these, but Mages are rare anyway.

This was also the first time I actually saw the Archmage. He was a tall black-haired man with an arrogance that looked like it flowed off him in waves. His aura rolled with power and it had large ugly patches flowing through it. He wasn't totally evil, but he'd definitely done some bad things.

His Soul stream was huge, it dwarfed mine. It even dwarfed Gregor and Nora's streams. When I looked at him I saw why everyone deferred to Gavin.

"Warren Grimes," The Archmage's voice was deep and it resonated across the Dome, "You stand accused of abuse of power. Do you understand and accept these charges?"

Grimes nodded, "Yes sir, I do."

"Then judgment will be carried out this day. You will be blocked from Pulling the Source now and forever more," He said with finality.

Five mages stepped forward, one in the lead and four standing in a line behind him. The lead Mage stopped in front of Grimes and the four flanked him. The center Mage Pulled. A tendril of power reached from the lead Mage to begin wrapping around the Soulstream of Grimes.

The tendril knotted around the stream and cinched down tight leaving a very small stream of life-force flowing into the man. Grimes gasped and slumped over a little.

Then the Mage Pulled a large amount of power and pushed the center of his tendril down into the Earth, right into the Source.

His aura dimmed as he countered the force of the Source trying to flow back into the tendril. The other four Pulled power and lay their hands on the lead Mage. The power they pulled was pushed into the lead Mage's aura which brightened again.

The lead Mage then tied the tendril off inside the Source and severed his Source Pull. The knot remained around Grimes' stream permanently fed by the Source.

"Sentence is passed," boomed the voice of the Archmage.

Chapter 16

I stood looking into the mirror at my Soul. The flows of power don't flow around in mine like most Souls do. The way I had designed my streams interface with my body actually makes my whole Soul glow brightly. All except the empty spot.

Right in the center of my Soul is an empty spot. I don't know what it is, maybe that's the reason I can see the streams. In all my poking around I'd never found any way for the empty space to be filled. It doesn't feel like it's a bad spot or anything, just empty.

I shut my Inner eye and shook my head. There's no use worrying about it. It's always been there and never hurt me yet.

I'd come back from a run outside on the Soulguard's trail. It was awesome. It ran straight up the mountainside and circled around up near the top, then right back down. It was a great run with lots of places to jump around like Kharl always fusses at me for.

Kharl had arrived the week before and the Guard was enthusiastic about his return, to say the least. He is a well-liked man in the Guard and I could see why. I've known him my whole life and he is the Soulguard personified.

The values he holds dear are the ones that make the Guard what it is, loyalty, honor, and duty. If I can be half the man he is, I'll consider my time in the Guard a success.

***

"Shield crafting is probably the most important skill a Mage can learn," Nora Kestril stated, "I'm a little more partial to shields, since that is my specialty."

"We will start with each of you, in turn, crafting a shield that covers a marked area in the floor. I will judge how strong the shield is and we can go from there. Focus is most important while crafting shields. Shields are crafted without Pulling from the Source and you always have to focus on the shield to keep it going. The larger the shield, the more focus it takes to hold."

She turned to Gavin Price, A tall, dark-haired man with arrogance flowing across his aura in waves. I glanced at the others in this class to see a wide variety of emotions about Gavin.

Darrel had distaste rolling across his aura. Paige Turner, the talkative red-head I had met when I first got here, was feeling about the same. Several of the others that I hadn't met yet showed fear and a few were loyal to him.

He walked to the center of a circle drawn in the floor of the Dome.

"Start," Nora stated.

A barrier of energy swelled from Gavin to surround the Mage. Then he pushed it out to the lines in the floor.

When he was done, Nora concentrated on the shield for a moment and nodded, "Very good, it's strong enough, But I wouldn't try to do much bigger.

Soulguard | Christopher Woods

You'll sacrifice strength for area and it could hurt you in the end."

"Paige, your turn."

Paige stepped into the circle as Gavin stepped out. Her shield took much longer and I could see it was a lot weaker as well.

"You'll have to practice on speed, Paige," Nora said as she concentrated on the shield, "And you'll have to keep the shield smaller to be strong enough to hold. But don't let it bother you, we need supports as much as we need Battle Mages."

I'd learned that what the other four Mages at Grimes' sentencing had been doing was to support the Mage doing the actual block. That is the function of support Mages, to help the one doing the action by pushing life-force into them.

I could see a bit of disappointment in Paige's aura. I guess support Mages are not very high in the hierarchy.

"Colin."

I stepped to the center of the circle and began weaving a shield from my stream. It took a moment to finish and Nora was looking at me with a strange look.

"That was very slow," She said, and I could see a sneer on Gavin's face, "But I've never seen a shield this strong in my life. I don't feel you Pulling."

Gavin's sneer was gone and I saw disappointment and jealousy flowing across his aura.

"Is this the kind of shield you used at Morndel?"

I nodded, "I had Mattie to help keep the Demons off while I crafted it though. I've been practicing, trying to get faster but its slow work."

"Can you describe how you make it?" Gavin's jealousy was growing. What the hell is it with the guy?

"I guess the easiest way to describe it is that I weave a shield straight from my Soulstream instead of Pushing it out from inside. It's slow but once it's done, I don't have to focus on it to keep it active. My Soulstream feeds it automatically."

Her eyes were widened in understanding, "And how did you learn to do this?"

"I was only Guard trained, I never even met A Mage until after the thing at Morndel. All I had to go on were descriptions from Kharl and Kyra and that wasn't much. But since I couldn't use the Source, I experimented with other things and this is what I came up with."

"Interesting," she said thoughtfully, "I'd like to see you later today if you don't mind. I want a detailed description of what you do. This could be quite beneficial to the Mages."

"Ok, Darrel," she turned back to the trainees.

I took down my shield by snipping the tendril that began the weave and the whole thing dissolved.

Darrel met me with a wide smile and I saw satisfaction in his aura. His shield was good, as fast as Gavin but not quite as strong.

"Can you show me how you do that?" Paige asked quietly, "I don't want to be just a support Mage."

"Sure I'll show you, and I've got a few more things I learned as well."

Chapter 17

"My focus is a little less than others but I have a photographic memory," Paige said, "If I see something I can remember it. It's like a curse here though, I can remember it if I see it but I never actually see it."

I could read the frustration in her aura.

"Hang on a sec," I concentrated and made my Soulstream glow.

She gasped, "Wow."

I slowly wove the shield around us as she watched avidly. Not a word coming from her mouth as she soaked it up. When I was done, the shield was glowing.

She laughed happily, "I can do this."

I snipped the tendril and the shield dissolved.

She concentrated and I watched her stream spout a tendril that wove itself around us as she repeated exactly what I had done. When she finished she clapped and bounced happily.

"I did it! I can feel it staying up by itself!"

"Now if you want to make it bigger, push out with your mind."

She pushed and the shield expanded. Then she pulled inward on it and it shrank in size.

"Oh thank you! Thank you!" She bounced around and grabbed me and kissed me. Then she laughed and snipped the tendril and ran out of the Dome.

I saw two female Guards whispering a little ways off but I could hear them with my heightened senses.

My face turned red as one of them said, "I'd give him a tumble, Mage or not."

The other one laughed, "Jaegher's kid... might be fun."

I headed for the exit with my face burning. I'm not the most experienced person with women. Well, actually, not experienced at all.

***

"Before any Mage Pulls from the Source, they must have an idea how much power it will take to do what the Mage is trying to do. When you Pull too much, it is dangerous," Nora said, "Here is where practice is essential. Today we will learn how much each of you need to shoot a fireball."

"The amount of force used in a Pull is different for each Mage due to the difference in size of the Soulstream. A Mage with a large stream doesn't have to pull as hard as one with a smaller stream."

"Some of you have already done this and I want you to go first. We'll start with Gavin. Gavin has practiced a great deal in the Dome and has shown a good deal of skill in crafting fireballs."

Gavin walked forward and faced the target dummy about forty yards from him. He shaped a round shield about two feet in diameter in front of him and Pulled.

Just like Gregor's had done, the power filled the shield to a certain pressure then ruptured the far side where a weaker section of the shield was placed. A fireball shot forward and hit the dummy.

It was soaked up by the shield around the target and I watched as the power flowed down into the ground and dissipated into the shield around the Dome.

"Our first effort will be to make the weakened area the right strength to hold until the right pressure. Darrel, I want you to make your shield and leave the weakness where you feel it should be. Then Pull and we will see."

Darrel stepped forward and crafted his shield. The shield was pushed out from inside of him like a regular shield, only it rests between the hands. I could see the excitement rolling through his aura. This was his first try at a fireball. He Pulled and turned the power into the shield. The end ruptured too soon and his fireball didn't fire in a straight line. It fell to the ground well before the target.

I heard a snicker from Gavin's direction, it could have been him or any of the four followers that trailed him everywhere.

Darrel's aura was rolling with embarrassment, anger and disappointment.

"That's ok, Darrel, now try to reinforce the weakness a little more. Don't add much at a time, the whole purpose today is to establish where the right level is for each of you."

Darrel repeated the process with a bit better success this time. The fireball reached the target but it wasn't strong enough yet.

"Just a tiny bit stronger now," Nora coached.

Darrel did it once more and the fireball looked much as Gavin's had. It was soaked into the shield. His excitement was back and satisfaction rolled through his aura as well.

I watched as seven people were shown how to fire a fireball. As they were doing that I crafted a shield from my stream. It rested about chest level on my Personal shield and I made an opening on the far side with a weaker spot in the shield just as everyone else had.

At the base where my stream was I put a portal much like the one for my personal shield. This would allow me to turn the thing down to a passive level like my shield or open it to shoot the fireball.

"Ok, good job. Now Colin, I'm combining the fireball training with your first Source Pull so we will work on both levels at the same time. First I want you to make your shield, and then I want you to Pull very gently. We'll see from there where the Pull needs to be adjusted."

I opened the portal for the fireballer and reached down into the Source and Pulled with my mind. The power surged up and I steered it into the fireballer. I already knew it was too much before it hit the fireballer but I couldn't do anything about it but let it go on.

The end of my shield erupted four times before the power was through.

"Crap," I mumbled.

"Way too strong, Colin," Nora stated, "but good for a first Pull. Now Pull softer and let's see what happens."

I Pulled just a tiny bit at the Source and the power flowed up my stream much slower this time.

It filled my shield and ruptured like it should this time. The fireball flew straight into the target and was absorbed like the others.

"Very good," Nora said, "Now there's one more thing. Sometimes there is a need for a more powerful fireball than is standard and each one of you will have to find the highest output you feel comfortable with. Each of you will pick a target dummy and practice. Increase your Pull a bit and make the rupture stronger. But never make the rupture stronger than the shield or it gets ugly."

She nodded at me, "Feel free to use the dummy you're already facing, Colin."

She turned to the group, "Do not look at this as competition, Some Mages are stronger than others. It's a fact of life. What we want to know is where you are comfortable at in using power."

I looked at my shield and made a portal on the other side of the fireballer, then changed my mind and made it like the other Mages did with the rupture.

Now is not the time for innovation, I thought.

The rupture I made was just a little bit weaker than the shield. I Pulled again about like I did the first time and power surged into the fireballer. It rolled around and around inside and I was beginning to worry a little when the rupture burst.

The fireball slammed into the target with a tooth jarring explosion. The shield soaked it up but I watched as the power flowed almost halfway up the Dome before dissipating.

"Holy crap," I mumbled. I turned and saw everyone looking at me. I saw a mix of emotions on their auras. The predominant one was fear. In Gavin's aura I saw jealousy and hate.

Why does he hate me? I'm just doing what I'm told. I guess I'll never understand some people. We're here to fight Demons. When you get a powerful ally in the fight shouldn't that be a good thing?

What's worse is he's never even said a word to me. I've said hello several times to be snubbed at every turn. He just decided he had to hate me so his followers do the same. But they're too scared to actually say anything.

***

"The greatest part to the personal shield is that it works as a privacy screen as well," I said to Paige and Darrel, "The portal allows you to set the strength of the flow into it. Just leave a trickle to make a screen and open it wide for the shield."

"Doesn't closing the portal kill it all together?" Darrel asked, watching my shield as I pointed to the different parts I talked about.

"Nope, if you actually cut it, it will dissolve, but just closing the portal leaves it intact. Everything I weave from my stream is still there unless I actually cut it loose."

"I can't light it up like that though," Paige said after concentrating.

"I'm not sure but that may be something special I can do. There's so much I don't know about my skills. Now that I can actually use the Source, I'm finding new things all the time."

I looked at Paige, "With a memory like yours, can you draw what you see. I've never seen an illustration of the things we do. Wouldn't it be so much easier to focus your mind on something if you could see what you want to create first?"

"Sure, I can draw this stuff. All the Mage things we are taught are based on simplicity. I'm sure someone has tried more complicated things before, maybe there are some things in the archives."

Chapter 18

It was my eighteenth birthday and I was about to report to Tien Yueh for a new butt kicking session. I thought Kharl and Kyra had been tough, but Yueh is awesome. The man moves faster than a cobra and hits like a truck at the same time. It really is a good reminder to anyone that there is always someone better.

I'd been at the Academy for three months now, and I'd been to weapon training with Yueh every other day for at least an hour. I liked the sparring, even though it was painful in the extreme. When I'm sparring I feel alive, I feel an exultation I've only felt once before. When Mattie and I were fighting real Demons, I had felt this feeling. It's like *this* is what I am made for. I don't know, maybe I'm a little off.

I left my quarters to head down and looked up to find Regina Worthington closing the door to Gavin's quarters. She looked back at me with a dazzling smile that would have melted me into goo if I wasn't looking at the hate rolling through her ugly aura. I forced a smile in return and turned away, toward the elevators.

As I approached the Dome I could hear Tien talking, "You must always keep your focus. If you lose your focus you make mistakes. Mistakes will kill you when facing Demons."

He looked up as I entered the Dome, "Ahh, the Mageguard finally shows up."

He'd taken to calling me that when I started training under him. I consider it a compliment. Most Guards have a low opinion of most Mages, but since they call me a fighting Mage, I'm accepted by them. It didn't hurt that they thought Kharl and Kyra were my parents either.

"I'm only a few minutes late, Master Yueh."

"A few minutes can be an eternity in the Soulguard, Young Man," he admonished, "Today we will practice with the swords."

Each day, it was a different style of weapon that he tested me with. Swords were by far my best weapon, but I had learned a great deal from Yueh about several kinds of weapons. Staves, daggers, clubs of various sizes, and even a huge battle axe that looks like it came straight out of a fantasy movie.

It was much too big for a normal person to wield but Soulguards are far above normal. It was actually pretty fun to use but the twin short swords are my favorites.

"Today I want you moving as fast as you possibly can, Colin. You have a bad habit of just moving fast enough to keep up with me. Today will be the test of your true limits," Yueh smiled as two more people entered the Dome.

Kyra and Jack Riordan both waved at me. Then they both entered the ring with us.

Oh crap, this is gonna hurt, I thought.

"A Soulmage has a Soul stream more than twice the size of a Soulguard," Tien Yueh continued, "It stands to reason he should be able to tap much more potential than a guard. Discovering that potential is what training is about."

The four of us took our place in a very large sparring ring and a Guard approached with an arm-load of practice wands. He looked at me with pity as he handed me two of them. The others each took two wands as I stretched my muscles to limber up.

"3...2..." The world slowed down, "1...Go!" the Guard's voice boomed.

We began the Dance and I was hit from three directions. I sped up and blocked Kyra's next swing, but Jack's still got me as well as Tien's. It's very hard to concentrate while three Elite Soul-guards whale on you. Faster and faster we danced.

One hit caught me close to the kidney and it hurt. Rage flashed through me for a split second, but with it came a focus I've never been able to achieve before this. The world slowed to a crawl, my Soul stream pulsing with power. I spun from the middle of the trio and landed three blows into Tien's mid-section. Before he could react, I was behind Kyra to land two blows in quick succession and spun away from her return to land four cracks across Jack's midsection.

I dodged around their swings and started to make another pass when I heard a voice speaking very slowly, "Halt!"

We all slowed ourselves back to normal. My chest was heaving and my muscles felt like they were vibrating.

"...You see that?...three of them...hit them all...fighting mage..." I heard whispers from the Guards who'd been watching.

All three Elites were sweating and breathing hard. Kyra's aura blazed with pride.

"I told you you'd be better," She said.

"I'm impressed," Jack agreed.

"Not better," I returned, "Just faster."

I was amazed at what had just happened. In all the years of sparring with my mother, I'd never gotten past her defenses. And I'd just gotten past her, Jack, and the Weapon Master of the Academy. Amazing.

"That is what I was looking for," Tien stated, "In America you are probably the best Mage with weapons. In the Far East, there are many more of what we call Mageguards. They train as a Soulguard, like you, and then a Mage. They have more leeway because they aren't directly under the supervision of the Archmage."

"He seems to think Mages are above this sort of thing and he's powerful enough to make his feelings policy," Jack agreed.

Kyra nodded and pointed at my hands, "You need to take a run to work off the excess energy you're carrying. You're vibrating."

"I think I will," I returned as the same Guard came to retrieve the wands. I saw amazement in his aura and a bit of fear. Why fear? I wondered.

I headed to the edge of the Dome and began running around the outside edge to work off the excess energy. I saw one of Gavin's followers, Kurt Yarden, as I passed and his aura was showing fear too. What is the problem with everyone? I wondered.

***

Soulguard | Christopher Woods

It seems that my birthday was to be filled with surprises. I returned to my quarters that evening to find Paige, waiting for me. We'd been practicing with shields over the last few months and I had not only shown her the shield but taught her the way I made the fireballer. She was a lot higher in the standings now to become a Battle Mage.

"I heard it was your birthday," She said softly, "and I owe you so much for all you've done for me. I thought I could do something special for you."

I saw several things in her aura, none of them fear, and my eyes widened in surprise as she stepped toward me, wrapped her arms around me and pulled me close.

Sex amongst the Guard is not only allowed, but actually encouraged because of our need for secrecy. If it's kept in house it's much easier to deal with.

As she pulled me toward the bed, tendrils of our Soulstreams intertwined. I was clumsy at first but it's a great advantage to be able to see the reactions of everything you do. We fell asleep in each other's arms afterward.

I have to say it was the greatest birthday I'd ever had.

Chapter 19

"Not much is still known about the man who created the Soulguard around eight hundred years ago," Nora Kestril said, "He was born around 1200 AD maybe a little later. He was a Knight in one of the Crusades until he came back from the wars to find his home ravaged by Demons. There had been some witnesses and Greyson Kent had started his own Crusade to find a way to battle these monsters."

"It's not very clear how he learned to do the things he did, but he discovered how to knot his Soulstream and he trained anyone he deemed worthy to join his cause. He called them the Soulguard and they began the fight to save Humanity from these Demons. It's not clear what skills he possessed, but they called him a Soullord. Maybe it was from being the man in charge or he may have been something other than a Mage."

"Over the years the Guard has grown to a multi-continental organization. We have a central base on each continent, except Antarctica. There are two in Asia due to the size of the continent and the population there."

"We are not subject to the rule of any government because our Mandate is to fight Demons, not other Humans. We don't participate in Humanity's wars amongst themselves. When a person joins the Guard, they swear the oath to the Guard. It is an oath that is enforced by every Mage and Guard. If a Guard or Mage uses their power against Humanity, they are permanently tied from the Source and exiled from the Guard."

"If their crime is particularly severe, the penalty can be death by severing them completely from the Source. It is a horrible way to die. The body withers away and dries up into something resembling a mummy from Egypt. I've only seen this once and it was enough."

***

"Come on, you know you want to," I heard voices ahead of me, near the showers. I was supposed to meet Paige and go to dinner at the Mess hall together.

"I've seen you going into that Guard scum's room. Maybe you should try a *real* Mage out for a change."

"Not likely, you prick." I heard Paige's voice and the rage almost surfaced.

I've carried a rage inside of me for years. Very seldom does it surface, I keep it locked away because it scares me to know I can feel something so primal and revel in it. I had touched it at Morndel when the Demons had attacked but I never let it out completely.

It was surging dangerously close to the surface as I strode around the corner.

"Let go!!" Paige exclaimed, jerking her arm from his grasp.

"I'll show you..." He began as he dropped his privacy shield to let her feel his Power.

Soulguard | Christopher Woods

Her Soulstream is about six inches in diameter and his is around ten. The power difference is more than that sounds. He's actually about three times as powerful as Paige and he intended to intimidate her with it.

My stream is actually fifteen inches in diameter, I'd actually broken down and measured it one day, which means I'm probably about three times as powerful as he is. I did probably the dumbest single thing I've ever done in my life. If I'd known all the repercussions from this one act, I might have done things different. But I didn't.

Paige saw me an instant before I reached Gavin Price. I grasped his shoulder and spun him around. He turned with a snarl, then a sneer as he recognized me. I let him get a good look and dropped my screen.

"Never touch her again," I said softly, my eyes crackling with the Soulfire my rage was sparking.

His aura flooded with shock at what he could sense and then with terror as he realized exactly what I could do to him. He turned in terror and fled down the hallway.

"Oh my God," Paige murmured.

She wrapped her arms around me and some of the intensity of the moment eased and I pushed my rage back down inside.

"Oh Colin," she shook her head, "You shouldn't have done that. He will never forgive you, now. There's nothing but trouble for anyone who makes an enemy of the Archmage. And if you're the enemy of his son, you're his enemy."

"I couldn't let it go, I'm sorry," I returned, the rage subsiding.

"You don't need to apologize to me," she laughed softly, "But there will be trouble for you after standing up for me. He couldn't do anything more than intimidate me, or, Archmage's son or not, he would face the penalty for abuse of power. Possibly stronger charges."

"Sometimes I just can't abide things," I said, "and the bastard's arrogance and attitude have been grating at me for months. I'll face the repercussions when I have to. Now I think we were supposed to have dinner together. I think I've had enough of arrogant Mages, shall we eat in the Guard Mess?"

"That would be nice, if they don't mind the company of a couple of Mages," she returned and locked her arm in mine as we walked down the hallway toward the elevators.

Chapter 20

Paige put her fork on her plate as she finished her dinner. She, Darrel, and I met in the Guard's Mess hall every Tuesday and the Guards were used to us by now. Darrel didn't really understand why I always wanted to eat there but he got along with the Guards much better than he used to.

"So, I found something interesting in the archives about Greyson Kent. One of the manuscripts mentioned that the way he chose his Soulguards was to look into their Souls. If they were deemed worthy, he recruited them. Maybe that's part of being a Soullord," she paused to take a breath.

I held my hand out to Darrel.

"Man, I hate you," he said and handed me twenty dollars.

"What was that about?" Paige asked.

"He bet me you wouldn't stop to take a breath for thirty seconds after you finished eating and started talking," Darrel pointed at me, "I figured maybe ten seconds, but thirty?"

She glared at me then at Darrel, and back at me as the seconds counted down, "Piss off, the both of ya"

"Aagh!" I handed him back his twenty and he beamed.

"He also bet you'd not wait more than five seconds to give some rude remark, I chose fifteen," He said snidely.

Her mouth dropped open and she turned to the Guard on her left, "Do you believe this?"

102

The Guard hid a smile, "I was shooting for fifteen on both bets."

She turned back to us, "Hmmph, guess who's sleeping alone tonight? Care to bet on that?"

She stood up and with her head held high, carried her plate to the counter and walked out, not even glancing our way.

The Guards around our end of the room burst into laughter and I jumped up, "Wait a minute, Baby, you know I was kidding."

As I left the room I heard the Guards' laughter all the way down the hall.

***

It had been two days since the incident with Gavin and I'd only seen him once. Hate and fear had rolled across his aura at the sight of me. I was sitting in the Guard Mess hall when Allen Denton walked in and approached me.

"You've been summoned to the Archmage's office," He said with some satisfaction. He'd said it loud enough for the few Guards present to hear it. I guess I was about to be an example.

Rage boiled inside me, under the surface as I stood and followed Denton out the door. I felt dread as I followed the man to the elevator and quietly rode up to the upper level where the senior Mages all had offices.

He showed me to the door and said with an arrogant sneer, "He's expecting you."

I opened the door and walked into a very opulent office. The desk was of some beautiful wood and it was huge. The Archmage sat in a chair behind it with power rolling around in his aura.

"You are new to the Academy, Colin," He looked at me with dead eyes, "But even you should know better than to threaten my son."

"He threatened my girlfriend," I returned evenly.

"Did he?" surprise flowed across his aura.

"Neglected to tell you the entire story, I see," I returned.

The Archmage sighed, "Be that as it may, no one threatens my son, and especially not some jumped up Guard. I don't think you really understand who I am."

He dropped his screen and I could feel the waves of power rolling off of him. I'd never felt anything so terrifying in all my life but the rage was beginning to surface.

"So basically you're saying that what your son wants, he gets."

He looked at me with those dead eyes and gave a small nod.

"That's fine with me," I answered, "He can have anything he wants."

My eyes were smoldering and I was seeing him through heat waves, "Except what's mine."

"I don't care about you, I don't care about your son, and I've never said one thing out of turn to the man. But because the lady decided to be with me, he feels he must try to take her."

"I'm not here to compete with him or you or anyone else. I'm here to learn to kill Demons. Who's

in charge of this place? You or the spoiled brat caus-
ing problems?"

I dropped my screen also and faced the
Archmage squarely. My rage speaking now, "I know
you're strong, but I wonder how much of that you
can handle without flaming out. I know for a fact I
can use every ounce of what I have and if that's the
way you want it, bring on the fire! You'll know I was
here."

I had no idea if I could actually back my
words, but my rage was in charge of this one. I
turned my back to the most powerful Mage in the
world, who was fuming, and walked out of his office
without another word.

Chapter 21

I entered the dome with the two swords gifted to me by my mother. Rage still boiled in me so I went to the end where the shielded dummies stood and drew them. My anger seethed as I began the Dance. Fury fueled by the sheer absurdity of the situation.

Had I really just threatened the Archmage? What the Hell is wrong with me? Where does all this rage come from?

I danced the blades faster and faster Pulling the Source as I sped up more and more. My swords began to glow with the Soulfire coursing through my body. Faster and faster I spun until finally with a scream of pure fury, all of the power pouring into me surged down my blade and screamed across the space between me and the targets in a razor sharp arc.

It destroyed three shielded dummies before weakening enough to be absorbed by the Dome shield. Power fluctuated all across the shield as it dissipated.

I stood dead still in shock staring at the splintered dummies as the shields began taking their shape once more.

A voice rumbled from behind me, "Damn, Son."

I turned to see Kharl standing with five other Guards who were staring at me in awe.

"Your meeting with the Archmage went that bad?" he asked.

"You could say it went bad, but it would be an understatement," I returned sadly.

"Tell me."

***

"You did what?!" Kyra looked at me like I was an idiot. Which I probably am, by the way.

I'd followed Kharl back to the Guard barracks out in the front of the mountain the Academy is carved into. We were sitting in the quarters shared by Kharl and Kyra. The subterfuge that we were using about my parentage meant that they were a "couple".

I don't think it bothered them at all, having spent the last eighteen years together.

She stared at me like I was a strange experiment that might have to be destroyed.

"I know," I shook my head, "I don't know what I was thinking."

"I said don't make waves not Hey why don't you threaten to rip the Archmage's son a new one and while you're at it, tell the Archmage, the most powerful Mage in the *world*, to piss off. Friggin Rourkes, they're all the same," she began pacing around the room, her hand to her forehead, "Jump right in the deep end, no clue how to swim, just jump right in!"

Kharl was looking at me like I had never really seen before. With the respect of one man looking at his equal. Not that Kharl would look down on anyone, but I was that crazy kid he was raising. Now he looked at me with more respect than I'd ever seen him give anyone but the Elites and Gregor.

"Oh, calm down," He rumbled, "He said what everyone else wants to say and doesn't have the nerve to. The truth, something we've always been advocates for."

"But you've made a powerful enemy in the Archmage. One day, the repercussions will be felt. He's a hater, son, and he's got patience. The son doesn't have patience, he's the one to worry about for now."

He sighed, "Well, on a lighter note, some friends of yours will be here next week to start training. Maybe they'll be able to curb your enthusiasm to take on the Mage Academy, single handed."

"You've seen Trent, you big ox, he'll probably ask to roast hotdogs in the fires as the Academy burns to the ground," Kyra snorted, "and while everyone's not looking the girl will probably stab someone."

"Yeah, that's what I'm saying, they'll curb his enthusiasm. I mean, I'm pretty sure that's less severe than what this one's already done."

"You've got a point," Kyra returned. "I could just beat the shit out of Gregor, 'interesting times', he said."

Chapter 22

"You had a meeting with the Archmage, didn't you?" Paige asked, "I heard you went up to his office and everyone felt it when he dropped his screen. It was about the other day wasn't it? It would have been better to leave it alone."

I nodded.

"What was that you did in the Dome afterward? Some of the Guards told me you did something with a sword and destroyed three dummies right through the shield."

"I was venting some of the frustration from my meeting with that self-righteous bas... the Archmage."

She looked at me for a few minutes but I wasn't about to tell her what the Archmage had said to me in his office. She might just do what they want to protect me and I couldn't live with that. I know how I am and I would do something monumentally stupid if that happened. It's not that I'm a jealous person, but she doesn't want to sleep with Gavin. If she wants to, she's free to do what she wants. But to be forced by someone else or even circumstance is unacceptable and I would probably kill Gavin Price, damn the consequences.

"On a different note," I changed the subject, "Did you get a chance to draw any of the shields we talked about?"

"I drew the personal shield exactly like yours," she reached into a black satchel she carried and pulled out a stack of papers, "and I started on the fireballer. I found some things in the archives, but no diagrams, there were just descriptions. There were surprisingly few papers in there about Mage skills. You would think there would be more. Everything has been passed down over the years by instruction alone. I don't think new things are discovered very often because of the danger of experimenting with the Source."

"I think it was what Greyson Kent showed the first mages," I said, "Think about it, it was in the 1200's so if you wanted to create a strong weapon, what would you base it on? Maybe a catapult, throwing huge balls of fire."

"That makes sense, but you would think there would be some change over the years," she returned.

"I think there are some new things, I bet most Mages have skills that other Mages don't know. Like a personalized skill that only you know. We need to talk to some of the other Mages and discover some of these things so we can do diagrams of them too."

"I can't see their things to draw them, Colin."

"I can see them. If I learn these skills I can show them to you. You can draw diagrams and every Mage can learn."

"I'll talk to some of the Mages, you talk to some of the Guards. I bet they've seen all sorts of things you might be able to use for this. Some of them are over a hundred years old and I know they've seen a lot."

"Do you think a Guard could make the personal shield? It doesn't require a Pull and I can see great benefit for them. I'd like to take your diagram to the Guard barracks today and see if I can get some volunteers to try it."

She nodded in agreement, "Oh, Yeah, the Guard will definitely be able to use it. They learn as much focus as we do and they manipulate their streams to knot them like they do. I would almost guarantee that, at least, some of them could use the shield."

She pushed the papers away from her and looked at me, "It looks like we have a couple of hours before reporting. What could we possibly do to pass the time?" she said with a finger twisting a curl of her red hair.

"I'm sure we'll think of something," I answered with a smile and leaned toward her. All the worries of the Archmage and his son, shield making, and Mage craft faded as our souls began to intertwine.

***

"Today we will test your proficiency in the use of shields and the fireball. We will be testing speed and strength of both."

I'd spent the last few months practicing and a few weeks ago I'd had an epiphany. If I can carry around a personal shield ready to be activated, why can't I carry a fireballer and a few different kinds of shield as well? The answer, no reason whatsoever. I designed three different shields with a portal to feed each one. They all had the same size feeder tendrils. Each could be used separately, or all could be used together to add to the strength. It all depended on the situation. If I was completely on defensive I could use all three. If I need less I can use one or two at a time and conserve the energy for offense.

When I Pull I channel the energy before it reaches the shield so it doesn't explode out like the one at Morndel. Or I can let it do just that if I so desire. I like it, it's fast and strong.

"We'll start with Darrel."

Darrel stepped forward.

"First make a shield when I say go," Nora stated, "3...2...1...go."

Darrel projected his shield from inside of himself. He wasn't quite comfortable with making them from his stream yet, but he was working on it.

"Very good," Nora approved, "Now we'll try the fireball. First I want a standard shot, then I want a power shot."

We call the shot where you use all the power you are comfortable with a power shot. Darrel brought his fireballer up. This he had gotten the hang of now. When his portal opened the fireballer was active. He'd designed two of them, one for a standard and one for a power shot. The standard rolled with power for a second and his fireball shot true.

He closed the portal to that one and opened the powerballer and power flowed through it to roll around inside the shield for a few moments until a much more powerful fireball screamed down the range to hit the shielded dummy. It was a strong shot and took a moment to dissipate.

"Excellent, Darrel, a great improvement," Nora smiled and glanced at me. There was an approval in her aura as she looked toward me. Most Mages don't share their skills with others and she could tell that I had been working with Darrel and Paige both.

"Paige," Nora turned to her and motioned for her to start, "First, a shield."

Paige, like me, had designed her shield with a portal and raised it in an instant. It was a powerful shield for someone with a small stream, and Nora smiled.

"Very good, let's see the fireballs."

Paige had done the same as Darrel and designed two fireballers and she let fly with the first one. It was a standard shot and flew true. Next she let fly the powershot. It rolled for a moment before it shot true as well. It was much more powerful than the first but it had taken some time to build up.

"I see a massive improvement there Paige," Nora said with another glance at me, "Gavin."

Gavin took his place and projected a shield much like he'd done before. Then he let fly his fireball. It was perfect like always. His power shot rolled in his shields more than he was comfortable with, but he refused to be beaten by someone with less power than himself, so he pushed himself. The powershot shot true and he sneered at Darrel as his was stronger.

If Gavin would try to be halfway human, I could show him the stream shields as well but he wouldn't even look at me. Much less try to learn something from me.

Nora called several more names and critiqued their performances. Most of the trainees did well, without incident.

"Colin," She motioned for me and I stepped forward. I'd spent some time with Nora, going over the shield techniques and she was familiar with my shield by now but I had added the triple shield since then and she was surprised when I raised them. First I raised the outer shield then number two and pushed it out to slam into number one. Then the third to do the same.

Her eyes widened and surprise rolled across her aura, "You've been experimenting again, I see. That's the strongest shield I've ever seen, Colin. And it seems that you've fixed the speed issue. Very good. Now let's see the fireball."

I opened the portal to my number one fireballer and Pulled. My fireball flew true and I opened the powerballer. It rolled for almost fifteen seconds before it ruptured and roared downrange to slam into the shielded target dummy. It was about like the first one I'd shot several months ago.

"That's not any more powerful than the first time, Colin, you're holding back. We need an accurate read on your powerful attacks to know where you need to be in the Mages. Now do it again and don't hold back."

I frowned, I had already alienated half of the trainees because of the first one and I had enough problems with Gavin already. But I guess she was right so I opened another portal and shut the powerballer. This was something I was experimenting with. I had created a triple shielded fireballer. On the side with the rupture, I had also formed a rifled barrel.

With a small shrug, I Pulled fairly hard and sent it into the fireballer. It rolled inside the shield for a full minute before rupturing and hurling down the rifled barrel. It had enough force to push me backward almost ten feet. Once again I broke several dummies through the shields before the shot weakened enough to be absorbed into the shield. Power surged across the dome as it was absorbed into the shield and I heard several gasps behind me.

"That's more like it," Nora looked at me, "Now you get to come in after the tests and show me exactly how you did it. Was that a gun barrel on the front of it?"

Paige was looking at me with one eyebrow raised. I hadn't shown that one to her yet. I glanced at the others and saw fear flowing around their auras and Gavin's ever present hate as well.

"Yeah it's a rifled barrel to put a spin on the projectile. Makes it shoot farther faster," I answered.

"Interesting," Nora said thoughtfully, "Interesting, indeed."

Chapter 23

"I've got something you may be interested in, Master Yueh," I said after sparring with the Weapon master, "It's something I think any guard can do but I wanted an opinion from you, first."

"What might that be?" he asked, "I hear your innovations are quite, interesting, to say the least."

I grinned and went over to the folder I brought with me. I pulled out the sheet with Paige's diagram for a personal shield. It showed a person from three angles. The shield was very detailed, Paige does very good work and her memory is amazing. I handed the page to Tien. He was quiet for a moment and looked up at me in surprise.

"Even if I didn't know you, Colin, this one act would prove, beyond a shadow, that you are more than any other Mage to ever walk these halls," he said quietly.

My face turned red, "It's not just me, Paige Turner made the illustration and Darrel Barnes has been right there, working with us."

He looked at me, "Never has a Mage done something like this for the Guard. Not even Gregor Kherkov and he's been a friend of the Guard for many years. This will revolutionize the way the Guard does everything. I don't know if you truly understand the scope of what this is."

"Yes, I do," I answered with a steady gaze. "It will save lives and make us better at destroying the Demons. I don't have much practical knowledge of fighting the Demons but what I have learned showed me what it would have meant if I had been using one of these."

I motioned toward the ugly scar down the left side of my face. As I had gotten to know the Guard, I had seen many of the scars from their battles. A wounded Guard is not as deadly as a healthy one, if you want to look at it coldly.

"Perhaps you do," he nodded, holding up the paper, "How did you describe this much detail to someone else for them to draw this?"

I looked around to see only Guards around us in the Dome. I turned back to Tien and concentrated. My personal shield lit up and I didn't need an aura to see the surprise Tien felt.

"I can see everything without lighting it up, but I've been able to do this for almost every shield I've been able to make. Paige has a photographic memory, so I don't have to do this very long for her to get the details."

Tien was smiling, "You can see them without lighting them up?"

I nodded and turned the lights back off. He was looking at me with a wide smile on his face.

"I never thought that it would happen in my lifetime," He said softly, staring intently at me, "Colin, I'm two hundred and forty years old and I've seen things no one else has ever even thought of. I've studied every manuscript I could find and I know what you are."

I looked at him in surprise, "What do you mean?"

"You know you're different from other Mages. A long time ago there was a man they called

Soullord. He could do amazing things and he's the one who taught the Mages their skills."

"Greyson Kent," I nodded.

He nodded in return, "Most people don't know it but he could see the Soulstreams and the Shields and all the power flows of the world. One of my ancestors was one of the Mages who worked with him. My family learned several new ways to use shielding from him."

I smiled, "The shiny cover that keeps me from looking in."

He nodded with a small smile, "At least, I know for sure it works, now."

"So I'm a Soullord? Paige has found a few references that might turn our thoughts in that direction, too. I'm not sure what that will mean later but for now, I'm just a Mage," I said and changed the subject a little, "We've been working on some new Mage innovations as well as this shield for the Guard. I tried a rifled fireballer yesterday."

"Fireballer, heh, I heard about that. At the rate you're going, there won't be any more test dummies by the end of the year." He laughed, "Have you got more copies of this diagram?"

I smiled, "Oh yeah," I reached into the folder and handed him a stack of them, "I was going to give each Guard one. If they choose to try it, anyone who needs it is welcome to come to me and I'll help in any way I can. I can see what they are doing, whether they can or not. I'm willing to help any of you."

"The Guard will be forever in debt to you for this, Colin, Thank you," there was respect in his voice and it felt good.

118

***

"I wonder how long a shield can stay active once the link is cut to it," I muttered to myself. I was alone near the test dummies at the lower end of the Dome.

I created a shield about two feet around, like the fireballer and disconnected the link. It stayed active for a second then dissolved.

"Hmm," I rebuilt the shield and Pulled a small amount of power into it. Then I disconnected and the shield held for several seconds. "Hmm, I say."

I crafted a shield like the second one, with power in it but there was no weak spot in it. I rolled it across the floor. it dissolved about ten feet away. I tried again and I rolled it harder than before. It dissolved about thirty feet from me.

"That should do it," I mumbled but I opened the portal on my personal shield, just in case.

I crafted another shield ball and powered it. Then I Pulled and channeled enough power for a fireball into it. I pulled my arm back and rolled it. There was a huge explosion and a brilliant flash two feet in front of me and I felt like I was hit by a truck.

That was about when I realized I hadn't anchored my shield, because the world was spinning as I was flipped through the air and across the Dome. I hit the shield wall of the Dome at the other end about thirty feet in the air and it felt like a second truck had run into me. I hit face first and upside down, and then fell straight down right in the middle of seven Soulguards who'd been playing dice.

I know all this because I watched the memory of it in one of their auras a few minutes later. As for me, I had my eyes screwed shut and was screaming all the way across the Dome.

I opened one eye and looked around at seven faces looking down at me. I felt around on myself to make sure all the parts were still there, and then opened my other eye.

"Ouch."

A tall black haired Guard named Riley snorted, "I'd say."

I stood up and, as nonchalantly as I could, walked back to the scene of the crime.

There was a roar of laughter behind me from the Guards and I made it a point to not look in their direction.

Perhaps I could leave the tendril that feeds it connected till it was farther from me.

"Probably just blow myself up again," I muttered.

I had been concentrating and hadn't seen the Guard who coughed behind me to get my attention. I jumped and turned around to see a blonde haired Guard I'd seen several times around the Dome. She was usually sparring when I'd seen her before. Now she was trying to hide a grin.

"I usually wouldn't interrupt a Mage when they're talking to themselves," she started, "But when you started talking about blowing yourself up, I figured I better talk to you before you try that again."

I laughed, "What can I do for you? Before I blow myself up, I mean."

"The Weapon master said that we should come see you when we get the new shield built and have you check it out before we try to use it much. Would you mind giving me a minute of your time to see if I have it right?"

"No problem," I said and opened my Inner eye. She had gotten it very close to what the picture portrayed. Her portal was closed at the moment.

"Ok, open the portal just a tiny bit and let's take a look at the flows."

"You can actually see the flows?" she asked and surprise rolled through her aura.

I wasn't hiding it from the Guards, "Yeah, I can see them. There are certain people that I don't really want to know this. But I trust the Guard, I was raised by two of the best."

She smiled and I saw approval roll through her aura, "You're right there, Jaegher and Nightwing are two of the best. And Guards don't talk a whole lot with the people who *don't* need to know, now do they?"

"True."

She opened her portal and I watched the energy flow through her shield. It was pretty even except a small area in back where the weave hadn't been as tight as it should be.

"There's a spot right here that is weak and needs to be tighter," I was pointing at the spot and realized I was staring straight at her backside.

"And just what do you think you're doing?" I heard Paige's voice and jumped, my face burning.

"I was just checking her shield for her," I stammered.

"I'm sure it was her shield you were checking," Paige returned looking at me with one eyebrow raised. I seem to get that look from everyone, because the blonde woman was giving me the same look.

"Really, I was," I couldn't think of anything better so I concentrated on the Guard's shield and tried to light it up like I do mine. Everyone's mouths dropped open, including mine when the blonde's whole stream, aura and shield became visible. The gap in the shield was plainly visible, and the Guard easily adjusted it with her mind.

I felt dizzy and I broke out in a sweat so I Pulled a little from the Source into myself. The dizziness went away. Apparently, what I was doing took some strength to hold.

"Holy crap," I mumbled.

"You can say that again," Paige returned with surprise and awe in her aura.

"Holy crap," I repeated and she gave me the look again. I let the Guard's aura disappear once more, and stopped Pulling energy into myself.

"Please try not to blow yourself up," the blonde looked at me with gratitude rolling across her aura, "You don't even know how much this means to the Guard. If you need anything at all, don't hesitate to ask for it. Thank you."

With that, she nodded at me and headed back toward the exit to the Guard barracks.

"Blow yourself up?" Paige asked looking at me with her head cocked to the side a little, "Experimenting, are we?"

"Nothing that can't wait," I answered, "Wanna go get something to eat?"

"Sure," she locked her arm in mine and we headed for the Mess hall, "Admit it, you were looking at her ass."

Chapter 24

"So what were you experimenting on?" Paige asked.

"Oh, I was trying to make a fireball that wouldn't bleed off any of the actual fireball's energy to fire," I shrugged and took another bite of the fried chicken leg in my hand, "I think I may have it figured out but I need to try it later in the Dome. You want to come see me get blown up again?"

"What do you mean, again?" she asked with her fork paused inches from her mouth.

"Oh, I'm sure you'll hear about it soon enough," I returned.

I heard several Guards come into the Mess hall and I kept my head down. I could hear them plainly.

"He flew all the way across the Dome flipping about four or five times to slam into the Dome. Then he fell right on Jake's dice right after his roll."

"Bullshit."

"I'm not kidding! I swear it looked like something out of a freaking cartoon."

A third voice joined in, "You know what he said?"

"What?"

"He just said 'Ouch' and he got up and walked back over where he started and scratched his head."

There was good humored laughter from that side of the room, "Oh, shit there he is." the first voice said quietly and the voices dropped a bit.

Paige was staring at me with her mouth hanging open, "Really?! You really blew yourself up, today? Why? Why do you do things like that to yourself?"

Her voice was higher than before, I was pretty sure everyone in the room heard her.

"Well, no one's gonna let me do it to *them*."

She sighed and I heard more laughter from the Guards.

***

Once again, I was at the end of the Dome where the test dummies were and as soon as I'd gotten there, everyone who had been in the area found some reason to be somewhere else. I looked around at Paige.

"What? What'd I do?"

She let out a long slow sigh and shook her head. Then she turned and headed for the other side of the Dome, where a bunch of Guards had suddenly crowded. I saw money change hands several times.

"Hardy freaking har," I mumbled.

I opened my portal all the way and anchored to the floor this time. They better not be betting on my trajectory, I thought, I wasn't going anywhere.

I shook my hands and popped my neck, "Ok, here goes," I muttered.

Once again I formed the shield and channeled power into it from the Source. This time I left the tendril that had powered it up attached. Then I Pulled again and filled the shield with power.

I cringed as I threw the ball toward the test dummies. It didn't blow me up this time, though. It rolled about forty feet away from me, next to a group of dummies and I snipped the tendril. The shield weakened and there was a large explosion that made my ears ring. Three targets were splintered through the shields, before the shield soaked up the rest of the power and it dissipated.

"He shoots! He scores!" I yelled with both hands pumping in the air.

"What is it with you and blowing things up?" I heard a familiar voice and turned to see Trent Deacons walking toward me. Alongside of him was Mattie Riordan.

"It must just be a guy thing," she added, "It's good to see you again Colin."

"I don't know if it's a guy thing or a Colin thing," I heard Paige comment as she walked up as well, "You just disappointed a lot of Guards, Hon, I think they wanted to see the flying act again."

"Once was enough," I grumbled.

"Flying act?" Mattie asked, "What's he done now?"

"Oh, according to the Guard, earlier he decided to blow himself up," Paige reached her hand out to Mattie, "By the way, I'm Paige Turner, you must be Mattie and Trent. I've heard a little about what happened at Morndel, but this one won't say a whole lot."

Mattie shook Paige's hand and said, "Let me tell you all about it..."

The two of them headed back across the Dome talking back and forth with many hand motions that looked like possible examples of explosions.

"I haven't really blown that many things up," I started, until I looked at the shielded targets. Eight of the twenty targets were destroyed. Three with the sword arc, two with the triple shielded powerball, and three from the Soulfire grenade. "Well..."

"You broke all those? Aren't they supposed to be shielded so they won't get broke?" Trent asked.

"Umm, Yeah."

"Did you really blow yourself up? Some of the Guards are talking about you."

"Sort of, yeah."

He chuckled, "God this place is gonna be fun."

Chapter 25

I was lying beside Paige as she snuggled up beside me. She looked intently into my eyes, "I'm a little worried about you," She said softly, "Why do you have to keep pushing things? If your shields hadn't held up, you'd be a greasy spot in the Dome. They say you'll be another Kelvin Demonkiller."

I smiled and she leaned up on one elbow with a small frown, "That was *not* a compliment. The Demonkiller ran off on some one-man war against a clan of Demons after his wife and child were killed. He demonstrated what a Mage can do but he also showed us that we need each other to survive. He died because he went alone. That's not what you want to do, is it?"

I looked intently at Paige, "Can you keep a secret?"

"By now you know I can. What are you hiding from me?"

I lay there, quiet, for a moment, "My real name is Colin Rourke."

Paige gasped, "Oh my God, He was your father?"

I nodded, "He didn't run off for vengeance, and I believed he had for many years. He went out to die and make everyone believe it was vengeance."

"But why would he do that?"

"So that I could live without the Demons hunting me. They thought I was dead. He died for me and the reason I do what I do is to repay the sacrifice my father made."

"They found me at Morndel and another one hundred and twenty two people died because the Demons want me dead. They'll try again, but I'm going to be ready for them. No one else is going to die for me."

"If I can show half the courage and dedication Kelvin Rourke did, then I can hold my head up proudly."

She reached out and touched my face gently, "I'm sorry."

I kissed her softly, "It's ok, no one knows about him, except a very few, but one day they *all* will."

***

"What we know about the Demons is sadly not what we would like," Nora began her lecture, "We know they are from some other dimension or just a different planet. They come here through portals."

She looked at me, "Colin, you've seen one of these portals, as have some of the new recruits in the Guard. Most of the veteran Guards have seen these portals. The portals stay open as long as the Demons are here. You'll see plenty of these as you hunt them after you are posted to your station."

"It is theorized that the portals have to be open for the Demons to survive here. Possibly as an opening for their Soulstreams to flow from their planet to this one."

She paced across the area in front of us, "There are three kinds of Demons that we are familiar with. One, the Lesser Demons seem to act much like attack dogs. They come across and just slaughter anyone they come across. They're vicious and they have no fear. Soulguards can handle them in great numbers."

"The second type is the Wrathguard, or Soldier Demon. These are fast, strong and smart Demons. They also control the Lesser Demons, making them more dangerous than before." She paused looking at Yarden who was yawning, "I know most of you already know these things but some of this information may not be known by everyone, and it's important to know your enemy as well as you can."

"The third type is not as well-known as the first two. The Wraith is not a Demon we really see a lot of, but when there is one of them, serious problems follow. They can control Soldiers and Lesser Demons making them much more deadly. They are extremely fast and strong. They can destroy a Soulguard in seconds and it takes the concentrated power of a strong Mage or combined might of multiple weaker Mages to kill them, usually."

She stopped in front of us and looked intently at each one of us. Her gaze stopped at me last, "Everyone knows what happened when Kelvin Rourke became the Demonkiller. One Mage can do amazing things, but you will need the Guards around you and the help of other Mages to survive. Rourke showed us what a strong Mage can accomplish alone but he paid a dear price for his success."

I knew at that moment that Nora knew who I really was and she worried that I would do the same thing as my father. I could see the worry in her aura and I saw memories of my father flashing across it as well.

I felt almost ashamed for watching as I saw the emotions associated with my father flashed through her aura. Nora Kestril had been in love with him all those years ago, and I saw the loss and pain that his death had wrought in the Senior Mage.

"If you really want to know about your enemy, talk to some of the Elite Guards posted here. They have been fighting them for over a hundred years and they will know much that a new Mage would find useful as they take up their duties."

"There will be a prime time to learn from them tonight," she continued with a smile, "There will be an exhibition of martial skills, from 4 O'clock until 9 O'clock this evening. Anyone who wants to participate is welcome, Mages as well as Guards. I understand Colin is participating in a few exhibitions. I believe he is going to show some of his innovations to any who want to attend."

She smiled and nodded to me and I stood up, "I'll be showing any who attend how to build the Streamshields a few of us have developed and a few other things we've come up with. Anyone who wants to learn any of these skills is welcome to come to me. I'll teach them to anyone who wants to learn them." I looked directly at Gavin as I said this. I wanted to offer my own olive branch. Maybe we could move past all this bullshit that need not be there.

He just looked at me with hate in his aura.

***

Paige was as excited about the Exhibition as I was. We would actually get to distribute the illustrations to every Mage and Guard there. We had worked for a week straight getting all of the illustrations put together into booklets to give to each person who attended the event.

We were eating in the Guard Mess when a group of Guards I had never met came into the room. They were rotating through as they were being transferred to different posts. There were a lot of Guards being transferred this week and it was actually part of the reason we were doing the Exhibition today.

One of the new guys looked intently at me, "They say you're something else with a sword," he commented. I could see the disbelief rolling through his aura.

"I'm fair," I said between bites of the rib eye steak I was demolishing.

Simms, the Guard sitting a few seats down the table snorted. Paige laughed softly.

The new guy looked around suspiciously, "I knew it, they played me," He returned. "I put my name in to challenge you with a sword cause some people kept saying you were obnoxious and thought you needed taken down a notch."

He looked at me for a moment, "I think someone lied to me. I've heard rumors since then that you scored hits on the Weapon master in a bout."

Simms snorted again.

He looked at Simms, "How bad is it really?"

"Well, look at it this way, who are the best three Guards you've ever heard of with the sword?"

He ran his hand through his hair, "Yueh, Nightwing, and probably Jack Riordan."

Simms motioned toward me with his fork, "He scored on all three at the same time," he said and ate another bite of his steak, "My suggestion is to withdraw or get about ten or fifteen Elites to join you."

My face was red and Paige was laughing at me, "You just can't stand it when people compliment you," she turned to the Guard, "They already have a demonstration set up for the Guards. You might join in that if you want."

"What demonstration?" I asked.

"Oh, you'll see," she said with a smile, "It's gonna be so fun."

Simms perked up, "Funnier than seeing him blown across the Dome?"

"Maybe, that's hard to beat," She answered, "Have you seen the video, yet?"

I jerked in surprise, "Video?!"

"Oh, yes," She laughed, "They installed cameras in the Dome a long time ago. It even got a good angle. Sadly, there wasn't any sound but the video is excellent."

The new guy shook his head, "What've I gotten myself into?"

Chapter 26

The turnout for the Exhibition was a great success. There were fifty Elites stationed at the Academy and every one showed up. There were also twenty trainees and twenty five Guards in the process of transfer. All of which were there.

There were also twenty-five Mages present, five of which were Senior Mages. All of the trainees were present, even Gavin Price. Many of the Mages I had not even met yet.

I was familiar with a few, though. Nora Kestril, Gregor Kherkov, Allen Denton, Regina Worthington. The Archmage wasn't present, he was on some sort of overseas trip, visiting the other central bases.

As every person entered the Dome, Paige handed out the booklet with our shield designs and fireballers. Some of the Mages looked at them and surprise rolled through many auras.

"We're going to have to start paying you instructors pay, too," Gregor said behind me with a chuckle, "I thought you were trying to keep your skills a secret."

"Just parts of it," I answered, "What can be used by all, I'm perfectly willing to share."

"Well I guess it's time to start this circus and guess who gets to be the ringmaster?"

"Heh, at least you don't have to be one of the exhibits."

Gregor stepped out into the Dome in front of everyone, "Ok folks, we have an interesting evening planned for you. Before we start the Martial display, I welcome a new Mage who has brought some really great innovations to the Academy this year. Colin Jaegher."

I walked out to the center. I was a little nervous, to be honest, "Hi everyone, we just wanted to show you some of the things we've come up with so far. Paige has given each of you a booklet that has illustrations for all the things I'll demonstrate today and then some. Feel free later to approach either of us for help if you so desire."

Everyone was quiet as they looked at the drawings. I saw many emotions rolling across auras, surprise, shock, and gratitude were present on a lot of them.

"I want to start with the basic privacy shield and the personal defense shield." I concentrated and lit up my privacy shield and portal switch. "The portal is how I control the amount of power flowing through the shield. You may be more comfortable with some other type of control. I like the portal."

I opened the portal wide and my shield hardened. I pushed the bottom down into the earth to anchor it and nodded to Kharl. He approached with five more elite Guards.

"Most of you know Kharl Jaegher, he is going to demonstrate how powerful one of the Stream shields really is."

With that all five Guards opened up and pounded on my shield and I didn't move an inch. They pounded for a few minutes then stepped back and Gregor stepped forward.

Before anyone knew what was happening, he Pulled and threw a fireball at me. There were gasps and a few yells. It really feels weird to look down the barrel, so to speak, of a fireball. The fireball slammed into my shield. I felt the jar but my shield held nicely.

"It's strong and it's versatile," I said, "But it's only as strong as your stream allows it to be. Mine is stronger than the average Guard will be able to raise, but any shield beats what the Guard had up until now."

"Mages should be able to make them as strong as this. The beauty of the thing is that you don't have to focus on the shield after it's crafted to keep it active. The portal lets you shut it down to a trickle that makes a great privacy shield without having to project one."

The Guards and most of the Mages applauded loudly and I saw Paige's aura glow with pride. I looked to Kharl and his was much the same.

I shut the shield down to the trickle charge, still visible.

"Next I'd like to show you Mages a Protective shield with much the same qualities," I opened the first shield portal to a trickle and lit it up, "I have several shields crafted that are much like the privacy screen, on a trickle charge you can feel it but it doesn't stop anything. Push it out to where you want the shield and open the portal."

I opened the portal after pushing the shield out to about twenty feet from me. "My stream is large enough to feed three of these at once if need be."

I opened the second one and slammed it against the first, then I opened the third and did the same with it.

"If I'm totally focused on defense, I can run the triple shield. Or if I need both defense and offense," I dropped the inner shields and left the outer one up, "These shields are strong but they do weaken, the larger the area covered. It depends on stream size, more than anything else."

The crowd applauded once again. Some of the Mages were paying very close attention, now.

"All that we've come up with is in the illustrations, and I know some of you Mages have special skills you've developed over the years. I would love to see some of these so we can add them to the guides. If anyone has even seen something that looks like it would be useful to a Mage, please tell me or Paige about it. We are trying to put together this book so all Mages can benefit from the skills that are discovered."

I shut down my shields and opened another portal, "Now this is a fireballer directly fed from my stream as well, all it takes is to open the portal..."

Everything went great until I came to the fireball grenade. As I described how to make it, Gregor walked back out to the center where I was.

"To have an idea how much power is in one of these fireball grenades he is speaking about, let's just take a look at some video footage that Miss Turner has made available to us."

"Oh crap," I muttered as a large screen lit up with a video of the Dome where I was experimenting. There were gasps as the grenade blew up just as it left my hand. It really does look like something out of a cartoon. I flipped at least five times as I flew across the Dome.

When I got up and went back over scratching my head, looking confused, the whole crowd roared in laughter and applause.

"It didn't deter the young man, though," Gregor said through his laughter, "He was back in the Dome and trying again before the day was through."

Chapter 27

"Our next participant will show us something that hasn't been seen in this place for nearly twenty years. Kyra Nightwing will perform The Dance of Blades." The lights dimmed except around the center of the Dome.

Kyra walked out to the center and turned to the crowd of Guards and Mages. She wore a black body suit and her twin swords gleamed with silver.

She opened with the first stance of the Dance like she would when we do this together but the focus wasn't on speed. Her body flowed into the moves with a fluidity that made it so much more.

As she spun through several of the moves, Paige, who stood beside me sighed, "She's so beautiful."

I hadn't realized how beautiful Kyra really is. Combined with the grace and poise of the Dance, I could see why everyone was sitting in silence with amazement flowing through their auras. The people who had actually seen her perform this had satisfaction and some had other emotions I won't talk about. She is my mother.

She began to speed up, twirling her blades into a fighting stance she uses on me quite often. Faster and faster she danced. I could see the deadliness of every move, but the beauty of the Dance masked the lethality and made this a completely new experience for me.

The Dance ended with the same move I'd finished a while back only she didn't throw an arc of power at anyone.

The applause lasted a long time and I was clapping right with them. There were several wolf whistles and Kyra bowed to the audience and made her way to the exit.

"That was awesome," Paige said in my ear, "It doesn't look the same when you do it. Yours is scary as hell."

"It was beautiful," I chuckled and put my arm around her shoulders, "You ever see Kyra fight Demons you may rethink how you see that Dance."

"Now let's welcome Bravo Squad of the Elites," Gregor's voice boomed. I wasn't sure what all had been planned beyond my part and Kyra's dance.

Twenty Elite Soulguards entered the central area and lined up in a straight line. With a single sound, forty swords were unsheathed from the scabbards on their backs. All the Guards wore black uniforms like I hadn't seen up to this point and each sword gleamed silver.

With another single sound all forty swords sprang to life with Soulfire. Then began the most intricate performance I have ever seen. Each sword wove the exact same pattern around the guards. Every one in synch with the others.

Another shout, and the Guards began weaving in and out around each other, swords blurring with speed. Not a single Guard stepped out of the pattern. I was amazed and just stood there with my mouth hanging open.

Another shout sent every Guard up into the air, swords still weaving the pattern in synch. They landed in a diamond formation, the front twenty facing forward and the back twenty facing back. The swords never slowed. This continued for a second and with another shout each Guard performed a perfect spin kick to land exactly in the same formation.

It didn't stop there, the second they touched down every one of them launched another and another. I couldn't see a single one miss a beat as they stayed in synch. The focus alone was amazing I don't know how long it took to perfect this maneuver, but it was awesome.

Another shout sent them airborne, once more to land in a perfect circle, their swords weaving the pattern and the spin kicks began again, just as before.

This continued for a moment until with a final shout, they sprang into the air to land in the perfect line as they had started, with swords outstretched to the sides. Each sword tip was bare inches from the next Guard's sword tip.

The whole line bowed to the awestruck spectators and, as they straightened forty swords were sheathed in unison.

Never in my life had I seen something so awesome. The audience seemed to agree because everyone who was seated stood and the applause continued for quite some time.

"Wow," came a voice from behind me. I turned to find Trent approaching along with Mattie, "That was better than I thought it was gonna be."

"Kyra was awesome," Mattie said, "I want to learn that dance, it was beautiful."

"He can do it," Paige motioned toward me, "But it's not as pretty. His version tends to blow things up."

"Why doesn't that surprise me?"

"It was only the one time," I protested. All three laughed.

We were interrupted by Gregor, "Our next presentation is from Gary Kahn."

A very large man I'd met training with Tien entered the circle with the biggest battle axe I have ever seen. It was at least five feet long and the huge double blades were four feet across. It must have weighed a couple of hundred pounds. But Soulguards are strong and Kahn wielded it like it weighed nothing. He began an intricate performance with the axe, spinning it around him like someone usually would a sword. It was slower but impressive, nonetheless.

"I got to get me one of those," Trent said in awe.

"It figures," Mattie replied.

"It's better than those little toys you carry around," He said.

"She'd cut you twenty times before you could swing that thing," I laughed.

"But it looks so cool."

"I'd worry more about getting your new shield figured out, you big ox," Mattie said, then turned to me, "He's having a hard time with the shield because he hasn't finished focus training yet."

"It'll come a lot easier after you get the hang of the focusing techniques." Paige said, "We usually keep a new Mage training for a year before they begin anything else. Colin's the first that jumped right past that into regular training. Of course, he cheats."

"It's not cheating," I protested, "I got skills."

"Yeah, keep telling yourself that if it lets you sleep better at night," she said.

Gary Kahn finished his performance to another round of applause and Gregor strode back into the circle, "Ok, our next demonstration needs a Mage to volunteer."

"Ah, Colin seems to have stepped forward to volunteer."

I looked to my right and left, everyone had stepped back a step, leaving me where I was. With a long drawn out sigh, I returned to the circle where Greg waited with a huge smile. I heard the laughter of Guards and Mages alike.

"Over here will be fine," Gregor motioned to one side of the circle and a Guard ran out to give me two of the practice short swords. His aura rolled with anticipation and that was a good sign I wasn't going to enjoy what was coming.

"The opposing side of this demonstration is twenty-five veteran Guards." Gregor's voice boomed and I knew I wasn't going to enjoy it. "Anyone receiving a 'killing blow' drop where you are and let us see what we will see."

A killing blow is a blow to the midsection that would "kill" someone in a real battle.

"If you receive a crippling blow, the appendage is rendered useless."

At that point, the twenty-five Guards filed in. They lined up in an arc along the other side of the ring. I saw the Guard who had talked to us in the Mess hall on the left flank and the woman who had asked me to check out her shield, her name was Daphne Cavanaugh, on the right flank. I recognized many of them but there were some I hadn't seen before as well.

I stretched to loosen up and prepare for this. I knew this demonstration wasn't just for me, but for the Mages, in general to keep in mind. A lot would be for me though, to remind me that no matter how good you are, you can be beaten.

Just knowing I would lose didn't bother me but it isn't in me to lose without a fight. They'd know I'd been there.

"Ready?"

I nodded when Gregor looked at me and the guards nodded when he looked at them.

"3…2…" The world slowed to a crawl, "1…Go!"

They launched at me but I was already amongst them. It was a short fight, but I'd landed seven "killing blows" and ten "crippling blows" before the first one got through to me. The first person to hit me was the guy from the Mess hall and the second was Cavanaugh.

"Halt!"

Everyone stopped as Gregor entered the ring again, "The point to this demonstration is that, no matter how good you are, numbers can still overwhelm you. This goes for Guards and Mages alike. But let's see what happens when there are two Guards aligned with the Mage and see what happens."

He turned to me, "Pick any two of your opponents to join you."

It was an easy choice, I picked the two who had hit me first. The man smiled and Cavanaugh chuckled. As they approached my side, the man said, "I didn't get to introduce myself earlier, I'm Rictor Hughes."

I nodded and Cavanaugh said, "Keep your eyes on the match and not my ass and we'll do fine."

My face turned red and she laughed, "What's your plan?"

"It may not be what you guys really want to do, both of you are aggressive fighters. But if you'll trust me we'll win this."

"What do you want?"

"I need one of you on each flank and using pure defense. If I don't need to worry about my flank defense, we'll go through them faster than you would believe. Just trust me to take care of offense."

I could see the doubt in Rictor's aura but I didn't see any in Daphne's. She'd seen me fight the Elites, she knew I wasn't just bragging. I saw acceptance roll through his aura and I began to loosen up once more. Two more Guards joined the other side to bring the number back up to twenty-five again.

"Ok, we'll be moving fast, we don't stop for anything, right flank first and we'll work our way to the left."

They both nodded and we moved to our positions. The countdown began once more and the world slowed to a crawl again.

"Go!" rang out and we were moving to the right in a flash. The only way one of them could get to me was the flanks but Rictor and Daphne are a couple of the best Guards with swords I had ever seen. No one was getting through their defenses. Guards received "killing blows", one after another until all of them were down. We hadn't received a single hit.

"Halt!"

The crowd stood and applauded, while Gregor made his way back out to the center if the ring.

"Just two Guards made a great difference in that bout. This tells me that one person no matter how good can be beaten, but a person with support can do so much more."

Everyone began putting the practice swords back on the rack until I started to put mine away.

"Hold up just a minute there Colin," Gregor said and I felt another sense of dread. I swear they all love to do this to me. I thought it was just Kharl and Kyra, but everyone was enjoying this too much to just be them. I think all of the Guards must have a sadistic streak in them.

"The final demonstration will be a one on one match between Colin, here and a friend that came over from China, just for this exhibition. Let me introduce you to Len Yueh."

A man walked out into the circle and smiled at me. His Soulstream was larger than mine and he carried two practice swords like he was a pro.

This was the other shoe I'd been waiting to fall. I knew there was something planned for me but I thought it was the bout with the Guards. Len Yueh approached me and placing one of his practice wands under his arm, he held his hand out to me. I did the same and shook his hand.

"Shall we give them a show?" he asked in perfect English.

I nodded and he smiled again, "You know the Dance?" he asked.

"Kyra taught it to me."

"Good, she was always my best pupil. Let us Dance the Blades together," he said.

This is the guy that taught Kyra? This is going to be interesting, I thought.

"Let us start slow and speed up as we go."

"Ok"

We moved to the starting squares and loosened up. Once more the countdown began and the world slowed.

"Go!"

We met in the middle of the ring at a moderate pace and began the Dance. Every attack was parried, both his and mine. We moved with the fluidity Kyra had shown earlier.

"Faster,"

We sped up and continued, every time he sped up I matched him, our swords blurring with the speed at which we were moving.

"Now we give them a show," he said softly, "Pull and let us see how fast we can go."

I Pulled from the Source, my swords flared to life with Soulfire, as did his and the world slowed once again. We Danced the Blades, glowing with Soulfire and I'd never felt so good in all my life. Times like these are the only time that the rage that festers below the surface of my mind can be used. I use it and I become more than I was before.

But I can't let it out completely, I'm not sure what would happen. So I use what I can and it feels good to be able to release it.

Around the ring we danced until we heard in an incredibly slow voice, "Halt!"

When we stopped and turned to the crowd, amazement and awe rolled through auras and everyone stood in applause. I saw Kyra at one side and there was pride rolling through her aura.

"The point of this demonstration," I said after the applause ended and before Gregor could say anything, "Is that no matter how good you are there is always someone better."

I nodded in respect to Len Yueh, who, from the moment we had started, held back to match my skills to make this a performance. Then I returned my practice swords to the rack and returned to where Paige, Trent and Mattie stood.

"I hope everyone enjoyed the exhibition and I would love to have more of these in the future. If anyone has any questions about any of the new techniques Colin demonstrated earlier, feel free to come to us and we will either answer the question or send you to the one who can."

Chapter 28

"So, how many of you actually asked any of the Guards about Demons yesterday?" Nora asked us after we had gathered together once more. "My guess is, not many. But any of you who did, can share what you've learned."

"Demons are partial to caves and most of their attacks are at night," Darrel offered, "They seem to try to cultivate secrecy as much as we do. This shows that they aren't just monsters, but they have a plan in place to deal with Humans."

"Yes this seems to be so," Nora said, "We haven't been able to ascertain this plan, yet, but we keep trying. Kurt?"

"I was told that they've left children alone for the most part and that they've left pregnant women alive even when they witnessed the entire attack," Kurt Yarden said, "There are very few incidents where pregnant women have actually been attacked by Demons."

"This is true. But there are a few of these attacks we know of," She looked at me, "Such as the attack on Rhayne Rourke. Maybe someday we can find out the reasons behind the few attacks that have happened on pregnant women."

I had a sneaky suspicion I knew why those particular women had been attacked. Perhaps they had all been children who would have been Soullords. How the Demons could have known this, I don't know. Maybe it was a just chance and bad luck, I doubt it.

"All right everyone," Nora said, "That will be all for today. Colin, Paige can you both stay for a moment?"

After everyone had left, Nora turned to me, "You said you wanted anyone with a special skill to add to your manual?"

"Anything you think may be useful, we'll gladly add to it."

"A few years back," she paused and chuckled, "Quite a few years back, I saw a Mage use something he called a Soul lance. It was a concentrated shaft of Soulfire that shot straight into a Wraith. It took a strong Pull to use it but I thought you might like to try it out."

As she was telling me what it was I was getting an idea for it. Almost like a flame thrower but more power, maybe. I was already crafting a tube that was about three inches in diameter with a feeder tendril to supply power.

"Ok, let's see if it works," I said and turned toward the remaining practice targets. I pulled and channeled into the tube, which shot a shaft of Soulfire straight at the target. The shield held fine until I Pulled hard and power pulsed into the lance, ripping through shields and incinerating yet another target.

"Do you realize how hard it is to build those shields?" Nora asked, "You've destroyed almost half of them already. We'll have to dismantle the shields to replace the targets and build them all over again."

"Exactly how does the shield work?" I asked, "There are two feeder tendrils to it. Why two?"

"That's something only Senior Mages learn," She said and looked at me for a moment, "But if I don't tell you, you'll start poking at it, won't you?"

I grinned and she sighed, "To tie a construct to the Source you need two tendrils to, basically, create a circuit. If there is something alive at the end of the tendril, you only need one, like the Soul-streams."

I saw what she was talking about in the shield I was looking at.

I reached out with a tendril like I had seen the Mage do when he tied off Grimes from the Source and wrapped the tendril on the left without touching it. Then I extended it to wrap the other, making a jumper around the shield. Then I squeezed the tendrils from the Source almost closed, while cutting the connection to myself immediately after the squeeze. None of the power had a chance to flow up my tendril into me. The shield flickered and almost disappeared.

"What did you just do?" Nora looked at me intently.

"I was just testing something," I said as I reached back out and loosened both knots to let the Source flow back into the shield. I left the jumper in place for an easy way to take down the shields when they needed me to. "I can help with the shields when you want to replace the target dummies."

Nora shook her head, "Sometimes I just want to pick you up and shake you. You do things we spent years learning in seconds. It makes us look inept and ignorant. The worst part is you don't even realize you're doing it."

"I just try to do what you want me to," I returned. "I'm not trying to hurt anyone."

"I know, Colin," she said, "It's just hard on us old-timers when you come in here at eighteen years old and continually show us up."

"I'm sorry."

"Don't apologize for being who you are, Colin," Nora placed a hand on my shoulder and squeezed softly, "Maybe this is exactly what the Mages need. A little shaking up won't hurt us. It's just hard to sit and watch sometimes. I think the Lance can be added to the manual, though, don't you?"

I watched all the emotions flow across her aura as she talked to me, I gained a new respect for Nora Kestril. Not only was she fighting the jealousy and frustration of dealing with me but her last question was asked in truth. She really wanted to know my thoughts on it. It felt good to earn the respect of people like Nora and Gregor or Tien. It meant that I was doing something right.

"I think it's good to add but it takes a strong Pull to really put the power in it. The shield itself is as simple as it gets, though. We may be able to come up with some finishing touches before we put it in the Manual. But we can definitely use this."

"It's powerful enough," Paige agreed, "But that was a strong Pull. Someone like me probably couldn't Pull enough to stop a Wraith with it but a powerful Mage will probably like it."

I lit up the new shield so they could see it too, "So can you see anything I can do to make it work better?"

They both began to examine the Lance. "Maybe if you make this part a little smaller it will focus more power in a small area..."

***

"3...2..." the world slowed, "1...Go!"

I met Kharl head on. There wasn't much technique involved at first. We just whaled on each other. He used several moves after a bit to try and throw me, but I was prepared for them.

"Much better, Son," He said as he fainted left and I went right. I don't know where he came from but the next minute I was flying through the air to slam into the new "Mat" that had my face print in it too.

"If you let me get ahold of you, you're gone," he chuckled.

I heard laughter from the side of the Dome where the new trainee Guards were watching the bout.

"Hardee har," I mumbled and charged back in at Kharl, using more speed than before.

"That's more like it," Kharl said, "Make me work for it."

I hit him five or six times before he connected again, but when he did I flew backwards into the Mat again.

"Halt!" came Tien's voice. We stopped and made our way out of the ring. Several of the Trainees entered and took their places in the ring for a

practice. I smiled as I saw that one of them was
Trent.

We both turned and watched as Tien
counted down for the Trainees. At "Go!" they
charged each other and began swinging. Both of
them were pretty good at boxing but Trent had the
reach to hold the other guy back far enough not to
get as much of a pounding as his opponent.

When Kharl and I spar it looks like we just
whale on each other, but really, that's what we do as
we look for the opening to do more. That's why the
Mat is there. When he does "more" I end up face first
in the mat. It happens less and less as I get better
though and I'd only hit the Mat three times in our
match.

Trent and his opponent were just whaling
on each other, there wasn't "more" but that would
come later. Trent is strong as an ox, He's stronger
than many Guards. But it has to do with the way I
taught him to alter his Knot so that it didn't leave the
body to distribute the power as much. He knotted
his quite a bit more than the regular knot is twisted.

Instead of one loop of the knot feeding his
right leg, there were three separate loops. The body
doesn't have to distribute the power as far so the
body was stronger.

"Halt!" Tien stopped the match.

"Andrew, when facing a stronger opponent,
don't just swap hits with him," Tien said, "You have
to push your speed and focus on not getting hit. If he
can't hit you he won't beat you. For example,
Mattie?"

"Oh no," Trent muttered, then said loudly, "Somebody make sure she doesn't have one of those knives, please."

"I'm not frisking her," a voice from the group of trainees said, "Friggin suicide."

Several of the trainees laughed until Mattie looked around at them with one eyebrow raised. It got quiet very quick.

"She's damn good with those knives, Son," Kharl said quietly, "and almost as good with short swords. Jack's one of the best and he pushed her all her life. Scares the shit out of most of the Trainees and some of the Vets as well, Heh heh."

"I bet he doesn't get one hit in while she takes him apart," I said, "She's wicked fast, you should have seen her fight at Morndel."

"That ought to keep his head from swelling up too much," Kharl laughed, "Speaking of swelled heads, can you look at my shield without yours swelling up too much? They should be paying you instructors pay, too. Gregor says you've taught a lot more than you learned since you've been here."

I laughed, "Sure, I can look at it, and if my head gets too big, you can always throw me into the Mat again."

Over the last month, since the Exhibition, Guards had been coming to me on a pretty regular basis with the new shields. Most of them were fine, and the few who weren't, I lit up their streams so they could actually see as they fixed the problems.

About that time, the match started and we watched Mattie run circles around Trent. He would swing but she was never there when it reached its destination. She landed about twenty powerful blows before Tien called a halt.

"Speed trumps power under most circumstances," Tien said, "Power is very useful in a nest of Demons, though. Numbers can counter speed easier than it can counter power."

Mattie was smiling evilly at Trent who was looking a bit worried. I laughed at my friends. Speed doesn't always trump power, if the powerful one has close to two hundred years of experience, speed just makes you able to last a little longer.

Kharl and I made our way across the Dome toward the showers. We stopped, away from the others and I turned to him. I opened my Inner eye.

"Ok let a trickle charge into it."

Kharl opened the portal just a tiny amount. It looked good all the way around.

"Looks good, Dad," I said, "Open it up."

He opened it up and I said, "See if it interferes with the Soulblade you make."

He flipped his wrists and his Soulblades burst into being. They seemed as powerful as they always were.

"I don't see any problems with it."

"Great," He said and the swords disappeared, "Ky has hers done too but she figured she'd get you to look tomorrow after dinner. Man, I'm glad we can eat somewhere else now. I think she was trying to kill us all those years."

"If it doesn't kill you it'll make you stronger," I laughed.

"I guess you could put it that way," he said, "I'm heading out to the trail, see you later."

"See you."

Chapter 29

The last few days had been rather peaceful, I'd worked on the Soul lance a little and I'd checked five Guards' shields.

I'd only seen Gavin once and he was still radiating hate, but there was something else there too. He was anticipating something, maybe he would be getting his first assignment soon and we'd be rid of his arrogant ass.

I'd also checked Kyra's shield and she'd woven a tighter shield than I did. It was quite good. She's always had a lot of focus, and you could tell with the shield. Most of the Elites had come through over the last month and a half. They'd all gotten the shield right. I guess focus comes with age.

Almost everyone at the Academy had a personal shield by then. I'd even seen Gavin sporting the new and improved privacy screen. I felt good about that, he was such a prick, I was afraid he wouldn't even try because I had been the source of it.

I passed Darrel as I headed to my quarters, "Darrel."

"Hey Colin," He said, "I got that Soullance thing crafted. If you don't care, will you take a look at it tomorrow?"

"No problem."

"Thanks man."

I found a note pinned to my door. It was from Paige.

It said: Colin, meet me on the Guard trail, near the top of the mountain. I have a surprise for you. It was signed with a capitol P.

I smiled and went into my room to change into clean clothes and I put my twin swords on the rack.

I should oil them, I thought, but I can do that after I meet Paige.

I left my quarters and headed to the elevator. I ran into Daphne Cavanaugh in the elevator.

"Hey, Daffy"

"Colon."

We had been calling each other names like this since Trent and Mattie had gotten here and Trent dropped his favorite name for me in the Mess. Thanks a lot, Buddy.

"You find out where you're going, next month?" I asked.

"Yeah, they're sending me to New Mexico."

New Mexico was the station where my real father and mother had been posted back when the attack occurred. After the Demonkiller legend, it had become the cherry of postings. Only the best got stationed there.

"Good, you deserve that post. You seen Rictor around?" I asked, "He was supposed to get his new post too."

"I haven't seen him, but he must have pissed someone off, I heard he got Knoxville, Tennessee."

"Why is that a bad thing?"

"Oh they had to pick somewhere to send the troublemakers and the rebels. So someone picked the Knoxville post to be the one. The Guards there aren't that bad but they are Characters with a capitol

159

C," she said, "The problem is they send the worst Mages there and the Guard doesn't mesh very well with them."

"Ahh, I guess I'll have to give him my condolences next time I see him."

She chuckled, "I'd give him a bottle of whiskey, he might get some use out of that."

"I might just do that."

The elevator hit the bottom floor and we exited. She headed into the Dome and I headed outside. It was late September and all the trees were changing colors. I like this time of year, the cold weather doesn't bother me much. Soulguards aren't prone to be bothered by temperature. Cold is still uncomfortable to us but not like it is to a normal person.

I saw several Guards beginning a run up the trail and I followed along. I didn't recognize any of them, they must have been some of the others transferring through to other postings.

I reached the top of the trail just behind the Guards who suddenly stopped. I looked past them to see someone slumped under a tree. I saw the flaming red hair and leaped to Paige's side. Something was wrong so I opened my Inner eye.

Her Soul was dim, and I looked down to see a tendril from the Source, wrapped around her stream.

"Paige!" I knelt beside her and felt someone Pull on the Source. I looked down to see a tendril clamp onto my Stream about a foot from where my stream entered my solar plexus and squeezed. My stream almost closed off and I fell beside Paige.

Son of a Bitch was blocking me from the Source! Rage clawed its way out of the pit where I keep it trapped. I clawed at the knot, around my stream and actually untied it. I threw it aside as power surged back into me. I turned toward the source of the tendril and flipped my wrists, calling forth two Soulblades. The fire was a dark red just as my rage was in my aura.

I looked to the tendril that had just sank into the Source to tie me off and smiled as the Source, with nowhere else to go, surged back through that tendril into the cluster of Mages back in the trees. Then the screams began. The Source is not forgiving, It will rip your body apart and burn you to the ground. This is just what it was doing to Gavin Price and four of his followers who had connected to him as supports. I felt a savage joy but it felt wrong and I beat my rage back down and pushed it back in its cage.

I looked down at Paige to see her looking at me in horror. She'd seen my reaction and it horrified her. I felt shame course through me and I turned back to the tendril. Maybe I could cut it with the Soulblade.

I swung one of the blades and severed the tendril. The Source stopped surging into the group of Mages, but it was too late. I watched as Gavin Price flamed out along with Dahlia Morgan, Steve Corum, and Donald Sheldon. Only one of the four didn't flame, Kurt Yarden was screaming in agony.

"Release it!" I screamed at him.

He looked at me with bloodshot eyes and released the power out of him. In the blinding light, I saw the horror-stricken face of Regina Worthington.

161

The blast washed over her and she screamed as she was burnt by the raw energy that had exploded out of Kurt.

I winced and turned back to Paige who had watched in horror as four Mages died in that inferno. She looked at me with accusation and I knew in my heart that Paige would never feel the same about me. This was all my fault, they wouldn't have targeted her if I hadn't stepped in those long months ago.

Now she was blocked from the Source. The one thing she truly loved was being a Mage, and because of me it was gone.

I reached down to her, "I'm so sorry."

She flinched as I touched her and I felt a pit open in my chest. I saw fear roll across her dim aura. She was afraid of me. Oh my God, she was *afraid* of me.

Chapter 30

"Oh my God, Colin," Kyra held her head in her hands, "This is bad. The Archmage will be after blood."

I stood up, "I didn't ask for any of this. I've just tried to do what I was told. I don't understand why they did this. What did I do?"

"You were just there, Son," Kharl answered. "Sometimes that's all it takes."

"They'll try to put this on you at the hearing," Jack Riordan said, "Make sure your story is straight."

"It can't get straighter, I'll tell the truth. I didn't start this and they died because they were frigging stupid. Not because I had some nefarious plot to do anything."

"The question is, who taught Mage trainees to do a Source Block?" Kyra asked, "Only senior Mages know how to do that. The Archmage is, conveniently, overseas."

"They've planned this since my visit to the Archmage's office. Even the timing was planned."

We were interrupted by Gregor entering Kharl and Kyra's quarters.

"This is a little beyond 'interesting times', I'm beginning to regret those words," He said, "They sent for Guilefort, the truth seer."

"Who's that?" I asked.

"He's the Mage who's a lie detector. He can always tell if someone is telling the truth."

"That's good news," I smiled.

"What?"

"No matter how they try to play this," I explained, "The truth is the truth. I didn't attack those Mages. They tried to block me from the Source and failed. Pure and simple. If there is a person there who can see the truth, then I'm not worried about this hearing. If they want to charge me with abuse of power, or even murder, the last person they want to be there is a truth reader."

***

"Ye stand accused of abuse of power and murder Colin Jaegher, How do ye plea?" the accent was a thick Scottish brogue.

This was the opening from the presiding Mage in the council, Lennox Flynn. He had flown in from the Scotland Academy, so that the presiding Mage would not be biased.

"Innocent on both accounts."

"Do ye' 'ave someone ye wish to stand as yer defender?"

I pointed at the Truth seer, "He'll be defense enough."

The Mage nodded and I saw respect actually flow through his aura, "As it should be."

"The way this works, the Council will ask ye questions and the truth seer will tell us if ye speak the truth. Do ye accept these terms?"

I nodded, "Yes I do."

"Ye may begin, prosecutor."

"We will start with some simple questions to let the Truth seer get a feel for you. Is your name Colin Jaegher?"

"No."

"Truth."

The prosecutor looked at me strangely, "What is your name?"

I stared at him for a minute, "None of your business."

"Truth."

The prosecutor turned to the judge, "This is outrageous. Require him to answer."

"He did answer and it was the truth. Continue questionin' 'im and don't ask wat isn't any of yer business."

I could see amusement roll through his aura. That had been a new one to him and he thought it was funny.

The prosecutor turned back to me with rage in his aura, "Did you hate Gavin Price?"

"Not until he blocked Paige Turner, an innocent Mage, from the Source. After that, yes."

"Truth."

"Did you kill Gavin Price and three other Mages three days ago?"

"No"

"Truth."

The prosecutor stepped back in surprise. "Then how do you explain to us what happened to the Mages?"

"They tried to block me from the Source and failed, this is on them, not me."

"Truth"

I was beginning to see amusement in the aura of the Truth seer as well as the judge. They were getting the idea by now that this wasn't a trial, it was a way to get rid of a problem, me. They'd brought the wrong person here if they wanted to dispose of me.

"Do you know how their attempt to block you failed?" The prosecutor was pacing back and forth in front of the Council.

"Yes."

"Truth."

"How did that happen?"

"I untied the knot."

"Truth."

The Council members turned to each other in amazement and several exclamations were heard.

Flynn slammed his gavel down, "Silence!"

Everyone stopped talking, and the prosecutor turned back to me, "How did you untie the knot?"

"With my hands."

"Truth," the truth seer said in amazement.

After a moment of silent amazement he continued, "What happened after that?"

"The best I could tell, they were trying to tie into the source when I managed to get free. A backlash flowed back into them and they died."

"Truth"

"According to a Guard you called up Soulblades as soon as you broke free. Is this true?"

"Yes."

"Truth."

"Guilefort, just pipe up if 'e lies," Flynn said, "Yer 'avin too much fun with that."

"Yes sir," Guilefort answered sadly.

"And what were you going to do with those Soulblades?"

"I was going to cut off their frigging heads."

"Truth," Guilefort popped out, "Sorry."

The prosecutor stood back and smiled, "I'll take that as a confession."

"No you won't," I said, "That's exactly what I would have done if the Backlash hadn't killed the bastard. Lucky for me I didn't have to. You can't convict me because I wanted to kill the stupid prick. Let me ask you a few questions. Is it not a crime, to block someone from the Source who hasn't been tried and found guilty by the Council?"

"Yes, but..."

"Truth."

"Why am I here, on trial when I was just defending myself? Is it because the Archmage wants me out of the picture? Or is it that you are so scared of him that you want to hang me so that you can have a bad guy to give to him when he gets here?"

"I don't have to answer your questions!"

"I think ye do," Flynn interrupted, "Is it one of the answers the lad put forward?"

"No!"

"Lie!"

"This is outrageous!" the prosecutor exclaimed, his face completely red, "I am not on trial here!"

"And neither is this boy," Flynn returned as he stood up, "Every one of ye should be ashamed of yerselves. One, for lettin someting like this happen in the first place, and second for trying to accuse the victim of a crime. Yer foocking disgraceful and this hearing is over."

I stood up and my rage was trying to escape again. I nodded toward Flynn and Guilefort, then I turned and walked out of the Council chambers. There was one more detail I needed to take care of.

I saw Daphne and Rictor talking in the hall and I walked up, "Daph, you said if I need anything just to ask. Did you really mean that?"

She nodded.

"I need a group of Guards to keep me from being interrupted while I set these matters straight."

"You've got it."

"Meet me outside in ten minutes," I said.

"What's going on?" Rictor asked her as I walked away.

"He's got a crazy look in his eye," Daphne answered, "Whatever it is it's big and I gotta get the Guards together."

I opened my Inner eye and looked around for her Soul. I saw her outside, behind the Guard barracks, sitting under a tree.

I paced back and forth in front of the entrance to the Academy until a crowd of Guards exited and formed up. I turned and headed for her. She looked up as I walked under the tree and the Guards formed a circle around us.

"It's time to fix what I caused," I said softly.

"No Colin you can't..."

But she was too late, I reached a tendril out and untied the knot from her Soulstream. The Source poured up the tendril into me and I felt that burn like I had felt at Morndel, but I was prepared this time. I channeled it straight into the sky.

As the Source flowed through me I extended the tendril to wrap around the gentle stream of life going into the tree. As it touched, power flowed into the tree as well as me, When the power level had dropped enough, I severed my link and the Source fed the tree directly. Its bark turned darker and the leaves turned green in the Fall, and I swear it grew right in front of our eyes.

I turned around with my eyes smoldering from the power coursing through me. I saw on the other side of my Guards, almost everyone stood with awe and fear in their auras.

Flynn and Guilefort both stood out there with amazement rolling through theirs. I looked into Flynn's eyes as I released the rest of the power into the sky. I could see his aura as he realized why everyone was scared of me. And he saw the real reason the Council had wanted to throw me under the bus.

Chapter 31

"There is one more thing I need to do," I turned to the Guards, "We have to go up the trail."

We all bounded up the trail to the spot where they had tried to trap me. With my Sight, I could still see two tendrils sticking straight up out of the ground. Once you tie something to the Source it stays tied to the Source.

This time I thought a little before I acted and I wrapped my tendril around the nearby tree's stream first and extended the end to the first tendril. As the tendrils touched, Life force poured up the tendril and I cut mine before it even reached the tree. There was much the same effect in this tree as the one down at the bottom.

"What are you doing?" Rictor asked.

"Where Gavin tried to block me, there are two tendrils of Source power just sticking out of the ground. If someone were to accidentally touch one, they'd probably burn. I'm tying them to trees so they won't hurt anyone."

I repeated the same action on the second tendril. If I'd just done that with Paige's, I might not have terrified half the Mage Academy. I guess you live and learn. I just wish I could learn the easy way for once.

"Done, now we can go back down. Thanks guys, I wasn't sure if any of them would try to stop me from unblocking Paige. She didn't deserve to be blocked."

Daphne nodded with a strong respect flowing across her aura. I looked at the other Guards to see the same sort of reactions in them all.

We all bounded back down the trail to find several people waiting for us at the bottom.

"I see you've been busy," Nora said, "I hear you made the whole Council look like fools. Then just for kicks, came outside and unblocked Paige from the Source. Busy, indeed."

"Son, you're gonna give me a heart attack," Kyra shook her head in wonder, "Can't you just give us a little warning?"

Kharl snorted, "He's never given us warning before, why start now?"

"Sorry guys, it was kind of a spur of the moment thing."

"You need to go talk to her, Colin," Nora said, "She's not moved since you unblocked her. She just sits there."

I nodded and went back to the tree that was now, at least, three feet in diameter at the base. Paige was sitting there looking at the tree. There was regret and sadness in her aura, and more than a little shame and guilt.

She turned as I walked up to her, "You deserved so much better from me, Colin. I was so angry at you when it happened. Then I saw you smiling as they burned and it scared me so bad. I'm sorry I blamed you."

She reached out and touched my face with her right hand, I could see her emotions and just once I wish I couldn't because she was still scared of me and when she touched me she remembered what she had seen. I saw from her perspective what she'd seen and I understood the feelings that went with it more than before. Seeing my face with that evil smile watching four people burn to death sent shivers through me.

"You are right to blame me, It's my fault. My temper brought us to this and my actions will bring more grief on the people I care for. It's best if you distance yourself as far from me as you can."

I turned and walked away, hoping she would call out and tell me not to go. But she remained quiet and I felt a great loss as I returned to the entrance of the Dome.

Chapter 32

I walked toward the elevator, on my way to a meeting with Gregor, and everyone I met showed fear in their auras. Whether it was fear of me personally or just fear of the reaction of the Archmage when he returned, I don't know.

The Archmage had been informed of the death of his son but he hadn't flown straight back in like I expected. I almost figured that he would come flying back and attack me, but he didn't.

Kurt Yarden was tried and found guilty of abuse of power two days after my farce of a hearing. They didn't accuse Regina Worthington of anything, although I believe she was there to make sure they got it right. She got burned quite badly when Kurt released the power and her face bore the scars of it. Her outside looked much like her ugly soul now, fitting, in my opinion.

I met a group of Guards as I crossed the Dome and several nodded with respect. At least I hadn't alienated everyone, the Guard still liked me.

I entered the Elevator and headed to the upper floor where the offices were. When I exited the elevator, there was the same woman who had been there on my first day at the Academy.

"Colin," she said, "There is a seat outside Gregor's office. They're having a meeting at the moment and you can wait it out there if you want."

"Ok"

I headed down the hallway and found a comfortable looking chair outside of Gregor's office. I sat as I heard several voices from behind his door.

"If we leave him here, the Archmage will find some way to get at him," I heard Nora's voice say.

"I'm not so sure the lad is the one I'd be worried about," came the voice of Flynn. "Ye may be worried about the health of the wrong Mage. E's welcome to come back to Scotland wit me."

"I don't think he needs to be in the Academy any longer, anyway," Gregor said, "He's taught us more in the last three or four months than we've taught him. I say we graduate him and send him to a post. Maybe killing Demons will keep him out of trouble for a while."

"I have to agree. We've been looking at sending him to Knoxville. We need to address some of the problems there and he should be good for the place," Nora said, "The Council will accept it, since it's the, supposed, worst posting. But Kharl has been arranging for some of the best Guards to be sent there, just for this."

"It looks like ye got tings well in 'and," Flynn said, "I'm not lyin when I say the lad scares the bejesus outta me. I can't 'elp but think there's someting more to 'im than just bein a Mage."

"There is," Gregor and Nora returned at the same time.

"Tien says he's a Soullord," Gregor said.

"Bloody 'ell! If the boy's a Soullord, then the Archmage better not try to take 'im on. I've 'eard things from me ancestors about Soullords. They can wield much more power than Mages can. Looks can be decievin, The lad's much stronger than ye think 'e is. Much stronger than 'e knows 'imself."

"He's supposed to be here by now, I'd say he's outside. I need to give him the news and settle his pay," Gregor said, "If you don't mind, I'll talk to you later, Flynn. I want to know what you know about this Soullord thing."

"No problem, Greg, I'm 'ere for another week before I leave."

"Well," Nora said, "Let's get out of here and let Greg do his thing. Lord, I hope he does all right in Knoxville."

"He'll do what he thinks is right," was Gregor's response, "That's something we can always depend on. Jaegher hammered that sense of right and wrong into that kid from the day he was born. He doesn't know any other way to be."

"Tis the way 'e should be. The way we all should be," Flynn returned.

The door opened and I tried to look as innocent as I could, but Nora chuckled and said, "I've seen that look too many times to be fooled, young man. Eavesdropping, were you?"

"I would never..."

"You don't lie very convincingly, either," she said, "Gregor is ready for you."

I stood up and entered his office. Flynn had held the door open and nodded at me as I passed. He pulled the door shut behind me, leaving me with Gregor.

Gregor smiled, "Well, Colin, since the Council couldn't hang you, we're gonna promote you instead. We usually have a ceremony for graduation but no one has ever graduated in less than a year, we're just gonna skip that part. Will that be a problem for you?"

"No sir, I hate ceremonies anyway."

"Good," He relaxed in his chair, "We're sending you to Knoxville, Tennessee. I'm sure you've heard it's a sorry post, but it really isn't. The Council thinks it's a lousy post for Mages, because the Guards there really don't like inept Mages. I have a feeling you'll fit right in, considering how you feel about inept Mages,"

I laughed, "I really don't know what you're talking about."

"Sure, keep telling yourself that," he returned, "By my calculations, we owe you ten months of trainee pay. But we decided, after the innovations you've taught everyone here, that we will pay you as a posted Mage while you were here. It's not as much as you deserve, but it will show, at least, some appreciation on the part of the Academy."

He handed me a large envelope, "This has your check and your written and signed orders to report to the Guard post in Knoxville. The address is in there and you have two weeks to get there. You can hitch a ride on the Guard jet, but you would have to leave today if you use it. There are ten Guards being sent to Knoxville today and a new Guard Captain. I think you've met him, Rictor Hughes."

"There are also a set of orders for the Mage Captain in Knoxville that I'm not very happy with. But the Council has the right to do it, so I have to let it go."

I looked at him worriedly and he sighed, "They are recalling the Mage Captain and three Mages for 'retraining'. This leaves you as the most powerful Mage in Knoxville. Which also means, you are left in charge as the acting Mage Captain. Rank in the Mages is rated by power, not experience, as you well know."

"That's a lot for a new recruit to handle, so try to work things the best that you can. They probably look for you to make mistakes that they can penalize you for. For some reason, the whole Council dislikes you greatly. It might be because you made them all look like fools in front of one of the most respected Mages in the world. Personally I don't think they needed help looking like fools but there is always someone else to blame, if you know what I mean."

"Yeah, I think I do."

"Good luck, Colin, and remember, you've made quite a few Mages very proud and we'll be doing what we can to help you. And the Guard will always back you. Never underestimate what that support means."

"I understand, Sir."

"Go spread your news, and try not to blow up Tennessee."

***

"...keep him alive for a year and he'll be the best you've ever seen," I heard Kharl's voice as I came around the corner from the elevator into the Dome.

"I'll do my best," Rictor Hughes answered with his back to me. Then he laughed, "This might be fun."

He turned to walk off and saw me and greeted me with a smile, "Blown anything up today?"

"It's only ten o'clock," I answered, "I've got plenty of time."

He snorted and walked on past me, "See you in Knoxville, Colin."

"I'll be there in a few weeks, don't kill all the Demons before I get there."

He laughed again, "There's plenty to go around, believe me," He waved as he left the Dome for the elevator.

"I guess you knew already, huh?" I asked as I turned back to Kharl.

"Yeah," He answered, "Been making preparations for the last few weeks. I sent some good Guards there to back you up. Not that I think you can't do the job, but it will help to have some people you can depend on until you get set. I really didn't see the move by the Council coming, and it'll make things harder on you. But I have a feeling you'll surprise every one of em."

"Thanks, Dad."

"I'm proud of you, Son. And, no matter what anyone says, if you hold those convictions and morals that you've shown here, you'll always have the loyalty of the Guard. If you need anything at all while you're there, just holler."

"Thanks, that means more than you could know."

"I have a present for you as well," He smiled broadly, "You never once asked what happened to your truck back at Morndel."

"I parked close to the gym," I said sadly, "I didn't need to ask."

He pulled something out of his pocket and handed it to me. It was a set of keys to a Chevrolet.

"It's a few years newer than the last one but I think you'll like it."

Chapter 33

"It's all the years he spent being the poor guy at school that did it," Trent stated as he reached for another roll, "He's trying to make up for it by destroying everything in the Academy."

"There's just no call for that kind of attitude, Colin," Mattie said, "I hope they don't have too many things in Knoxville he can break."

"Hey," I said, "at least I helped put the targets back after I broke em."

"True, but Tien said that they'd been there for forty years without any trouble till you came along," Trent added.

"Did you see the size of that tree behind the Barracks?" Mattie asked innocently, "Colin, have you seen that tree? It's huge and it's green, with snow on it."

The two of them loved to pick on me about anything. Most people avert their eyes when they see me. Mattie and Trent would poke at me for the same things the others were scared of me for.

I hadn't spoken to Paige since the day under the tree and I still felt the loss. I wasn't in love with her or anything, but she'd been my closest friend for the last ten months and it hurt when I had scared her away.

"Oh, he's got that look, again," Mattie said, "Don't beat yourself up about it Colin, she made her choice and you've got to stop blaming yourself.

Those guys deserved everything they got and then some."

I can always count on Mattie to cut to the chase and she sees things in black and white. There are no greys. They attacked me and failed, they paid the price and now it was over.

Paige saw all kinds of shades of grey, and she'd seen a part of me I'm not proud of that day. But it *is* a part of me and that's what she can't deal with. I understand better than most because of the skills I have. I'd seen her memory and felt the emotions. She can also look to the future and see that aligning with me puts her in the crosshairs of the Archmage. And he's a very big gun.

Mattie would probably slit his throat in his sleep. Black and white. He's the bad guy. Simple.

"She doesn't really have a choice, Mattie," I returned, "The Archmage is here and she's here for at least another year. She's already been targeted twice now because she was with me. The smart thing for her to do is stay as far away from me as possible."

"Doesn't make it right."

I couldn't even argue the point.

"I bet you can't wait to get to Knoxville so you can eat some real food," Trent changed the subject. Trent acts like a clown a lot of the time but he is a smart man and he knew that Paige was a touchy subject for me.

"What do you mean?" I asked, "This is great. I eat here every day and I love it."

"That's only cause Kyra used battery acid in her food. This is just bulk foods to fill up hungry trainees. You should go to a nice restaurant as soon as you get there, then you'll see what I'm talking about."

"This is the only food you've had?" Mattie asked incredulously, "This and Kyra's food?"

"Yep, that's why I eat here three times a day. If I wasn't a Guard, I'd be fat as a cow. Morndel's lunch was this good, too."

She laughed merrily, "Oh my God."

***

I stood and looked at the new truck. It was a 2004 Silverado with four doors and Kharl had jacked it up and added the steel on the front and back like my old one. I opened the rear driver door and saw a set of Bose speakers mounted under the seats.

"Didn't skimp on the stereo system," I mumbled in appreciation.

I placed my bag in the back seat. Everything I owned fit in a single bag. In the field, we don't have uniforms, exactly. Mostly we try to blend in with the populous. There are some times when we wear a black uniform of sorts, but they are provided at the outpost.

I'd looked at my check and been astounded. What was I going to do with thirty-five thousand dollars? I guess I could afford to do what Trent said and eat at some restaurants. There is a dormitory at the Knoxville Guard post. It is provided or there is a stipend provided if you want to get something for yourself.

I shut the truck door and heard a cough behind me. I turned to find Paige standing there. I left my Inner eye closed and walked to her.

"I'm sorry, Colin, I'm just not strong enough to be who you deserve. But I want you to know I do care about you and I'll miss you," she wrapped her arms around me and I held her for a few minutes.

"I'll miss you, too. Keep pushing the Mages to learn the new things and I'll keep in touch. If I come up with some new things I'll let you know. It's time for a Mage upgrade, whether they want one or not."

She nodded as she stepped away and I climbed into my new truck.

"Goodbye, Paige," I said and started the truck. She waved as I pulled out and headed down the dirt road that led back into the mountains and the Academy from one of the state roads.

It would be a long drive to Tennessee but I'd discovered a new band to break in the new system with, Five Finger Death Punch. With the music pounding in my ears I left the Academy behind.

Section 3
Lord

Chapter 34

I followed Trent's advice and the first thing I did when I got to Knoxville was to find a nice restaurant and get a meal. On the way across the country I'd stopped several times at fast food joints. They were awesome. If a regular restaurant was that much better, I knew what my money would probably be spent on.

I took an exit from I-40 that took me to a road that ran alongside of the interstate. It was called Kingston Pike and there were restaurants all over the place. I decided to try one called Olive Garden. It looked nice and there were a lot of cars in the parking lot.

Kharl had given me a good bit of cash to last till I got to Tennessee where I could open an account with a local bank with my back pay. I still had three hundred dollars of that money in my pocket.

As I entered, a pretty girl greeted me, "One in your party?"

Her eyes strayed to the huge scar that ran down my face. I'd been getting that look since I'd left Montana. It does stand out a bit.

"Yeah," I answered.

Another girl came and led me to a table in the corner, "Someone will be here in a minute."

I had gotten a few looks as I followed the girl to the table, but most people didn't pay attention to me. The few who did averted their eyes when they saw the scar. I wasn't used to that, everyone at the Academy knew where the scar came from. But it wasn't a big deal, so I just looked through the menu.

I had no idea what to try so I asked the waitress when she came to the table and I followed her suggestion of a dinner with steak and chicken cooked on skewers with some potatoes and some kind of squash. She brought breadsticks and a salad out for me to start on and it was awesome.

That was probably the best thirty dollars I'd ever spent.

"Come again," the greeter said as I left.

"Count on it," I answered and waved.

From there, I drove around Knoxville for some time before I found Middlebrook Pike, the road I was looking for. I checked the numbers of the addresses and turned left. Shortly, I came to the one I wanted. It was a two story building off of the road a bit with a lot of cars in the parking lot.

According to Kharl, most of the Guard post was underground, like at the Academy.

The name on the building was Spirit Enterprises, and I had to laugh. At least some of the older Mages had to have a sense of humor. It seemed like most of the Mages were too caught up in themselves to have a sense of humor. Gregor, Nora, and Paige were exceptions to the rule. Darrel was better than he was before I got there but he was pretty stuffy.

Maybe some of the Mages out in the field would be easier to get along with than most of the ones at the Academy. Everyone at the Academy had been running scared of the Archmage.

I pulled into the parking lot and shut off the truck. The song by Slipknot ended abruptly and my ears were still throbbing. If I wasn't a Soulguard, I think I would be half deaf by now.

I stepped out of my truck and walked around to the passenger side to retrieve the envelope from the glove box with my orders. I left my duffel bag in the back until I got settled.

When I entered the front door a Soulguard who sat behind a desk looked up at me, "Can I help you?"

"Colin Jaegher, reporting for duty," I answered, feeling a little off without a uniform on. I'd worn a uniform for the last ten months and regular clothes still felt odd.

"I've also got some orders for the Mage Captain that they sent with me."

"We've been expecting you," she said, "The new Guard Captain said you'd be here in the next few days."

She was a woman of medium height with brown hair and eyes. She wasn't beautiful but she was pretty. She stood and extended her hand, "I hear we have you to thank for the new shields, the Captain brought with him."

"A few of us put the book together several months ago and I'm glad Rictor brought some. I brought a stack of em with me, just in case."

I shook her hand as she said, "I'm Andrea Prada. I got stuck playing receptionist today. Our actual receptionist had an appointment for her kid with a doctor. So let me be the first to say, welcome to Tennessee."

I swear, Guards are so much easier to get along with than Mages, "Thanks," I answered.

Soulguard | Christopher Woods

"I'll call someone to show you to the Mage Captain so you can get the orders settled."

"That'd be great."

She paged someone named Jacobs and I went to the front windows to look outside. Tennessee is a beautiful state, even in the winter. I had learned to like the whole mountainous look in Montana, and Tennessee had those mountains, except not quite so big. The city was located amidst several ridges and it circled around them. It gave Knoxville an interesting look.

When Jacobs, a short, stout man with red hair, arrived he looked me over, "You're the one they say beat the Weapon master with a sword?"

I nodded, "His brother, Len Yueh, came in later and showed me what a Mageguard can really do though. The man is amazing."

For some reason, what I said sparked a sense of approval from the man. Maybe because I admit I'm not the best, I don't know.

"Well, follow me," Jacobs said while giving Prada an evil look.

She snickered, "I get to be a secretary, you can be a guide."

As we walked down a hallway he muttered, "Evil woman, she knew I was in the middle of a poker game."

Chapter 35

"Do you know what's in these orders?" The Mage captain asked as he finished reading them.

"I know the gist of them, Sir."

"You've pissed off someone very high up in the Mages, Young Man."

Rictor, who had been summoned when I was introduced to Sam Keller, the Mage Captain, snorted.

Keller looked up at Rictor, "What did I miss?"

"More like *everyone* high up in the Mages."

"Really?" he sat back in his chair and looked a bit closer at me. I saw the instant the realization hit him and I saw a memory flash across his aura, of a man who looked strikingly similar to me.

He sat up straight, his face pale, "Dear God, are you Kel's son?"

All that I had seen of this man's aura said that he was a good person and I was almost to the point of not caring anymore if everyone knew who I really was.

"Yes, he was my father," I answered, "but I was raised by Kharl Jaegher and Kyra Nightwing."

"Those are two names I haven't heard in some time," he looked at me for a moment and turned his stare to Rictor.

"So what did he do to piss everyone off?"

"From what I gathered, it started when they entered Colin in the Academy while the Archmage's son was considered the top Mage trainee. The arrogant little bastard decided that Colin was the enemy. Then the..."

As Rictor told the story of my last ten months, I watched Keller's aura. I watched the full spectrum of emotions flow through the man's aura by the end of the tale. Somehow Rictor had even heard of the confrontation I had with the Archmage, and it said a great deal about Keller's character that Rictor told the whole story to the man.

"I didn't think it was possible to piss off more people than I have but I stand corrected. You've not only done that but done it in less than a year. I'm impressed."

He shook his head, "You know the Archmage will try to bury you for what happened to his son. But, he'll wait a while to do it. He's a patient, evil son of a bitch but he's so strong, no one will stand against him."

"I know," I returned, "All I can do is my best. I'll face what I have to when I have to."

"They've actually done you a favor, sending the other two Mages with me. They're arrogant pricks and would be more trouble than they're worth to keep here anyway. They think you'll be swamped with running this place but they don't know about my secret weapon."

He smiled broadly, "Recently they blocked a young man from the source and sent him here. He's a frigging genius when it comes to running the business end of the place and the two Mages they did leave you have been running the Guard base for me for years. You can focus on the Patrol which is what Rictor here says you are well suited for."

I felt a great surge of relief when he made these statements because I have no idea how to actually run anything.

"I'll let Rictor show you around and you can get settled. Then I'll introduce you to Warren and the twins. I can postpone leaving for about three days, I'll try to give you as much information as I can in those three days. You should do fine with the help that's already in place."

"Is that Warren Grimes?"

"You know him?"

"They blocked him from the Source the second day I was at the Academy. I didn't expect he would work for the Guard after that."

"That man is as dedicated to the Guard as anyone, he just wasn't suited to fighting demons. They should have just allowed him to do something like this as a Mage and he wouldn't have arranged for the block to happen. I talked to him for ten minutes after he got here and I put him in an important position where he's thrived."

"I just wish the block didn't make someone so weak. A blocked Mage doesn't live long under much stress. A regular human has a much stronger stream than a blocked Mage or Guard."

I definitely needed to talk to Grimes, I might be able to help him out and still not violate any oaths.

***

"We've got more than ten businesses based out of this hub alone," Warren said, "The Guard has businesses located all around the world. Unlike the government, they can't tax the populous to provide the money to pay the Guard."

I nodded, "And you are the head of this hub's business ventures?"

"Yep, I've been running this part for the last nine months. I had a pretty hard time after they blocked me from the Source, but I have a purpose again and it helps me deal with the loss."

"Listen, I've met with you a few times and I see what Keller saw in you. If you could have at least, some of that back, would you take it?"

He looked at me suspiciously, "I arranged for this to stay away from the front lines. I'm a computer nerd, not a warrior. I can't do what you and Sam do. If I was a Mage again, that's what they would want of me. I just can't do it."

"If I give you some of it back, so you can be at least like a normal person, you won't have to face Demons. Just do what you do now. I think you should be as strong as a regular person, even if you don't want Mage power again."

"That would be great, except you just can't reverse what was done," He returned sadly, "It's called a permanent block from the Source for a reason."

"You talk to the Guard Captain about Source blocks. Then if you're interested, come see me," I said, "and while I'm here, I need some advice."

"What do you need?"

"It seems I have a good bit of money and I don't know what to do with it. I have thirty thousand dollars and what I draw from the Guard makes it where I don't need to use it to live on or anything. I talked with Sandy and Randy about my pay yesterday and I'm making more than twice what a Mage recruit makes because of the Acting Mage Captain rank. I really haven't got a clue what to do with it."

Sandy and Randy Quincy were the twins who ran the base for Keller, or for me now I guess.

"I can do some investing for you, if you want or possibly start some sort of business for you if you want. It never hurts to have more income than the Guard provides in case you end up blocked from the Source or something," he laughed bitterly.

"I don't know, how bout I make the funds available to you and you do whatever you do with it. I can invest thirty thousand now and probably, as long as I'm getting the higher salary, another five or six thousand a month."

"I can definitely do some good for you with that if you want. I'll have to get some papers together for you to sign but we can set something up."

Even with giving him that much each month, I would still draw several thousand for myself. I was amazed at the amount of money I was making. I'd never really had any money before, but I'd never really needed any either. And now I didn't need much for myself, I had moved into one of the Mage quarters at the base, so the only bill I had was the money it took to feed me.

***

Soulguard | Christopher Woods

It hadn't been a whole day since I talked to Grimes when he entered my office with hope rolling through his aura.

"Is it true," he asked in amazement, "Did you unblock a Mage at the Academy?"

"Yes," I answered, "I can unblock you, but if I do you're a Mage again. What I think I can do is loosen the bind so that you have as much stream as a regular person. If you choose to knot it, you have to take the Guard Oath to never use your power against another human. It will be your choice. I'll tell you now, you can't hide it behind a privacy screen from me. And I will hold you to your Oath."

"Understood."

I stood up and approached him. I reached out my hands like I had done when they tried to block me and slowly loosened the knot until it expanded to about three inches. You could see the paleness leave his face as life-force flowed into him again.

"Oh that feels wonderful. I've felt like a shadow for the last eleven months. You won't regret this, Sir. I won't let you down."

In his aura, I could see that he meant every word he spoke.

Chapter 36

"So how do the patrols work?" I asked Rictor. "I think I have the other stuff in hand. Keller was right about Grimes and the twins, so now I can get down to business with the patrols."

"We have a hundred Guards stationed in Knoxville. Half of them are on duty at any given time. There is always a rapid response team of twenty Guards ready to go at once to join a patrol. Typically there's a Mage on duty at all times too, but there's only one of you, so we have to do the best we can."

"I'm supposed to stay here with the rapid response team?"

"Ideally, yes," He looked at me with a grin, "Somehow I don't expect it to work out that way so we got you a sat phone. It picks up anywhere and you can get some experience with the patrolling aspects of the job."

"A patrol is two guards who, basically, drive around looking for trouble. You know as well as I that we can feel them if we get close. The first thing we do when we sense them is call in the RRT. Then, when they arrive we wipe out a nest. If we find one Demon, we follow it to the nest while the RRT is in route."

"I see," I said, "so the smart thing would be for me to stay with the RRT and come in with them."

"Yep, if you choose to patrol, I'd say keep it close to base so you can join the RRT when they get the call."

"How often are the nests found?"

"Maybe one or two a year," he said, "we don't see a great deal of action but when we find one there's plenty of fighting to go around."

"How many Demons are there in a typical nest?"

"The ones I've been into had around a hundred or so with Soldiers controlling them. All except one, it had a Wraith and about a hundred and fifty soldiers with around three hundred lesser demons. We took forty Guards and two Mages down into that one."

"Ok, I'll be around Knoxville for the most part. If you need the RRT I expect to be called. I think you should send someone east, though. I don't know why I feel this way but I feel that there's something to the east."

"Will do. You want to head that way with me?" He asked, "It'll let you see what we do in a patrol."

"Yeah I'd like to go," I hesitated, "But should I go? I really don't know what I'm supposed to do here."

"Keller went on a patrol at least twice a month, so it's not bad for you to go," He answered with a grin, "I know you don't want to stay here all the time waiting and it's alright. We'll get the call if the RRT is called in."

I felt relief because he was right, I wanted to go hunt down Demons, not sit and wait for them to attack. The researchers hadn't uncovered any missing persons reports or animal attacks recently, but a feeling just kept nagging at me. There was also a feeling from the North, but it was different. It wasn't evil, and I felt evil to the east.

"Tell the Guards to be ready," I said, "I've seriously got a bad feeling about the east."

He looked at me for a moment and nodded his head, "You got it, Boss."

We went to the armory and gathered the standard short swords for the Guard and some black body armor that was standard wear for a RRT. As we exited the armory, Andrea Prada saw us and turned our way.

"Are you two going on a patrol?"

"Thought I'd go out and show him the ropes," Rictor answered.

"Any chance I can go with you? The secretary called in again and I just know they'll want me to be her replacement."

Rictor laughed, "Rather fight Demons than answer phones, huh?"

"God, yes."

"Get your gear and come on."

***

We headed east and veered onto I-81 headed toward Johnson City. After driving for close to two hours, I began to see a darkness in the distance to our right.

"They're out here, all right." I said and pointed toward the hills to our right, "We need to head that direction as soon as we can."

"You felt this from all the way back at the base?" Rictor asked.

"I felt something evil in this direction. I can see them now, they have a darkness that surrounds them that I can see."

"That's gonna help when we send out patrols," He returned. His aura showed that he was impressed.

"You may as well call in the RRT, Rictor," I said. "That darkness is pretty big."

"You got it, Boss."

Prada didn't say a word, but I saw doubt in her aura as she glanced in my direction. Rictor must have read her mind, because he chuckled.

"You'll find, Andrea, that when the kid says something, it tends to be true," He said, "trust me."

She looked my direction again and I smiled, "You can always tell me 'I told you so' if I'm wrong."

She shrugged, "You're the boss."

I could still see the doubt in her aura until we reached the distance where they could feel the Demons themselves. She looked at me with surprise and amazement in her aura.

"I stand corrected."

We drove down some back roads to get a little closer, then pulled to the side and got out of the SUV. We went to the back and began putting on the body armor and I strapped my harness with the twin swords to my back. Excitement was coursing through me and my ever-present rage was building as I looked at the darkness ahead of us.

I looked closer and my rage grew, "They've got prisoners up there." I pointed into the hills ahead of us.

"I see human Souls very close to em."

"You see Souls?" Prada asked in amazement, "What kind of Mage are you?"

I jumped half the way up the hill, directly toward the darkness, my eyes focused on the human Souls clustered in the middle of the black souls.

As we got closer, I saw a cave mouth ahead of us and the darkness seemed to be centered in one large area under the ground. There appeared to be about twenty or twenty-five humans down there in the dark.

"How much longer for the RRT?" I asked.

"An hour."

"We can't wait that long, guys," I said, "We're gonna have to cut our way to the people where I can shield them till the team gets here."

"Can you sense how many Demons are down there?"

"A lot, and I see a very dark spot at the back of the cavern that has to be a portal."

Rictor had a grin on his face as I talked of cutting our way in, I realized that Rictor really loves killing Demons.

My rage was boiling dangerously close to the surface and I didn't see any reason to wait any longer.

"Let's do this, I'll take point. Ric, left flank, Prada, right flank. Stay with me till we get to the people so I can raise a shield."

Both nodded, Rictor wasn't surprised about me taking point but Prada was. But she knows how to follow orders and fell in at my right without hesitation.

"Go."

We shot into the darkness ahead and my swords burst into Soulflame, lighting our way. Seconds later, both Soulguard's swords lit up as well. The cavern was just ahead and I charged right into a mass of Demons. My rage soured and I began to dance the blades. It felt so good to let the rage free, even if it was only for a moment.

We reached the group of captives, who were screaming in terror, but they couldn't run from us. They were backed against a wall in some sort of alcove in the cavern. I turned and slammed a shield across the front of the opening, just before the Demons slammed into it.

My rage burned and I paced the inside of the shield, my eyes never leaving the Demons on the other side. I wanted out there. I felt like I was vibrating, I wanted out there so badly.

"Boss!"

I beat the rage back down inside of me and turned back to Rictor and Prada. The people in the alcove cringed as my gaze crossed them. I was still seeing through what looked like heat waves.

"Calm down, Colin," Rictor said softly, "We're in and the people are safe now. The team should be here soon and we can wipe this nest out."

Rictor thought it was adrenaline or just the excitement of my first battle. He had no knowledge of the rage I feel when I see Demons, or how hard it is to beat that rage back down once I let it out.

"I'm ok," I answered quietly where the captives couldn't hear me, "I just hate the waiting. I want them dead."

Prada was staring at me like I was some sort of crazed lunatic. She turned to the captives and sheathed her swords.

"You're safe now," She said softly and began to try to calm the terrified people.

People don't calm down when I try to calm them so I didn't even try. I left it to Prada and turned back to the shield and began slowly pacing back and forth in front of it while we waited for the RRT to get there.

I thought about throwing some Source grenades, but I was afraid it might collapse the cavern and that, I'm pretty sure, would be a bad thing.

Finally, after what seemed like forever, Guards poured into the cavern and the Demons outside my shield turned away from us.

"Let's hit em from behind!" I opened a portal in the shield and after we exited the shield, I left it attached to my stream and closed the portal we'd used as a door.

Then with a joyous cry, the world slowed and I began the Dance once more. It was one of the greatest feelings I'd ever had to destroy the monsters that had hunted me my entire life. They'd taken my parents, they'd killed hundreds of innocents. All to get to me. They'd regret it, now that I was ready for them to come. The hunter was now the hunted.

***

As it turned out the captives had been on a tour bus, coming down I-81, when the Demons attacked it.

Rictor sent several Guards out and had a bus rented and sent out to pick the terrified tourists up and take them and a few of the Guards back to Knoxville. I sat in the rear seat and no one sat in the adjacent seats. There were several scared glances in my direction.

Most of the people stayed closer to Prada. I guess she looked less dangerous than I did. They'd taken our SUV to go rent the bus and headed back to Knoxville already, so here we were riding a bus down I-81, back into Knoxville.

"Scary son of a bitch..." I heard Prada's voice whisper to the Guard next to her. She was unaware that I could hear her.

"He paced the inside of that shield like a wild animal in a cage. He couldn't wait to get at the Demons outside."

"I've never seen a Mage fight like that. Hell, I've never seen a Guard fight like that," another voice said softly.

I closed my eyes and lay my head back. I guess it's just how things are for me. Everywhere I go, people fear me. Normal people, Guards, and Mages all.

"Good thing he's on our side," Prada said.

Chapter 37

"Pull in up here," I pointed to a store up ahead, "I need something to drink."

"You got it," said Rex Louder.

It had been a couple of weeks since my first patrol and I worried about how the Demons had affected me. I think I had gotten a little carried away and I knew I needed to work on it.

I decided to go on another patrol, to get a better feel for things so I joined a regular patrol as a passenger.

We pulled in at a store that looked as old as the hills and I jumped out, "Want anything?"

Rex shook his head and I looked at Jenna Seymore, "You?"

"Get me a Coke."

I nodded and entered the store. The sign over the cashier claimed the best chili dog in Tennessee. I went to a cooler and got a Coke and a Dr Pepper.

"Let me get a couple of those chili dogs, too."

"You want slaw on em?"

"Coleslaw?"

"Yep."

I shrugged, "Sure, why not."

After I paid, he handed me two styrofoam containers. I slid the bag with the drinks under my arm and opened one of the containers as I walked to the door. The frigging thing was great! Who would have thought coleslaw would be good on a chili dog?

"Jesus, is he eating again?" I heard Jenna ask from inside the SUV.

"Looks like it," Rex answered, "I've never seen someone eat as much as this kid."

I got in the car as I finished the first one and handed Jenna her Coke, "Man, these things are awesome. You ever put coleslaw on a chili dog?"

"Eww," Jenna said, but Rex looked thoughtful.

"It might actually be good, but we just ate two hours ago. Where do you put all of it? Is one of your legs hollow?"

"It's like we're patrolling with a baby, you gotta eat every two hours," Jenna shook her head.

I opened the other container and waved it under her nose, "Sure you don't want one?"

"And again, I say, eww."

I laughed, "I'll take that as a no. Rex?"

"Nah, you go ahead, boss," He shook his head.

He started the SUV and we headed toward Knoxville. It was only about an hour away and we were headed in from a week patrol in Kentucky and Virginia. I hadn't felt anything out there like the Demons. I was still feeling something to the north of Knoxville, though. It wasn't evil, and I had a feeling I should check it out sometime soon.

After we pulled into the base, we unloaded our gear and headed inside. Rictor was walking out and stopped dead still as he saw me.

"I've had Marines come in with blood on their uniforms," Rictor was staring at my shirt, "I've had Marines come in with mud, dirt and even grease on their uniforms. But this is the first time someone has come in with chili on their uniform."

He shook his head sadly and walked away. Rex and Jenna burst into laughter.

"What? What'd I do?"

***

I drew the blades Kyra had given me. They were a matching set of beautiful short swords. They were three feet long with double edged blades two and a half feet long. They were made with some exceptional steel and had intricate etching along the blades.

In the center of our miniature version of the Dome I started the Dance. It had been a few days since I had been able to do this. When I really get into the Dance I can let loose of the rage in me and use its focus to add to it

I started at a normal pace for a Guard. I hadn't noticed as several Guards had entered the Mini-Dome. And more began arriving as I proceeded into the Dance. After each completed run through the Dance, I would add speed and do it again.

I completed seven repetitions before I Pulled as I had done while at the exhibition with Len Yueh. My focus sharpened and I glowed with Soulfire. As I finished the last stance, sweat rolling from me, I noticed that there were Guards crowded into the Dome, watching.

It started on the far left when someone clapped, then the whole Dome echoed with applause. My face was burning a bit. I had been so focused, I didn't even know they were there.

"That's awesome every time I see it, Boss," Rictor said as he walked toward me.

"Thanks," I returned, "My mom trained me since I was five in the Dance. I didn't even notice anyone was here."

"I actually came to see if you'd take some time to make sure the Guards have gotten the new shield working right. But I saw you start the Dance of Blades and sent for the others to watch. It really is something to see and none of us have seen it except a very few. I'd like to get you to do it again sometime for the ones who haven't seen it."

"They should really see Kyra do it," I said, "She's a master at it."

"She's very good but she's not as fast as you," Rictor said, "I never thought I'd be saying that Kyra Nightwing is not as fast as someone but you move like fluid lightning."

I felt a mix of embarrassment and pride. I guess Paige was right, I have a hard time taking compliments. I just try to do the best I can and most times I come up short of what I should have done.

"Yeh, tell the Guards to come to me whenever they're ready for me to check the shields. And I'll do the dance again later if you guys want. Hell, if anybody's interested, I'll teach them the Dance of Blades. It looks like we'll be here for a good while, maybe some of em want to learn it."

Chapter 38

I still felt something to the north, it wasn't Demons and it felt more urgent than before. I opened my Inner eye and looked northward. Something tugged at my awareness and I turned my truck north on highway 33 heading out of Knoxville.

I drove for thirty minutes before I saw a glimmer of light from a very bright soul off to the left. I turned left on a small road and pulled the truck over. A small farmhouse stood in the center of a large piece of land in the distance, and inside that house was a beautiful Soul that glowed brighter than most.

I drove into the driveway and headed toward the house. As I got out of the truck, a little girl opened the door and looked at me, her aura flowing with awe. Her Soulstream was enormous and her eyes were wide as she walked closer to me.

"Are you a Angel?" she asked in awe, "You look like a Angel. You're light is so bright. I prayed for a Angel cause Nana is sick and the monsters are coming to get me."

"The monster got my mommy last year. But she got the monster too. Now there's another monster and it wants to get me."

As she said this, I saw the little girl's memory of a Wraith and a woman Mage explode in a fiery maelstrom of power. The rage began to build and I flashed back to the death of my mother.

"Ooooh, the monster got your mommy, too."

Then it hit me, she'd just read my memory like I do. She can see streams and memories, she's a Soullord.

"You're like me," I said in wonder.

"Nuhuh, You're a Angel. I'm just a little girl," she shook her head in determination.

"Where is your Nana now?"

"She's inside," the little girl started, then her head turned to the left and I read fear in her aura, "Oh no, the monsters are coming."

I looked the same direction she was and saw a darkness on the horizon.

"Let's get inside with your Nana," I said and pulled my cell phone out to dial headquarters.

"Yeah, boss?" Rictor answered.

"Ric we have a code Zulu north of Knoxville, possibly with a Wraith. Get mobile and get here as quickly as you can. You'll feel it when you get near."

"Gotcha boss, we'll be right there." the phone clicked.

I ran to my truck and pulled my twin swords from behind the seat. Then I followed the little girl inside. A woman lay on the sofa, her aura was dim. She was very sick I lay my hand on her shoulder and Pulled very softly into myself and Pushed some life force into her.

"Ooooh..." the little girl said as she saw what I had done.

"Can't do that too much or it will hurt her," I informed her.

I anchored to the ground and wove a shield around us.

"I can do that," she chirped and a smaller shield began weaving from her stream. "See?" she asked proudly.

I dropped mine and smiled at the girl, "If you keep that shield in place, the monster can't get in. Now let me outside of it."

"The monsters will get you," she almost wailed.

I smiled, "No, if I'm out there I'll get them."

"Scaary Angel," she said with wide eyes, "Do I take it down?"

"No, just open a door in the front and close it after I go out," I knelt in front of her, "The monsters will never get you, don't be afraid. Just hold that shield up so Nana will be safe. Can you do that for me?"

She nodded and opened a door for me. I smiled and walked out to stand in front of the shield. I opened my portal to turn on my personal shield and my swords flared with Soulfire.

"Ooooh..." the little girl said as if she had found a new toy.

I chuckled, she's gonna be a handful, without a doubt.

I saw the darkness grow close and the rage erupted in me. The end of the house was ripped away and the world slowed to a crawl as I began the Dance. In moments there wasn't much left of the house around us, nor was there much left of the pile of lesser Demons that had ripped through the walls. The little girl stood, wide-eyed inside her shield, unhurt.

Soldiers loped across the fields toward us and with a savage exultation, I went to meet them.

"Look, Nana, the Angel is killing the monsters!"

My swords blurred as I danced the Dance of Blades amongst them and more demons fell. I felt the Wraith before it got there and turned to meet it. I felt the little girl Pull and I felt fear. Fear for the little girl.

But she was fine. A fireball hit the Wraith in the back of the head and it screamed and turned from me.

"My Angel! Not yours!"

It started for her and I leapt in front of it and opened up my Soullance. I still hadn't perfected it but for sheer power it was unmatched.

"Not today," I said and Pulled.

The power shot straight out the end of the tube in a huge lance of Soulfire. The Wraith screamed and tried to come closer to me. I poured more power into the lance and the Wraith roared one last time before exploding.

"Ooooh..." she said again.

Yep, she's gonna be a handful.

"More Angels!" she clapped in excitement as Rictor and twenty Guards came bounding across the fields.

I turned to the rest of the pack of Demons and charged into them. Rictor roared in pure glee as he slammed into the back of the pack of Demons and the Guards went through them like a hot knife through butter.

In moments it was over, all the Demons were dead and Rictor walked over to me, "You're a shit magnet, Colin, everywhere you go..." Rictor saw the girl behind me, "Stuff happens!"

210

I laughed and turned to the little girl, "Rictor, this is," I paused, "What's your name little Angel?"

"I'm Lyrica Jayne and this is Nana," she introduced the woman who had managed to sit up on the sofa. "Nana, this is the Angel, He killed the monster and the monster didn't get us."

I nodded to the woman and looked again at Lyrica, "You can take down the shield now, it's safe."

"Did I do good?"

"You did real good," I answered and she ran up and gave me a hug. She pulled me toward Nana.

"Thank you, Young Man," The older woman said with gratitude rolling across her aura, "You saved our lives and we will be forever grateful. But what do we do now? There will be more of them, there's always more."

"No there won't. I'll take you somewhere safe," I couldn't think of anywhere safer than the compound in Montana. The Elite Guards were there and Gregor and the Mages were there.

As I thought of Kyra and Kharl, Lyrica gasped, "You got a *new* mommy! Do you think I can get one? I really miss my mommy."

I knelt in front of her again, "I think you may get a lot of new mommies Lyrica Jayne. And I will gladly share mine with you."

She wrapped her little arms around my neck and cried for the first time since I'd seen her.

Chapter 39

Lyrica and Georgia, aka Nana, were asleep in the private cabin, on the plane. I called Gregor.

"Hello, Colin," he answered.

"Greg, I'm on my way back to Montana with someone you need to see."

"Really?"

"Oh yeah, I've found someone like me, and we need to figure out how this is gonna work. They are *not blocking this girl.* You know I know how to prevent that, and I'll show her how. Demons have hounded her since she was born, they killed her mother and I want her trained to defend herself."

"Calm down, Col," He said soothingly, "I can't guarantee that. But you'll have to get here first to discuss this."

"Just mark my words, Greg, they'll have to kill me before they block this little girl from the Source. You've seen what I can do. Imagine how many lives would have been saved if I had been able to train in Mage craft as well as Guard. I know how many, One hundred and twenty-two lives, Gregor. That's how many people died at Morndel that didn't need to.

"This girl will *not* have those lives on her conscience, Greg."

"I understand, Colin," he paused for a moment, "And I'll back you all the way, boy."

"Thank you, Sir."

I hung up the phone and dialed another number.

"Hello, Son," her voice answered.

"Hi, Mom, I need a favor..."

***

As the door opened on the side of the plane, Lyrica peeked out to see seventeen women standing in a line waiting for the plane. The first in line was Kyra.

There were fifteen female Soulguards at the compound at the moment and all of them had come for this. There were also two Mages, Paige Turner and Nora Kestril.

Lyrica's eyes went wide as she saw all of them.

"They're here to meet you Little Angel," I whispered in her ear.

"Me?"

"Yep," I nodded, "Go say hi."

Lyrica climbed down the stair and walked hesitantly over to Kyra, who reached down to lift the tiny girl into her arms.

"My Angel said he would share his mommy with me cause the monsters took my mommy. Is it ok?"

"It's just fine you little sweetheart," Kyra answered and hugged her tight. The other women closed in and crowded around Lyrica and her Soul glowed brightly.

I smiled and felt a hand on my arm. Georgia stood beside me with tears running down her face.

"Thank you," was all she said.

***

"A fireball?" Gregor asked incredulously, "She's six, Colin."

"She's like me, Greg, She can *see* all of it. She saw her mother shoot fireballs at demons and watched how she did it. I can see myself at her age doing the same if I'd seen Mages do it."

"I got the approval for training," Gregor said, "Mainly because she scares the shit out of them all. She's got more power in her Soulstream than me and Nora both. The only Mage with more power than her is the Archmage."

"And when I hinted that someone already knows how to prevent a block, and might have told her how, they jumped right on the bandwagon. No one as very enthusiastic about having a backlash like a certain group of Mages did."

"That's a relief, Greg," I exhaled slowly, "I really don't want to start a war at home. I just can't stand by and watch history repeat itself."

"Have you seen her in the last week?" he asked.

"No, she's running around with the Guard," I laughed, "Mom says she's been attached to her like a leech since she got here. Once she figures out that she's really not leaving her she'll probably be a handful to keep up with."

"She got her Soulstream knotted in less than a day and she's been bouncing around Ky like another youngster she talked about," he laughed.

"You're the one in trouble, though," He smirked, "You're her hero and now you have to live up to that status. Never shirk in your hero duties and never show up without a special gift."

"Oh crap, what do I give a six year old? Where's a gift shop?" I was panicking a little and Gregor laughed aloud.

He handed me a small box, "Chocolate works for girls of all ages."

***

"Angel!!"

A high pitched Squeal assailed my ears followed by a high speed projectile. I caught her with my right arm and held my left behind my back. She squirmed and tried to look over my shoulder.

"What's that?" she asked, her neck stretching as far as she could.

"Stretch your neck any farther and your head might pop right off."

"Unh uh" she argued, but she pulled her head back down just a bit, just in case.

I finally relented and handed her the package.

"For me?"

"Yeah, for you."

She sat down on the ground and opened the chocolates. She shoved one in her mouth and chewed happily.

"I have to go back to Knoxville, Little Angel. The Guard is gonna train you to fight like me and the

Mages are gonna train you to use the Source. You pay attention to them and learn all that you can. One of these days you won't need anyone to protect you, You'll protect others."

She looked at me wide-eyed.

"It's an honor to become a Soulguard, but there's a big responsibility that goes with it. You listen to Mom and you'll do good, ok?"

She nodded, "Are you going to be someone else's Angel, now?" she asked in a tiny voice.

"I'm your Angel. No one else's. But I still have to go help other people. There are monsters out there trying to get people and I'm going to *get* them."

She smiled brightly and hugged me, then ran back over toward Kyra, "My Angel is gonna go chase the monsters away, Mommy."

My mother looked at me with a smile, "You don't need to worry about this one," She said motioning toward the child, "She's in good hands. You've done a good thing here, Son."

Chapter 40

`It was my nineteenth birthday and I was trying to make sense of how Warren had doubled my money in a few short months. The man was amazing at his job.

I don't understand how the Mages could even have a problem with the man doing this kind of work instead of killing Demons. Sure Mages are rare, but some people are more skilled in other areas. Grimes had made more money for the Soulguard than he ever would have been worth as a Mage.

"Warren, there's no use trying to explain it," I interrupted the man, "I'm a mathematical idiot. But just to be clear, you've doubled what I've given you already?"

"Yes sir."

"Don't call me sir, it sounds silly."

"Ok sir."

I sighed, "Whatever you're doing, keep it up. I've actually got some more to add to it. As a matter of fact, I'd like to set it up where you just receive all my pay except a couple of thousand per month. At least for the foreseeable future. Then you do what you do with it."

"How do you trust people so easily?"

"I can see into your Soul, Warren. How are you gonna lie to me?"

***

"Boss," Rictor stuck his head into my office, "we got another nest. It's up in West Virginia. It's about a four hour drive."

"Ok," I set the papers I was looking through down, "Let's get going."

We left my office and went to the armory to gear up. The RRT was ready and waiting when we came out to the SUVs. Rictor and I got in the same vehicle. There were five SUVs each with four passengers except ours had six. The rear of each vehicle was crammed with weapons and body armor.

"You gonna try to control yourself this time, Boss," Rictor asked with a grin, "Leave a few for the rest of us."

My face turned a little red. I'd been really wired up the first time I got to kill Demons. I would try to control the rage inside me a little better this time. Maybe I wouldn't freak out the Guards this time. Prada looks at me funny every time I see her.

"What you want to listen to on the radio, Boss?" Jacobs asked innocently and Rictor groaned.

"It just so happens I have some Drowning Pool here," I answered and passed my MP3 player to the front.

"It's no wonder you're so damn ready to fight," muttered Rictor, "The shit you listen to would drive a sane person nuts."

I laughed and Jacobs said, "By the time we get there, you'll all be aching to kill something."

I leaned back in my seat and closed my eyes as the speakers began to rumble. Jacobs was the only Guard on our base who liked the same music as I do and it tickles him when he gets to rub their noses in it.

Four hours of DJ Jacobs' music selections and the others would have gladly strung both of us up by our heels. But we were all sensing the Demons by then and the aggression could be sent in a safer direction. I'd been sensing them for hours but I didn't bring it up. No need in freaking' my guys out before we ever got there.

"Feels like a lot of em," Tyler, the driver, said.

"They're down deep, too," I said, "Nick said something about a coal mine?"

"Yeah," Rictor said, "Old abandoned coal mine. One way in, one way out."

We pulled in behind the patrollers SUV and exited the vehicle. Jacobs opened the rear hatch and started handing out gear. I donned my body armor and the harness that holds my swords to my back.

"Welcome to the party," Rachel Corey said as she walked out of the darkness, "They're down in a deep assed shaft right inside the entrance."

An idea began forming in my mind, I didn't like it very much. My rage had started building the second I felt their presence and I'd been stewing for several hours.

As we entered the front of the mine I looked deep into the earth with my sight and there were no human Souls down in the bottom of that shaft but there were hundreds of Demons.

I sighed in disappointment.

"What?" Rictor asked.

I ran my hand across my face and beat down some of the rage trying to break out, "I got an idea, I really want to go down there and kill every last one of those damn things, but it would make more sense to kill them from here, I guess."

"Sure, let's just kill em from here," Jacobs said, "What do you want to do, stand here and throw rocks at em?"

"Actually, yeah," I smiled and started forming Soul fire grenade shields. I managed to make thirty-five shields without losing any shield strength. They were on the edge of the shaft. I Pulled and filled them with power. A lot of power. Lastly I Pulled and reinforced the shields farther to make them last longer once they were separated from the Source.

"Kick em in the hole, and run like hell," I said, "Make sure you run like hell, I put a crapload of power in these."

The Guards moved up and all the grenades were kicked into the hole. We all ran back out the entrance and I kept Pulling into the shields as long as I could. The shaft was over a hundred feet deep, but I managed to hold them until they reached the bottom. I cut the tendrils and a moment later, the world shook around us.

At least that's what it felt like, anyway. It was a small part of the world but it still shook hard enough to throw us all around some.

"Hell Yeah!" Jacobs yelled.

I looked down into the earth and there were no ugly black souls left alive down there.

"They're dead," I said.

"You sound so disappointed," Rachel looked at me sadly, "Think about us, We've been sitting here waiting for four and a half hours just to watch you blow up a mountain."

I laughed and removed my gear and stuck it back in the SUV.

"You just wait till I tell the twins how much gas you just wasted. You could have drove the Toyota and saved over a hundred dollars in fuel. You're in so much trouble."

One of the other Guards said, "They got some good ski resorts up here, you know."

"I'm definitely not trying to explain a ski trip to the Twins," Rictor said, "But it's only a few miles over to the New River Gorge. I always wanted to see that bridge they have over it."

I slid into the back seat of the SUV we had come in, "Jacobs, how bout some Mudvayne?"

Everyone scrambled for the other SUVs and Jacobs looked around in disappointment, "I have to drive, now?"

Everyone had found a different SUV than ours.

Chapter 41

I heard the commotion before it reached my door. I was sitting behind my desk with some of the paperwork that the Twins needed signed so we could get more supplies.

I hate paperwork, but it's part of the job, I guess.

A head poked around the edge of my door. It was connected to a pretty little girl who ran in the room as soon as she saw me. She cleared my desk in a bound and landed right in my lap with her arms around my neck.

"Angel!"

I hugged her back and said, "Happy birthday Little Angel."

She turned around and froze as she saw the giant teddy bear beside the door. It was six inches taller than she was.

"That bear's looking at me."

"That's your birthday present Little Angel."

She looked at it for a moment as Kharl and Kyra walked into the room. Then she looked at me, "Is it a Bearguard? It's got a Soulstream. It's got two Soulstreams."

"Go check him out."

She leaped from my lap, across the room and tackled the bear. The two of them rolled out into the hall and all we heard was giggling.

Kyra sat down in one of the chairs and sighed, "Lord, that girl is a handful."

Kharl laughed and sat down in the other chair, "Possibly, worse than a certain person, who bounced everywhere for a year. I don't know what his name is but his initials are Colin Rourke."

"What was she saying about the bear having a Soulstream?" Kyra asked.

"I experimented a little bit and made the critter a lot tougher. She won't tear him up that way," I shrugged, "I interlaced a light shield into the teddy bear that makes him almost indestructible. Then I tied it to the source so it would stay that way."

"You say things like that as if it's something everyone does," Kyra laughed, "Wait till I tell Gregor."

I laughed, "There are several messed up bears in the armory right now that show it wasn't an easy thing. There's actually one in our Mini-Dome that we use for target practice. He's solid as steel so I put one of those practice shields around him and there we go."

"How many bears did you have to buy?"

"Thirty-two."

Kharl laughed loudly, "You don't give up, easy. So what's this I hear about you blowing up a mountain in West Virginia?"

"Yeah, I think I upset some of the Guards with that. I'm not sure if it was the four and a half hour drive with no fight or the fact we listened to heavy metal all the way there that bothered them more."

"My bet would be the music, if you can call it that," Kharl said.

Lyrica poked her head in the door, "Can me and Bearguard go look around?"

"Promise to stay out of trouble?" Kyra asked.

"Ok," she frowned, "I promise."

"Then you can look around some."

She turned and walked down the hallway dragging the bear.

Kharl looked at his watch, "Her record is ten minutes."

"Ten minutes?"

"Until she gets into something," he said with a chuckle.

After eight and a half minutes, we got up and headed out to see what she was doing. I opened my Inner eye and looked for her Soul. She was going into the Mini-Dome, which happened to be on the same level as my office.

"This way," I said and led the way.

When we entered the Dome, she had Jacobs bent down listening to her, "That's Bearguard's brother. He fell to the dark side and I need a light sabre so I can stop him."

I turned to Kharl, who was looking around innocently, "Been watching Star Wars?"

Jacobs looked at me, "Can she have a light sabre to take care of our dark side Bearguard problem?"

I looked to Kyra and she sighed, "Practice wands, get the long daggers."

Jacobs headed for the rack and took down two practice wands that were about two feet long. He presented them to Lyrica with a bow.

"Your weapons, Milady."

Lyrica took the wands with a giggle and looked over where she had leaned her bear against the wall, "This is how we deal with Bearguards who turn to the dark side."

In the next instant, she was bouncing around the other bear with her blades looking suspiciously like little green light sabers.

"I should have fast forwarded through the scene with Yoda fighting Dooku. She bounces around more than you do." Kharl shook his head sadly. "She's even got Ky jumping around when they spar. It's just not right."

"You're just mad cause you can't catch her," Kyra said with a smile, "She's faster than Colin was."

By then there was quite an audience watching from the side with us.

"If any of you guys start showing up with light sabers, I'm making you spar with Colin," Rictor said from behind me.

"I'm not sparring with him," Prada returned, "I was on the first patrol, too."

"What'd you do on your first patrol?" Kyra looked at me with the one eyebrow raised.

"I got a little carried away," I answered with a red face.

"Carried away!?" Prada continued, "He scared those poor people so bad they wouldn't sit near him on the bus back."

"I guess you sat all the way in the front for moral support?" Rictor asked.

"Hell no, he scared me worse than them."

Everyone's eyes jerked back toward Lyrica when she suddenly Pulled. She was facing the bear with her back to us, so I didn't see exactly what she shot. The bear's head flew straight up in the air as whatever she threw tore right through the shield. Then the lights flickered and went out as the projectile went through the shield wall, too. There must have been some wiring behind that concrete wall across from us.

I made my personal shield flame brightly as a light source to find Lyrica standing with her head cocked to the side.

"Oh no," she turned to me with guilty look, "I broke it."

I could see fear rolling through several auras around us, but the look on her face was priceless. I began laughing and walked to her.

I reached down and picked her up, "It's ok, Little Angel, I broke a lot of stuff at the Academy. We'll fix it."

"I'm sorry."

"What was that, anyway?"

"Fireballs are too big," She explained, "I can't see around em so I squished it flat and shrunk it to Lyrica size."

I understood as she said it and I liked it. I was smiling and Rictor sighed, "Oh God, another one."

I walked out of the Dome with Lyrica whispering in my ear, "Everyone is scared of me. Why is everyone scared of me?"

"The same reason they're scared of me, Little Angel," I whispered back, "Most people are scared of what they don't understand. And not many people understand us."

"You're not scared of me."

"That's right, and you're not scared of me. You never have to be scared of me, Little Angel."

***

This wasn't the first time since we had bought our tickets to the Knoxville Fair that I wished for a camera. Kharl rolled across the floor in a bumper car being chased by a small figure in another one. Lyrica was joined by a horde of other kids in similar cars and all of them were aimed at Kharl.

"That is a Kodak moment," I said as I walked up behind Kyra.

"Oh, I got pictures," She held up her cell phone, "I'm showing them all to the Guards, too."

"Hehe."

"Are you eating again?"

"Yeh, these things are awesome," I raised an Italian sausage with onions, peppers, ketchup and mustard out to her, "Want one?"

"That looks decidedly unhealthy," she said, "I'd love one."

I handed the sausage to her and she bit into the end. After a moment she said, "How did you eat the crap I fixed for seventeen years without complaining?"

"Kharl told me I was the second kid you guys tried to raise and the first only made it seven years."

She snorted and almost choked on her sausage, "It's all his fault, I swore after the first year of living with him that I would never cook a good meal

227

again until he offered to make dinner just one time. He never offered and I never cooked a good meal."

I'd stopped chewing my sausage as she said this, "You mean to tell me, seventeen years of battery acid was because Kharl wouldn't make dinner."

"You make it sound so bad when you say it that way."

"I have to work out every day in the Dome to keep from swelling up like a tick because of my eating habit. I just can't stop. It's so good. And it's all your fault."

She laughed and raised the camera, "That's a good one. The look on your face is priceless."

The children all caught Kharl and seven bumper cars tangled up at one end of the ring. There were squeals of joy as Kharl was cornered and brought down by the pack of youngsters. Kyra snapped another shot of them.

"Son, thank you for bringing that little girl to me."

"Who else would I trust to teach her the right way to live? You and Kharl are the reason I'm here today."

"She's a sweet girl," Kyra said, "And she's had a rough start to life. But she's safe and now she gets to be a kid. That's something you never had, and I'm sorry. We never were safe enough to let you have the childhood you deserved."

"I wouldn't trade a minute of my childhood with you and Kharl for anything. The only thing I would have different would be Mage training and it just wasn't possible. That's the one thing I demanded of Gregor when I brought her to Montana."

"How did you manage that?"

"I told him I taught her to stop a block and it would be better for all involved to train her," I left out the threat that they would have to kill me first.

"Did you?" she asked, "Teach her to stop a block?"

"Yes I did," I said, "But I showed her how to do it without burning down the Mages who were blocking her. It's a matter of timing."

"Angel!" we were interrupted by Lyrica as she ran up at a normal pace for a little girl. She stopped as she saw my Italian Sausage.

"I want one of those."

"Let's go get one, then," I said, holding out my hand, "You should try the funnel cake, too. Some-one was also telling me about a cheeseburger with Crispy Crème Donuts for a bun."

"I've created a monster," I heard Kyra say softly as Lyrica and I made our way to the sausage vender.

Chapter 42

Eleven of us were seated at several tables that had been pulled together by our hostess when we came into Ruby Tuesdays in Fountain City.

"To taking out the trash," Rictor raised his glass of beer. We'd finished cleaning out a nest of Demons down near Chattanooga and had returned to our base earlier today.

"Taking out the trash," we all replied with our glasses in the air. Every one of them held beer except mine, I was only twenty, and I don't like beer much anyway.

"Let me tell you," I said, "If there's one thing Kyra Nightwing's cooking accomplished, it's to teach me to appreciate food. This was the best steak I've ever eaten."

"Really?" Andrea Prada asked, "You should try the steak at J Milton's in Middlesboro."

"They're good," Rictor said, taking a sip of his beer, "I like the rib eye you can get at Pete's Place in Maynardville."

"The Chop House is great," Janacek offered.

As the Guards started talking about where to get the finest steak my eye fell on a little girl, she was probably ten. There was something off about her so I opened my Inner eye. Her soul was dim, but it didn't seem to be from illness. I think this girl actually wanted to die.

Now why would that be? I wondered, until I saw the man sit next to her and she cringed. Fear and loathing rolled across her aura and I looked at the man. His aura was disgusting, it was vile. Then he looked at the girl and a memory rolled through his aura.

The things that man had done to the girl were hideous, and the rage began trying to claw its way out of me.

"Boss!?" Rictor had set his beer down as he saw my eyes begin to smolder, "What is it? Code Zulu?"

He looked the direction I was looking and then back at me, "Andrea, Janicek, get him out of here he's about to melt down!"

The two nearest Guards grabbed my arms and pushed me out of the restaurant. I was shaking all over as they steered me away from the front and toward the two SUV's we had driven in.

"Colin," Andrea asked with a note of concern in her voice, "What is it?"

Several more of our patrol strode out and headed in my direction. They were looking around for the Demons everyone expected to show up any minute.

The memory was burned into my mind along with every emotion that twisted bastard had felt as he beat and raped that child repeatedly.

Rictor stood in front of me and grabbed my arms, "Snap out of it! What the hell is wrong?"

I did something I had never done before, I took a memory and Pushed it into another's aura. Actually I Pushed it into all ten Guards' auras. They witnessed what I saw and they felt what I felt, all of the rage that was boiling inside me.

I finally beat the rage down and looked to see Rictor, his eyes bloodshot and his arms were shaking. Each of the Guards were looking at me in a mix of fear and fury. My fury and their fear.

Rictor managed to calm himself, "How did you keep from blowing up the whole place, Boss? I've never felt anything like what you just felt in my life."

"It's my curse, Ric," I said and held my hands over my face as I bent my head forward.

"That's what you feel when we fight?" Andrea asked softly.

"Every time."

"Damn," muttered Wilson.

"I can't let that man live another day, Ric. My Oath says I can't do it but I have to."

"Ever since that day at the Academy, you've asked me to trust you. Now I'm gonna ask you to trust me. It will be dealt with. This isn't the first time we've come across circumstances like this, and no one's Oath will be broken. Just trust me."

My Sight was still active and I saw truth in his aura and I saw the worry he felt about what I might do.

I nodded and Rictor turned to Wilson, "Bring the other truck after you find out which vehicle is his. Get a tag number and the rest will be handled."

"Gotcha," Wilson answered with a vicious look on his face. They all had seen what that bastard had done.

"You're sure he did this and wasn't just wanting to do it?" Ric asked.

"I don't read minds, Ric, I see memories."

He nodded and pushed me into the SUV, "All right then, It'll be settled soon then."

232

***

Rictor and I stood outside of a house on Emory Road. We stood well out of range of any lights, back amongst the trees.

I watched as that evil, disgusting soul wandered through the house. The child's dim and damaged soul was alone in a room at the back of the house.

In the darkness I almost missed it as another soul approached the house. I'd never seen a soul like this. It was pure black, not ugly or vile, just black. It held a beauty of its own, not like the brilliant color of a normal soul, but a beauty, nonetheless.

"He should be here anytime," whispered Rictor.

"He's here now," I answered quietly, "Who is he?"

"I met him in Afghanistan. He was the man they sent when they absolutely had to have someone disappear. The Afghanis had a name for him, The Whisper in the Night. That's all his target hears, a whisper out of the darkness and then death."

I watched as that black soul entered the house. The ugly soul entered the room with the girl and I saw the fear flare up in her soul. Then our man was in the room and that vile soul flickered once and disappeared.

I felt the rage stop beating at the walls to be free as I saw that soul extinguished.

"He was offered a place in the Guard, but he refused. He said that there were monsters out there that we're not allowed to fight and he would fight them while we fight ours."

The girls fear was replaced with hope as she neared the black soul. Then the two of them went out of that room and parted ways. The man left and the girl called the police. I could see her through a window dialing the phone.

"Justice is served," I mumbled.

"Yep."

Chapter 43

I was sitting in my office at HQ looking at a computer screen. I was trying to decide what to write in a letter to my parents. Some things I just can't say over a phone line, not after the events at the Academy. I can't give the Archmage an excuse to remove me, or worse an excuse to remove Kharl and Kyra.

"Hey Boss," he looked at me with a worried expression, I didn't need to see his aura to know that something was bothering him.

"Ric, what's up?"

He reached back and shut the door, so I opened my Inner Eye to better read the situation. Ric wouldn't have shut it if it wasn't serious.

He took a deep breath and let it out, "I need you to do me a favor. What you feel, that rage, there's something not natural about that, Boss. People just don't feel that much rage unless something is wrong."

"I know, I can see what people feel and I've never seen anything like this in others. Sure, there's rage in some people but I don't think it's like this."

"That's what I'm saying," he sat down in the chair across from my desk, "The thing is, I know a guy. He works for us when we need a doctor for, let's say, sensitive matters. If I get him to come out here, will you talk to him? Just let him see if there's something wrong."

I looked at Ric and the genuine worry he had in his aura. He wasn't worried because he was picked by Kharl to be my watchdog or because he was worried for himself. It was because he was my friend. That, more than anything convinced me to nod.

"Yeah, I'll see him. I need to know what it is. It started when I was about thirteen but it wasn't bad then, I just had a bit of a temper. The bad part started after Morndel, after I killed Demons." I met his eyes with my own, "Bring on this doctor, maybe we can get some answers."

"All right then," Ric stood up and turned toward the door, "I'll call him today."

***

I Pulled as I Danced the Blades in our training Dome at HQ. Faster I danced with my blades weaving around me in a blaze of Soulfire. As the Dance ended, I landed in the finishing stance. The Soulfire faded and the world came back into focus around me.

"That looks as awesome as it did the first time I saw you do it," Rictor's voice came from behind me. "You're mom looks a lot better doing it though. You just look scary."

I laughed and looked at the ex-Marine, "If you saw her kill Demons with the Dance, you'd know it was scary when she did it too."

"That may be true," he answered and ran his hand across his buzz cut hair. "We need to talk, Boss."

"Results from the Doc?"

"Yeah, he's here. He's in your office."

"Well, let's get it over with then," Doctor Terrence Pickney had done a great many tests on me. I don't know what they were called, but there had been a lot of them.

I followed Rictor out of our Mini-Dome and we made our way to my office. Pickney was seated across from my desk and rose as we entered, his hand outstretched. I shook his hand and moved around my desk to my seat.

"So what's the prognosis Doc?"

"I found something interesting when I ran your DNA." The doctor spoke in very precise words, English was not his first language and he spoke without accent of any sort that I could detect.

"I have found this same anomaly three times before. I was the man who was responsible for the autopsies after Demon attacks for many years. The first time I saw this was in 1970, in Berlin. After a pregnant woman had been killed by Demons, I found this anomaly in the body of the unborn child. There had been Demon blood in the umbilical cord from the slaughter. It had made its way into the child."

"After finding the Demon blood in the chord, I checked the child to find that a very small amount of the unborn child's DNA had been altered before it too died."

I could see where this was going already and I really dreaded the rest of the story.

"The second time was in 1981, with much the same results. The interesting thing is that the third time was in 1990, when the Demon's killed Rhayne Rourke. This same thing was found there, but there was no baby. It was presumed that a Demon had eaten the child. But that's not true, is it?"

I looked at the Doctor for a moment and shook my head, "No, I'm Colin Rourke. Kelvin Demonkiller was my father and Rhayne was my mother."

"I do not know how many changes this event has done in you, except to say that your DNA is not exactly human any more. Physically, everything is fine. But this rage you feel may be from a non-human heritage that we know very little about."

"If the Demons are driven by this sort of rage," I said softly, "they'll never stop coming, no matter how many we kill."

"That could very well be, but now we know some of what drives them and that is more than we knew before. The only thing I know that would help you is to retire to some peaceful spot where there is no stress to trigger your rage. Or whenever you face the Demons, embrace that rage so it has some outlet. It is very dangerous to let the rage build inside of you without an outlet."

He stood back up, "With the profession you have chosen, the second option is your only hope for now. I will do the research to try to find something you can counter this with but I will not give you false hope. The problem may not be able to be treated. Release your rage any time you can safely do so. Lives may depend on this."

I sat back in my chair as the doctor strode out of the office with Rictor. That's just great, I'm part Demon. It's probably where the hole in my soul comes from too, I thought. How the hell do I put that in a letter home? Hi mom, everything's going great out here and, by the way, I'm a freaking Demon spawn.

Chapter 44

"The Dance isn't set in any one stance. Each stance you use in battle can be a part of the Dance," I stood before a group of twenty Guards, "The Dance is not the stance but the flow from one stance to the next."

I was surprised that so many Guards had shown up to learn the Dance of Blades.

"The change from stance to stance becomes effortless after you practice enough times. The more different stances you are actually using, the more complex the Dance. Kyra taught me a great many stances so I can do a complex Dance."

"In battle, the key is to know what stance you need for what you face. Each moment, that need may change and you must be able to flow into the next stance without effort."

As I spoke, I worked through five different stances in front of the Guards. My movements flowed like water. There was no noticeable spot where my stances changed. They flowed together seamlessly. Well mostly seamless.

"Kyra is much better at the changes than I am, but I do ok."

Prada laughed, "He does ok," She said and shook her head.

"Each of you pick two stances you are familiar with and begin switching between the two. I will come by and we can see the best way to minimize the energy used in the change."

Prada had two stances she was switching between. One had her two wands poised for an attack from down low on the left and high on the right. She switched from that one to a stance with a powerful thrust with both swords combined with two steps forward to add emphasis on the thrust.

"The switch is good but there are several of the movements that aren't necessary. Part of the Dance is to remove any unnecessary movement between the attacks."

I took the same beginning stance and showed her where I would trim the moves down and assumed the second stance with a seamless flow.

She nodded and repeated the moves I made, "That was easier, it felt more natural."

"The Dance is all about feeling the natural flow in the changes. Keep using those two until it comes natural to you to use those moves to accomplish the change. After you are comfortable with it, add another stance."

I moved to Janicek, the next Guard in line, "If you lower the left one just a bit, you'll find it feels better."

He followed my advice and smiled as he felt the difference, "It is better."

"Most of the Dance, you figure out as you practice. I spent hours a day for thirteen years to learn what I have and I saw a man who came to the Academy that made me feel clumsy and inept. He was the most awesome swordsman I've ever seen and if I ever get the chance to learn under him I'll jump at it. He said he was the one who taught Kyra the Dance."

I looked to the door to the dome to see Rictor motioning for me.

"Excuse me guys, duty calls. Keep going and you don't have to accept my way as a rule. Each of us is different and the movement that works for me may be totally different than the move needed for a six and a half foot tall ox," I said as I motioned in the direction of Lawrence Davies.

He chuckled and kept on with his movements.

I placed my wands on the rack and headed toward Ric. As I reached him I opened my Inner eye to see that he was worried.

"You got an official visitor, Boss," he said, "Some guy from the Council, Guilefort I think."

"That's the truth seer," I said, "What are they after now, you think?"

"They want you to fail, Boss. There's no telling what they're after this time."

"Let's go ask him."

"Lead on, I'm right behind you," Rictor said with a laugh.

Guilefort stood as we entered my office and extended his hand to me. I shook his hand and motioned for him to return to his seat.

"So what can I do for you, Mr. Guilefort?"

"I'm here at the behest of the Council, and I have a list of questions that they demand answers to."

I could see the emotions rolling across his aura, doubt and unease with his assigned task flashed through him.

"All right, just cut to the chase, Mr. Guilefort," I said, "We both know you have orders and have to follow them. Put the questions out there and we'll see what we see."

He chuckled, "As straight forward as you were the last time we met, I see."

"The truth is the truth Mr. Guilefort."

"It's Simon, I feel ancient when you keep saying Mr. Guilefort."

"Ok, Simon," I leaned back in my chair, "Let's hear these questions the Council demands answers to."

"Number one. Are you familiar with Franklin DeRosa?"

"No."

"He was found dead in his home on Emory Road two weeks ago," he said, "He was also discovered to be a pedophile and child abuser."

"Oh," I said realizing who he was talking about. I'd never even asked the man's name, "Then I am familiar with him."

Guilefort nodded at the truth, "Second question. Did you kill him?"

"No."

I saw the relief in his aura. He had been worried about that answer.

"Did you violate your Oath to the Soulguard in any way pertaining to this man?"

"No."

I saw the relief once more. Guilefort was definitely rooting for me in this whole situation.

"Fourth question. Did you participate in any criminal activity pertaining to the death of this man?"

I turned to Ric, "Were we trespassing where we were standing?"

243

"Nah, too close to the road to be considered trespass."

"Then, no."

Guilefort smiled. Those had been the four major questions that he feared the answers to.

"Wait, is it illegal to see a crime and not report it?" I asked.

"No it is not," Guilefort answered.

Guilefort really wanted to hear what had happened but he didn't want to ask as a Council representative. The curiosity was eating at him and he was biting his tongue not to say anything.

"Oh, ok," I said, "you'll tell Gregor for me, right?"

He nodded and his curiosity was flaring through his aura.

"It started at Ruby Tuesdays..."

***

"Can I talk to you a minute, Boss?"

I looked up from the reports I was going over to find Orrick Wilson standing in my door.

"Sure," I said, "What's on your mind Orrick?"

"Sir, I just can't keep doing this," I could see the shame and embarrassment flow through his aura, "I've been reporting to the Council and I feel like I've betrayed you and the other Guards here. I would like to request a transfer because I can't keep it up."

"Why not?"

He looked at me like I'd lost my mind, "What do you mean, why not? I knew the Council wanted to hang you and I reported your actions to them."

"Were you ordered to report to the Council by someone of higher rank than you are?"

"Well, yeah. But..."

"Then continue to do so," I said, "The first thing you need to understand, Orrick, is that I won't hide anything from the Council. The only thing they don't know about me is my real last name. It was and is none of their business."

"You are not betraying anyone by following the order to report to the Council, as long as you are telling them the truth," I paused and looked at him for a moment, "I should have brought it up before now and saved you a good bit of angst. They want to bury me, yes, but if they plan to destroy me, they better stop sending a truth seer for their evidence against me."

"You knew about me?" he asked incredulously, "and still you trusted me in your patrols?"

I smiled, "Orrick, I'm a Soullord, I can see into your very Soul. Do you think I can't tell what sort of man you are, regardless of the fact your mother's maiden name is Denton. You're a Soulguard and that's enough for me."

I could see many emotions rolling through his aura ending in a flash of fierce loyalty to the Guard and to me personally. I shut down my sight because it was a bit embarrassing to see that sort of loyalty to me. What would spark something like that? I'm just a half crazed Soullord with Demon DNA, anger issues and a firm belief in the truth.

"Continue reporting to the Council and don't report anything but the truth. They'll never succeed through this sort of thing to destroy me. If they want to get rid of me they'll just have to come and try to do it themselves."

"Not one of em has the balls for that, Sir." Orrick turned to leave and looked back over his shoulder, "Thanks, Boss."

Chapter 45

On my twenty-first birthday the newest batch of recruits from the Academy arrived at the base. Fifteen new Guards were added to the roster but there were still no Mages. And no replacement for me as Mage Captain, either.

Rictor was looking the new recruits over and I joined him. The first recruit I saw was Trent Deacons and I waved to my friend as I entered the Dome. I recognized several of the others as well. All of them were at the Academy when I was there.

"He's the one..."

"Unblocked that Mage who was attacked..."

"Hell on wheels with a blade..."

I heard the whispers from across the Dome but acted like I couldn't. No point in embarrassing anyone so soon.

"The first thing I'll tell you," Rictor said to the recruits, "is that here, you'll definitely find Demons to kill. Our Mage Captain has been particularly good at sniffing out the bastards. He's pretty damn good at killing em, too."

He noticed me off to the side and laughed, "Speak of the devil. Anyway, we've logged more nests in the last year and a half than many Guard bases log in five years. They're either getting more plentiful or Colin, over there is just better at finding em. I'm thinking it's a bit of both. Regardless, you'll see action at this posting and we train hard here, because a mistake in the field will kill you and kill your brothers and sisters of the Guard. Welcome to Rourke's Rednecks."

Soulguard | Christopher Woods

I had heard rumors that the Guards had decided to give themselves a name for our unit, but this was the first time I'd heard it. My Guards have a sense of humor, that's for sure. My money was on Jacobs as the culprit who'd come up with that one. I was still known as Jaegher to most but my Guards know me for who I really am.

***

I awoke from a dead sleep. There was a feeling of evil to the west. I jumped from the bed and got dressed then headed out the door to find Rictor. I found him with the RRT. We had made it a point to have one of us awake with the team.

I walked in to find everyone laughing as Trent described something. Since everyone shut up as I walked in, I assumed it was some sordid tale about me.

"Don't believe him," I said, "He's a notorious liar."

"Honestly, how can you say something like that about me?" he returned, "It hurts my feeling."

"I'm so sorry I hurt your only feeling," I said with a smile. Then I turned to Rictor, "We've got something in the west."

"We get a call from Prada?" Jacobs asked.

"No, but we probably will," I answered, "But I don't need a call. I feel the bastards from here."

"Load up, men," Rictor ordered, "Let's go kill some Demons."

He turned to me, "Can you tell if it's big or not?"

I shook my head, "I can just tell it's there. I say we load for bear and if it's overkill, it'll be like a working vacation."

"Gotcha," he nodded and turned back to the team, "Load the whole team up. You heard the man, let's get on the road."

We were loaded and leaving the base in less than fifteen minutes. Five black SUVs loaded with weapons, armor, twenty-one Guards, and one sleepy Soullord. I leaned my head back on the headrest.

"Wake me when we get there," I said.

"Uh, Boss," Janicek said, "You're the one with the directions."

"West," I pointed toward the evil feeling, "Prada should call soon enough with specifics. She was supposed to go all the way into Arkansas. Surely she'll come across it, if not, I'm sure I can't sleep through it if we get closer."

"You got it, Boss."

As I dozed off I heard Janicek, "At least, if he's asleep we don't have to hear that racket he listens to."

I managed to doze for close to six hours before the evil presence sparked the rage inside and I jerked awake with my eyes smoldering. I was looking at a startled Guard named Nikoli. His face was pale as he looked into my eyes. Fear rolled through his aura but it eased as he saw I wasn't freaking out or anything.

I beat down the rage and looked around, "Where we at?"

"Just went through Memphis and Ric just got the call from Prada," Janicek answered, "Sometimes you're a scary bastard. You felt them all the way past Little Rock. Prada wasn't surprised at all that we were already on the way. She says it's a big nest."

Prada had quit being surprised a while back and just accepted my abilities.

"They're still some ways off," I said to Janicek with a smile, "I brought some new music to ease the ride a little."

Janicek groaned. I laughed and plugged my MP3 player into the jack for it.

"I don't think you guys have heard Godsmack yet."

Chapter 46

Two and a half hours later we pulled in behind Prada's SUV. She was right, the nest down in the cave system below us was large. I could see hundreds of ugly souls down there. They weren't bunched together like the ones in West Virginia had been. No Soulbombs this time.

"There's a crapload of em down there," I said to Rictor as he walked over to our SUV. I was buckling the straps of my armor and I reached down and pulled the twin shorts words out of the back and slipped them into the sheaths on my back. "They're scattered all through what looks like tunnels down there. There's one spot that they're bunched together. Must be a central cavern or something."

"We'll have to do it the hard way, it looks like," he said with a grin. Marines are so cool. Rictor lives to fight and loves it.

"Do me a favor, Ric, this is Trent's first patrol. Put a couple of vets around him, I don't want to lose him on his first patrol and he may get a little overzealous."

I heard a snort from behind me, "That's the pot calling the kettle black," Prada said, "At least there are twenty of us around his overzealous ass, there was just two around yours."

I laughed and turned to the cave mouth we could see in the distance, "That one didn't turn out too bad, let's try to make this one a little less exciting."

As we entered the cave, I took point and raised a shield across in front of us. No surprise attacks from the darkness. We worked our way down into the earth and the large cavern was closer than before. They had to be aware of us by now but they waited, instead of charging into the tunnels after us.

That was ominous, that sort of control was usually the influence of a Wraith.

"Odds are there's a Wraith down here," I warned, "keep a sharp eye out for it."

The large cavern was right around the bend and we turned to find ourselves facing a horde of silent Soldier Demons. At the sight of us they roared and charged. There was no time to look around for the Wraith. We formed a wedge formation with me on the point and the world slowed to a crawl as I began the Dance.

Many of the Guards had been learning the Dance as well and we tore into the horde of Soldiers. Demon blood and parts flew through the air as we cut our way into the crowded cavern.

Something slammed into me from behind and launched my forward across the cavern. Fire burned on my left side. Whatever it had been it went right through my shield. Pain ripped through me and the rage burst free. The world slowed again and everything was moving in slow motion. I turned my head back to see the Wraith that had hit me, except it wasn't a Wraith. It's clawed hands were glowing with an ugly purple and black flame and its Soulstream was nearly as big as mine. Power was pulsing up that stream. The damn thing was Pulling.

I saw it Tear through Janicek's shield like it wasn't there, raking those burning claws through his chest. It grabbed Wilson and literally ripped him in half and turned for the next. It's eyes rested on Trent Deacons as I felt the wall approaching behind me.

I flipped and landed with my feet against the wall and Pulled as hard as I could. I Pushed against the wall as I sprang back out into the air and shot back across the cavern with Soulfire pouring through me. I raised my swords in front of me and crossed them. Then I poured power into them.

The Demonmage was inches from grabbing Trent and Trent was turning to face it. The way Trent had knotted his stream made him much faster than the average Guard, but this thing was moving faster than a Wraith. Fortunately, I was moving like a burning comet and flew right over Trent's head. I pulled my crossed swords apart just as they connected with the thing's shield and they sliced through the shield and its neck both. The head flew up and I saw the wall behind it coming fast.

I Pushed against the wall with power but it wasn't good enough. I dropped both swords and raised my arms to protect my head and slammed into the rock face with a sickening crunch. Pain lanced through my body as I felt my right arm break and something gave in my shoulder.

As I fell to the floor in a pile, I saw every Demon in the cavern scream in fury and they all looked dead at me.

Oh crap.

They all charged at me, not even paying attention to the Guards. There were so many, the Guards were bypassed and they came straight at me. I struggled to get me feet under me and pain lanced through my body.

Then Trent was standing before me and his swords were blurring with speed as he stood his ground and held off a horde of Demons alone. He was struck several times but he didn't stop. He was freaking awesome. Then Prada was there on his left. And Rictor was on his right. Then the others arrived and they formed up with Trent Deacons at the point position. The Demons kept coming, and they all were staring straight at me with hate and rage rolling through their ugly auras. There was also fear because I had killed something very important to them.

I struggled to my feet, "I got one good Pull left in me, I soaked up a lot of juice back there. I can give you a good burst though."

"Yell when you're ready!" Rictor answered.

"Duck when I say to!"

"Got it!"

I opened my Soullance and aimed straight down the middle of the pack of Demons.

"Duck!"

The whole wedge went low and I Pulled hard, The lance of fire ripped across the Horde of Demons as I turned it back and forth across the front ranks, facing us. I kept it going as long as I felt safe to do it. I was feeling the heat from the Source building inside me and I shut it down.

The Guards were back up and ready long before any more Demons reached them.

"Trent, step back, check on Rocket Man," ordered Rictor.

Trent stepped back close to me and I saw blood all over him. He was bleeding from cuts everywhere and he staggered as he stepped close. I eased my back to the wall and sat down.

"Have a seat, buddy," I motioned with my left arm.

He slid down the wall beside me, "I think that's a good idea."

We sat and watched as the rest of the Guards cut through every Demon in the cave system. They were all pouring into the cavern aimed at me. The Guard only had to stay in formation and cut down every Demon as it tried to get to me.

"I think you pissed em off," Trent said, "You don't seem to have changed much, everywhere you go you make so many friends."

I laughed and it hurt like hell, "Don't make me laugh. Hurts when I laugh."

"He said Trent might get overzealous," Prada said as her sword severed a demon's head from its shoulders, "I told you, pots and kettles."

When the final Demon ran to its death on the sword of Nikoli, the Guards relaxed a bit. Every single Guard was wounded in some fashion. Some were minor and some a bit more extreme, but I was by far in the worst shape of us all. Three enormous gashes ran across my left side, although the amount of life-force still held inside me had stopped the bleeding. My right arm was broken and something was out of place in my right shoulder as well.

"Come on, Boss," Prada said as she helped me to my feet, "Quit sitting around watching us work."

Soulguard | Christopher Woods

Ric was helping Trent back to his feet, "That, my boy, was impressive." He said.

I looked toward where Janicek and Wilson had gone down and felt a great sadness. Wilson had bared his heart to me about what he had been doing for the Council. I felt the loss of a good Guard and a good man in him. Janicek had been a friend as well as a Guard and he would be missed.

We staggered into the tunnel that led to the surface and I stopped. Guards aren't buried, they're burned. We are born in blood and die in fire. Some believe our souls are not set free to go to the after-life until our bodies burn. Janicek had been one of these believers.

I turned back toward the caverns and re-leased the excess power out of my body in a flaming wave that crossed the cavern and set the bodies of the demons and our friends aflame. A weariness settled on me. It happens when a Mage draws too much power and has to release it as I had done. That is why a Mage tries not to build too much power up inside themselves. After release they are pretty much useless for some time.

"May the road to Paradise be paved with the Souls of your fallen enemies, my friends."

I turned to find every Guard right behind me, watching the fire.

"Prepare a place for us there, men," Rictor said softly, "We'll join you soon enough. Just not to-day."

Our group made our way up to the surface and Rictor called in to HQ. After he was through he turned to me.

"They say we have a doctor in Little Rock who can take care of the wounded," He said, "We'll head there first, I don't like the look of that arm."

***

"You should have come here as soon as it occurred, Young Man," the skinny old man said. "The bone has already started to heal and it'll have to be rebroken before I can set it."

"We did come straight here," I said, "I heal fast."

"You Soulguards never cease to amaze me," He said in wonder, "There's no way I can even put enough pressure on it to re-break it."

"Ric!"

"Boss?" was the reply from just outside the room.

The door opened and he walked in, "What's up?"

"He needs someone to re-break my arm and it's got to be one of you guys," I said, "But pain wakes the beast, so be careful."

He raised his personal shield and didn't hesitate.

The arm broke with a crack and the rage surfaced for a second and my other fist slammed into his chest before I could even think. He flew backward and crashed through the wall into the room beyond. I beat down the rage but I was still seeing through heat waves.

The doctor stood staring at me with a pale face as I got the rage under control.

"Ric! You ok?"

"I'm good, Boss."

"Sorry!"

"Sure, anytime!"

I heard laughter in the other room and turned to the doctor, "I'm all right now you can set it."

I looked at the hole in the wall, "Sorry bout that, I got rage issues. I'll pay for the damages."

He looked at the hole and back at me, "I see."

The resetting of the bone hurt but nothing like the re-breaking of it had. Putting my shoulder back in place had hurt some too but I'd kept it under control through that part. It was too late to get stitches in the gashes, they'd healed much faster than I thought they could and had already gone too far for that. Thank god for duct tape. Even with the tape holding the gashes closed, I'd have some pretty scars from this one.

"Thanks, Doc," I said to him, "Don't forget to send me a bill for the hole. Send it to the base in Knoxville for Colin Jaegher."

Chapter 47

"Why doesn't he ever try to jump in bed with any of the women around the base?"

I stopped as I heard the voice of Jenna Seymore around the corner inside the dome.

Prada's voice answered, "Ric said the last time he had a girlfriend, she was targeted by the Archmage. They blocked her from the Source just to get to him."

"That's horrible."

"Ric says that's why he stays alone all the time. He doesn't want to paint any more targets on the backs of people he cares for."

Ric is a perceptive man. I'm human and I want companionship as much as anyone else, but the more people involved with me, the more ways the Archmage had to come at me. He already had too many targets and I didn't want to give him more. I've seen several good looking Guards on the base and I am a Soullord, I can tell when someone is interested.

"That's so sad, but why would Ric be talking to you about it though?" Jenna asked in an innocent tone.

I almost laughed aloud as I pictured Prada's face turning red. I turned and went back the way I had come. I didn't want to embarrass the two women. They are my friends and they genuinely care about me. It gives me a nice feeling to know that my Guards care.

I walked around another hallway to get to the Dome. When I entered, Jenna and Prada were

259

across the Dome from me. There were several of the new Guards out in the center ring sparring and I stopped to watch. I turned my head as Trent walked up beside me.

He'd recovered fairly quickly from the damage he'd taken in Little Rock. My arm was still in a cast to keep me from using it. I'd Pulled the Source into me and my arm was almost healed but bones mend slower than flesh and I didn't want to Pull too much at a time into it.

"Hey, Boss."

"That sounds funny, coming from you."

"Still true, though," he said, "You've changed from the plain, unremarkable guy I knew in school. I know a lot of it was act, but some of it was just you. Now, you're harder. What you did in that cavern saved my life, but you'd have done it for anyone here."

"I seem to remember a single Guard standing over me holding off a horde of really pissed off Demons. You saved my life as much as I did yours," I said.

His face turned a little red, "I'm a clown a lot of the time but I'm not stupid, I hear what they're saying about you. Each and every one of these men and women would follow you into Hell and back you up as you kick in the teeth of the Devil."

My face was burning a little as well, "They'll do their duty as Guards. That's what we do. We go into Hell every time we enter those caves after them. Sometimes we die, sometimes we come back broken, but there's one thing we never do."

"What's that?"

"Soulguards never quit."

"Hoorah." I heard Rictor say from behind us. I hadn't even noticed him approach. "There's a Marine in you, Boss. If you weren't Guard, I could see you right out there in the trenches with em."

That means a lot when it comes from an ex-Marine Master Sergeant.

"So what's on the agenda for today, Boss?" Rictor asked.

"Thought I'd check out the new guys' shields, then I got a meeting with the Twins. Figured, as long as I'm healing up, I'd take some lessons about running the base. If the Archmage really wants to hurt me, he can recall the Twins. I'd be lost. I've learned a little over the last couple of years but, I keep putting it off. So I've spent the last week meeting with the Twins and learning as much as I can."

"That's a good idea," Rictor said, "At least you have a damn fine Guard Captain to handle the other part of the operation for you."

"Oh, hell, are they replacing you?"

He laughed aloud and slapped me on the back, "Catch you later, Boss."

As Ric walked away Trent shook his head, "Right there is living proof of what I'm saying. That man would follow you anywhere."

"He's a good man and a good Guard," I said.

"And one day you'll need us all. There's a day coming when you'll have to face that arrogant bastard in Montana. When that day comes, you'll have the whole Guard at your back. Know that," Trent said with a fierceness I'd never heard from my friend before. He turned and walked back out of the Dome.

I still don't know why the Guards keep placing that level of loyalty to me, personally, I just do what I've been trained to do. I learn new abilities all the time but I'm not learning them fast enough. I know that I could have done something to save Janicek and Wilson. I just have to figure out what it is, because the loss of those two Guards left a hole in my heart. They were my friends and I don't want to lose any more of them.

***

"Most of the actual running of the base is handling the pay of the men," Sandy said. Her twin brother Randy was sitting quietly as she spoke, "The equipment is low maintenance, unlike the Military's would be. We don't have to supply ammunition to the soldiers, for one thing."

"We do have a Mess hall but we closed it down when none of the Guards would eat there," Randy offered, "They'd rather draw the per diem pay and eat good food instead of that."

"I can definitely see that," I said, "I never knew food could be that good till I moved here."

"We've heard some of the tales of your bottomless pit," Sandy said.

"It's not bottomless, I just burn a lot of calories. Got a high metabolism."

"Sure you do, you must actually burn off the food with the Source or something."

I looked down at the papers in my hand.

"You do!" Randy laughed aloud, "That's how you eat so much. You really burn the food off with the Source!"

"I tried to work out enough to make up for it but I would have to work out every minute of every day to make up for all the stuff I eat. This is so much easier."

"Have you tried to just not eat as much?"

"But it tastes so good. Unless you've been raised by two evil Soulguards who made it a point to feed you the worst things in the world you wouldn't understand."

"You're saying Kyra Nightwing can't cook?" Sandy asked. Disbelief rolled across her aura, "They used to tell tales about how good that woman's cooking is."

"Don't you tell me that! I know why she cooked so badly, but don't even think of telling me she is some sort of Master cook. I will not be responsible for my actions if I heard something like that."

Randy was trying to hide his laughter but it wasn't working to well.

"Ok, let's get back to business then since you don't want to hear about Kyra's cooking skills after the time she spent in Italy."

Randy laughed harder as he saw the devastated look on my face.

"Where were we?" Sandy asked innocently, "Oh yeah, we were talking about wages of the Guards. A new recruit earns two thousand dollars per month then there is a Twenty five dollar per diem for food. If they choose to live off base, there is a monthly stipend of seven hundred dollars for living expenses. After a year, the recruit gains another

263

six hundred per month. By the time they reach five years they receive five thousand per month. This is veteran Soulguard pay."

"Do the per diems all stay the same, regardless of level of pay?"

"Yes, and the monthly stipend is the same as well." She answered. "One thing we spend heavily on is the body armor. We buy top of the line armor. And our swords are top of the line weapons. But swords are cheaper to operate than guns so we end up paying much less than a Military base would. Our money comes from our business endeavors ran by Warren. Whatever is left over is added to the pool of money available to the Soulguard bases across the US."

"How many bases do we actually have here in the US?"

"There are six bases in the US, Knoxville, Pittsburgh, Denver, Sacramento, the Academy, and don't laugh, Roswell New Mexico."

"Really, the base is in Roswell?" I laughed, "I knew it was in New Mexico but I had no idea it was Roswell."

"You don't listen very well, I said don't laugh and the first thing you did was laugh. I would have fed you awful things too."

"Now that's just mean."

"We also have two bases in Canada, one in Alaska, and two in Mexico. Each one has business ventures to support itself, but some make more money than others. All of the money is used worldwide by the Guard wherever it needs to be used. Warren is making Knoxville one of the highest earners in the US. We're only second to Pittsburgh right now. Soon this will no longer be the place they send screw ups, it'll be a base like New Mexico. People will be lining up to serve here."

"Not just because of the money either," Randy said in a serious tone, "More Guards are requesting to be sent here to serve under you than for the fact we are making money."

"I'm nothing special," I said, "Many Mages could have done what I've done."

"We had three Mages of your power level or higher, sir, and the only one who even had a semblance of the Guard backing you do was Sam Keller. And he was still just a Mage to them," Randy said.

"It's not that some Mages can or can't do what you do," Sandy said, "it's the fact that they don't do what you do. I know I can't marshal the strength to do your job so I try to do right by you by doing my job to the best of my abilities."

I nodded to the Quincy twins, "Thank you."

Chapter 48

"Damn, that kid's fast," Rictor said as we watched Lyrica bouncing circles around Jacobs. He was trying to catch her but she was a blur. She would occasionally stop and stick her tongue out at him.

Finally he turned his back to her with a grin and reached out and snagged her leg as she tried to jump back in front of him. He laughed as he dangled her in front of him and stuck his tongue out at her and blew a raspberry.

She was giggling uncontrollably by then and Jacobs actually let one slip out too.

"Did Ivan Jacobs just giggle?" Prada's voice came from behind me. "I think he just giggled."

Jacobs looked hurt, "I do *not* giggle."

"Looked like a giggle to me," Ramirez said from off to the left side of us where several Guards were enjoying the show. "Wasn't that a giggle, Trent?"

"Sure looked like a giggle," He said.

He let Lyrica loose and she shot off toward the test dummies like a flash, "I can't believe you guys would say something like that."

"Ooh, did we hurt your feeling?" Trent asked.

"His feeling? He's only got one?" Prada asked.

"Yep, and we hurt it."

I chuckled as the Guards kept up the razzing of Jacobs. I really enjoy just watching the guys and how they joke around with each other. It feels good to be a part of that camaraderie. It's much like a sense of family. The Guard has been the only family I've ever known. First, Kharl and Kyra who are Soulguard to the core. Then the Guards at the Academy, I felt the same feeling with the Guards there. And now the Knoxville Guard was swiftly becoming part of my extended family.

I know they have much the same sort of feelings for each other, I am a Soullord. I can see into their Souls and see what they're feeling. They are all brothers and sisters in arms. And it was a great feeling to be accepted as one of them. Most Mages don't even know what it is they are missing.

I watched as Lyrica bounced around the dome. Kyra and Lyrica had come in to visit after they heard I'd been injured. Lyrica had grown like a weed. She was a foot taller than she was when I'd seen her last.

She shot in my direction and landed near me without jumping in my arms like usual, "When are we going to eat?"

"Lord, girl," Prada said, "don't say that word around him. If I ate as much as he does I'd be as big as a house."

"I think we should move this little party," I said and then in a louder voice, "I'm buying dinner who's up for a visit to the Chop House?"

I called ahead. Somehow I figured they'd need a little preparation for seventeen Guards, two Mages and a couple of Soullords.

It's a good thing Warren was making me a crapload of money. This was gonna be expensive.

***

"Remember that crazy shield thing he made in Chattanooga?" Lewis asked.

"Yeah that was an easy run. We didn't have to draw weapons till the last little bit," Kim Salazar answered, "May have been the easiest nest I ever was in."

Prada snorted, "West Virginia was easier, all we had to do was kick a bunch of bombs in a hole."

"You gotta point," Jacobs agreed.

I looked at Kyra and saw a little smile on her face, "What is it?"

"This is what I missed when we left to hide," she said, "Not that I regret it but the Guard are a family. I'm so glad they made you a part of it instead of the way it usually is."

"I'm a Guard first, Mom," I said, "Mage second."

"How did you break your arm?" Lyrica asked.

"I ran into a wall, Little Angel."

"That's just silly."

Then I heard Jacobs start singing and I winced. He was singing Rocketman and I knew it would only be moments till they had to tell that story.

He stopped singing and looked at Lyrica, "You see, it happened like this..."

I knew she was watching his memories because her eyes suddenly lit up and she turned to me with her mouth hanging open.

"You were fl..."

"Absolutely not."

"But..."

"No."

She squirmed, "But..."

"Definitely not."

"What?" Kyra asked.

Lyrica turned to her and with amazement flowing through her aura said, "He flew."

The whole group of guards erupted in laughter. Jacobs paused to wait it out and finished his story. Kyra turned and looked at me with the look that she always gives me, one eyebrow arched. Then she turned to Lyrica.

"Absolutely not."

"Aww," Lyrica pouted.

Sandy and Randy Quincy were sitting quietly on my left and I could see that they were actually enjoying being a part of this group. My Guards look at Mages totally different than they did when I got here. Perhaps I have done a little good since I arrived.

***

"You know it wasn't really the right thing to do don't you?" Kyra asked.

"Not the smartest or the best decision," I said, "But it was the right one. If it were to do again, I'd still do it. My Guards don't get killed when I can stop it."

"I know, Son," She said, "but there will come a time when you have to weigh the consequences. And sometimes the lives have to be spent for the greater good. I've been around for a hundred and ninety years, most of them fighting Demons. You can't save us all and sometimes it's necessary to hold back to use your power for the things only you can do. You can't do those things if you're broken and laying on the floor."

"I hear you, but I don't know if I can do that."

"And that's why they love you, that's why they'll follow wherever you lead. And when the time comes they will give their lives for you. It's a heavy burden to bear, but bear it you will. Always keep the values and morals you have shown. That's what makes someone worthy of the loyalty of men and women like these. Just try to keep the consequences in mind as well."

"I will."

"Good," She hugged me and Lyrica ran up to hug me as well.

"Bye Angel, next time you can spar with me after you get better. Ivan is way too slow."

"Yes, Ma'am."

She giggled and ran up the steps into the plane.

I turned and made my way back to the SUV. When I returned to the base, it was nearly midnight so I headed to my quarters. Just as I started to close my door, Andrea Prada stepped inside and I saw what was flowing across her aura.

"I can't..."

She kissed me fiercely, "Shut up and accept what's offered."

She pushed me backwards into the room and our Souls began to intertwine. Paige had been soft and gentle with her love making. Prada was very...energetic.

Chapter 49

"I've got how much money?" I asked in amazement.

"With all the money you've added over the last four years to the initial amount, I've been able to do some more investing and you just passed a million dollars over what is tied up in businesses. We just bought a lot of foreclosed properties around the area for next to nothing and you should be able to net a substantial amount from those when the economy picks back up."

"Foreclosures?" I interrupted, "I don't want to be a part of putting people out of their homes."

"These homes are already owned by the banks, we don't have anything to do with them before that."

"Still I feel we should try to help people instead of take advantage of them. Make some sort of donations to help some of the people around here. Maybe take one of the properties and give it to a family in need. That would be doable wouldn't it?"

"You can't save everyone, Colin."

"True, but no one can say we don't try," I said, "Look up the people before you do the deed, though. I don't mind helping the people who are in genuine need. I'm not interested in helping the useless ones who won't try to help themselves."

"You've been talking too much with that Shoffner kid, haven't you?"

"He's from this area and he's shed a lot of light on how folks think here."

Patrick Shoffner was a native of the area and he'd just gotten here from the Academy. He was nineteen and new to the Guard but he was as dedicated as any of the vets stationed here. Everyone liked the kid, and when he was welcomed to Rourke's Rednecks he had fit right in.

I stood up and headed for the door, "I gotta go meet with the Twins, then Ric has some sort of thing going on this evening. I'll talk to you later."

"All right, Boss," he answered and I heard him muttering as I walked down the hall, "Crazy...give em away...too noble for his own good..."

I chuckled, it might be crazy, but I don't see why a person can't help when they can. I have more money than I'll ever need already. I can give some to the people in need. The Guard gives me what I need. I live on base, I make enough money to feed my eating addiction and that's really all the money I spend.

I passed Jenna Seymore as I walked down the hall and she smiled and nodded, "Boss."

"Jen." I smiled in return. The night before she'd been the one to visit my quarters. I'm pretty sure Prada and Jenna had planned the whole thing since it started last year. Every so often one of them would show up in my quarters. They kept it secret so that I wouldn't feel like I was painting targets on their backs. They genuinely care for me and they didn't want me to be alone. They are both wonderful women but I find it hard to be more than friends with someone who is afraid of me. It's hard not to see that all my Guards are afraid of me. They love me but they are afraid of me. It's something I've come to find in everyone around me. Only a few people in my life aren't afraid of me.

Maybe it's actually not fear of me, exactly, but fear of what I am. The skills I have as a Soullord, the rage from the altered DNA. These are what my Guards see when they see me. These are what they see when we go into the caves after Demons. It's like I'm two people. One they love, the other terrifies them.

So when either of those women come to me, I turn off my Sight so the fear isn't what I see. And I just feel the companionship of a woman.

I reached the office that the Twins share and entered.

"Boss," Sandy said as she saw me, "We've got some good news for you. You've officially become the youngest Mage Captain in the Guard. They can't deny that you've done an excellent job since coming here and now they have to make it official."

Randy laughed out loud, "I bet it hurt the bastards to sign this."

He handed me an envelope.

"I'd say Greg pushed this or Nora." Sandy said, "Both of them are strong advocates for your future in the Guard."

"I'd say so," I said, "What changes for me can I expect?"

"The only thing that changes is the pay, really," Randy said, "But there's going to be a respect thing with other Mages. Before, everyone knew it was a position to make you fail. Now they'll know you more than earned the rank, because you did it while they actively tried to make you fail."

"I did it because you two were here and Warren. I just killed Demons."

"Maybe," Randy laughed again, "But you do it very well. And we make you look good. Although, I think you could easily do our jobs now. That broken arm last year actually gave you time to learn something."

"Even if your math skills are atrocious," Sandy added.

"Let's leave my math skills out of this, thank you." I stood back up and turned to the door, "Math shouldn't have frigging letters in it, anyway. Math is numbers, not letters. I don't know who the crazy ass was who decided to put letters in it but they need to be dragged out in the street and shot."

Both Mages started laughing and I waved as I left the room, heading for my office. When I got there the phone was ringing and I answered.

"Colin Jaegher."

"Still going by Jaegher?" Sam Keller's voice asked, "Thought you'd be going by Rourke by now."

"Nah, my checks are still to Jaegher although I don't make it much of a secret about it anymore."

"You guys busy down there?"

"Not so much this year. We had a pretty harsh incident last year in Little Rock and the bastards seem to be laying low."

"Well I have a large problem and I could use your help."

"What do you need?"

"We got a pretty large infestation and I could use a lot more bodies here to help stomp it out. Too much area for me to get em all alone and I need the coverage for a large area."

"Not a problem, I'll leave an RRT here and bring the rest up there. Where do you need us to go?"

"I'll send a plane down to get you. Fly into JFK in New York and I'll meet you there. It should be able to get there by this evening."

"Will we have problems with bringing our gear?"

"It's our plane," he said, "There won't be a problem."

"We'll be there."

"I'll owe you one," He said and hung up.

New York, huh? That might be fun. I dialed Rictor's cell phone, "Hey, Ric, we got a job. For all the Guards we can bring."

Chapter 50

"You could have said it was the damn sewers," I said.

Sam laughed, "Then you wouldn't have come. I made that mistake with the Guards at the Academy. They just laughed at me and said to call you, cause you were closer."

"Which Guards?"

"Kind of funny, his name was Jaegher, too."

"He's gonna pay for that one," I said, "Mark my words, Kharl Jaegher will pay."

I heard a laugh from behind us, "It was so bad he even lost his appetite."

"No frigging way," I heard Jacobs, "There's no way he lost his appetite."

The tired Guards were making their way into the base in Pittsburgh. We'd spent two weeks straight killing out the nest of Demons scattered throughout the sewer system of New York. It was the nastiest job I'd ever done, and it was Kharl's fault. Maybe I could get Lyrica to set his hair on fire or something.

"After we get cleaned up," Sam turned to the Guards, "I think I owe you dinner at the least. How bout I order about fifty Pizzas and a truckload of beer."

The pizza didn't thrill the Guards as much as the beer.

"A big truck!" Holsey, one of the new transfers into the Rednecks yelled.

"A damn big truck!" yelled Jacobs.

"A damn big truck it is!" answered Sam.

***

"I had it made," Trent said, "I was picked for the RRT and I thought I'd miss something. Ramirez switched with me and now that smell is permanently embedded in my nostrils."

"That'll teach you," Jacobs laughed and bit into another piece of pizza.

"Why did your Mage Captain torch that whole room?" I heard a voice ask at the other end of the room.

"Finally found something that he couldn't handle," I think it was Jackson's voice, "Rats."

"After all the crap you guys have told us," another voice joined in, "How can the guy be afraid of rats?"

"I don't know if I'd call it fear, exactly. Let's say he has an aversion to sharing air with the little vermin," Jackson said, "He torched the whole room. It's not like he ran, screaming, back out of it."

"True enough. He wasn't screaming."

"It wasn't as bad as the time he blew out the whole wall in his quarters on base," Prada said.

"Why did he do that?"

"Sometimes he feels the Demons when they come over and it happened to coincide with some sort of bad dream he was having. He woke up Pulling and blew the whole wall out. It was right in front of a bunch of us. He was out in the hall with Soulblades and everything."

"Yeah," Kim Salazar said with a snort, "The Boss sleeps naked, too. There he was, butt-naked and his eyes looked like they were flaming. As soon as he realized where he was, he blushed from head to toe and ran back into his quarters."

I remembered that night. There were five women out in the hall and I'd really had a nightmare. But really, did it have to be about frigging Zombies? Really?

The Demons had been in Kentucky that time, so they were relatively close by and had triggered my rage. Needless to say, I began wearing clothes when I slept after that.

I looked at the other Guards in the Dome. They were downing beers as fast as they could in the attempt to actually get drunk. They laughed and joked and I soaked up the atmosphere. This is what I fight for. These are my family. It's all well and good to say you're trying to save the world from Demons but that's too big for one person to really cope with. But my family is large and we can say it without feeling overwhelmed because we're all in it together.

My thoughts were interrupted as the Guard Captain from Pittsburgh walked over to me. Anthony Caprida was his name and he was, if not an Elite, very close to one. His Soulstream was not much smaller than many of the Elites at the Academy.

"They tell me you learned the blade from Kyra Nightwing," he said as he sat down on the bench to my left, "Did she teach you the Dance of Blades?"

"Yeah," I answered and bit into a slice of pizza. I chewed and swallowed, "I've been teaching it to some of my Guards. Several of them are good at it too."

"I noticed some of them seemed to be Dancing as we fought in the sewers. Prada is really good," He said, "What impresses me, though is when you are leading a group of Guards, the whole group seems to flow with you. It's fascinating."

I wasn't aware that he'd seen us fighting in a group down in the sewers. I didn't remember being teamed with Caprida.

"I witnessed your patrol from one of the tunnels above you," He said and smiled. I thought, for a second he'd read my mind. "It was when you were in that central junction. Looked like a huge room, packed full of Demons."

"I remember where you're talking about," I said with a chuckle, "That's where Jacobs fell in the hole right in the middle of it."

"Did I hear my name?" came a voice from over with the others.

"Probably talking bout you coming out of that one place looking like a drowned rat," I heard Trent.

"Please don't talk about that, it was a horrible experience and should never be brought up again."

Caprida chuckled and shook his head, "I have to say, you're not like most of the Mages we deal with. It's refreshing."

"Thanks."

"Might I talk you into doing the Dance for the guys tomorrow, before you have to leave?"

"Sure, we might be able to get a few of the Guards to do it too."

"I would appreciate it," he said and stood up, "Some of these guys have never seen it and would really enjoy it."

"I'll come in the morning."

"Great."

As Caprida walked away, Trent made his way over and sat down, "You know, my luck is awful. First I thought I was winning when Mattie and me were given our orders. She got New Mexico and I got Tennessee. I was happy to get to come out to work with you after being trained where I could actually help."

He snagged a piece of my pizza, "Then, on my first patrol, I got the crap beat outta me. Then I talk Ramirez into switching with me so I wouldn't miss anything and I get two weeks in a sewer. I'm beginning to worry."

I laughed, "At least Mattie gets to work under Daffy, She's a hell of a fighter and I think she's a good Guard Captain."

Jacobs stopped dead in his tracks on his way over to where we sat, "Did I just hear you call Daphne Cavanaugh Daffy? *The* Daphne Cavanaugh?"

I looked at him for a minute and he shook his head slowly back and forth with his mouth hanging open.

"I think I finally figured you out, Boss," He said abruptly and continued over to where we sat, "You got no sense of self preservation. I mean, first you piss off every powerful Mage in the Academy."

"Not all of em," I protested.

He continued, "Then you Wile E. Coyote into a wall in Little Rock."

"Well, I kind of misjudged th..."

He held up his hand, "And you call the scariest woman I know Daffy."

"But..."

"No self preservation," he interrupted, "You're supposed to have a little voice that tells you not to do things. You don't have that little voice and I think I'm going over to the other side of the room before some of whatever you got gets on me."

He turned and walked back over to the other Guards. I looked back down to see that my pizza box was gone.

"He stole my pizza."

"Damn it!" Trent said, "I was trying to get at least one more piece of it."

He stood up and followed Jacobs, "Hey give me some of that! Why do you think I went over there, anyway?"

As Trent pursued Jacobs across the Dome to the other Guards, Sam Keller walked over and took a seat.

"I'm not the sort of person to get jealous," he said with a shake of his head, "but I really wish I had the rapport you have with your men."

"I was raised by two Guards that most of them sort of idolize. It gives me an advantage over most other Mages."

"It's not just that either," Sam said, "I go with my men into caverns just like you, but Caprida is their leader. I'm just the Mage. I saw how you work with your men, and don't deny it, they are *your* men. I was with Caprida when we saw you cleaning out that room. Every move you made was mirrored in your Guards. It was like you were connected on some level. Caprida was quite impressed, as was I."

"We've worked together a lot," I said, "they know how I work."

"It's more than that," he said "but you'll see it when you're ready. I think it has to do with being a Soullord, but it's just a theory."

He stood back up and looked down at me, "Just think about it a little and see if it makes sense to you. You know more about what you can do than I do. As for me, I'm turning in for the evening. Have a pleasant night."

"You too, Sam."

He could be on to something, I had Pushed memories into my Guards before. Was it possible that I was broadcasting to them as we fought? Maybe he was right.

Chapter 51

My birthdays always seem to go in one of two directions. Either I have something really wonderful happen or I end up with my face in a wall.

My twenty seventh birthday was bound to be one or the other. Since I happened to be perched on a mountain top, as far from civilization as I could get, and I was trying new skills that I just couldn't really do inside, I totally expected one or the other to occur.

I pushed a shield into a massive boulder at a passive level. It was a round shield much like what would be used to power a fireball. I was trying to ascertain whether I could make explosions inside rock to possibly cave in the caverns around whole nests of Demons at a time.

I had read that an enclosed explosive will do much more damage than one out on the surface. I really didn't want to try this inside the dome.

Everything was doing fine until I Pulled and sent it inside the shield for the Soul bomb to use. Unfortunately the solid rock and the Soulfire had a volatile reaction and there was a great big explosion ten feet in front of me.

It seems like a person who blows himself up on a regular basis would learn to anchor his shield. No, why bother with that when you can blow yourself off of a mountain top?

As I sailed backwards, I looked down to see the edge of the mountain receding away from me and the seriously long drop below me.

"Ah shit."

At that point, I was leaning toward a face in the wall day.

As I looked at the ground getting farther and farther away from me, an idea began to form. So I began crafting a shield around myself. I smiled as it took shape even as I began to fall after the blast's force wore off. Then I spread my arms and opened the portal on my new shield. The wings caught the air and I soared forward instead of down.

Maybe it wouldn't be a face in the wall day after all. It was the most wonderful feeling I had ever felt and the exhilaration of actually flying was awesome.

Unfortunately, I don't know jack about aerodynamics. So while I was reveling in the feeling of flight I neglected to see the cliff face to my right was getting much closer. When my wingtip touched the rock face it spun me right around to slam face first into the damn thing.

I decided as I bounced and tumbled the rest of the way down the mountain, this was never going to be spoken of to anyone, ever.

***

"I'm a little worried about the frequency of their attacks, this year." Rictor said.

We were both standing in the dome. I had looked at the blueprints of the Knoxville Guard base and found a safe direction to fire my newest weapons. I'd taken Lyrica's idea and flattened the fireballer down to a disk launcher. It put all the power of a fireball behind a razor sharp disk about two feet in diameter.

"Me, too," I answered, "I contacted the head of the Scotland Academy yesterday and he says that attacks have increased, both there and in China."

I turned and aimed toward the target that I had put a shield around. When I opened the portal to the disk launcher and Pulled, fiery disks erupted from the launcher to slam into the target.

"That's a hell of a lot faster than the fireball," Rictor said.

"The penetration is better, too," I returned, looking at the slices that covered the back wall behind the outer shield, "It might take out a Wraith faster. Give it less time to get to you."

"Or the Guards around you."

"The main thing I want to test is something I been working on, lately. I studied a little about lenses and I'm hoping to be able to focus power through one."

"Should I back up to a safer distance?" Rictor laughed.

"It'd probably be smart," I smiled and opened my personal shield.

He saw my shield come up and he took off toward the door, "Shield comes up, you cut a trail," he muttered and raised his shield.

I formed a small lens-shaped shield in front of me. It was barely visible because I wanted to see what happened. It was not much more powerful than a privacy screen to start with.

I formed a small feeder tube the same size as the lens and Pulled a very small amount through

it directly at the lens. There was no noticeable difference, so I started easing the portal to the lens open.
As it strengthened, the power changed shape on the
other side. It actually worked. The power was visibly
hitting a single point, then spreading back out.

"That wasn't worth running over here for,"
Ric yelled from the door.

"Just give it a minute."

I crafted another lens at the point where the
power was the most focused. This one was different.
It was designed to take waves coming in from an angle and make them turn straight once more. As I
strengthened the shield, the power was a smaller
stream but much stronger.

"Excellent!"

"Really?" Ric shook his head and started
back over.

That's when I opened my eight inch
Soullance and crafted lenses inside of it.

"This is the fun part," I said and Pulled gently till the power was focused the way I wanted.

Then I Pulled like I normally would and my
lance erupted with a blinding stream of condensed
power that pushed me backwards several steps. I
stopped and the light level lowered. I turned to find
Ric back at the door, looking like he'd never left that
spot and I laughed.

"That make you feel better?" I asked.

"Much more like I would expect."

"It took me years to figure it out, but if I test
on a small scale it's a lot safer when I do it on a large
scale."

"Yeah, but the other way was much more
amusing to everyone else," He chuckled, "You don't

even know how many times that video of you blowing yourself up has been played around here. If you'd copyrighted that tape you'd be a millionaire."

"Hardy Har."

I turned back to my target to find a three inch hole in its chest. I looked through the hole to see a hole in the wall behind it as well.

"Now *that* is a Soullance!"

"More like a laser cannon," Ric said, "This is what watching Star Wars will get you, light sabers and laser cannons. Next thing you'll want to do is change the name of the Source to the Force."

"You know, that would be..."

"Absolutely not," Rictor interrupted and turned around. He walked back out of the dome without another word.

"What? What'd I do?"

***

"Have you heard what happened in California?" Randy Quincy asked.

"No, what is it?" I answered.

"Our illustrious leader sent the son of Lucien Salvador out to Sacramento. The boy has the spine of an eel, but his father is one of Price's staunchest supporters."

"This doesn't bode well."

"It gets worse. The first nest cleanup he goes out on, the shit hits the fan and he runs away. Four guards injured and one died. It was a small team because there was a Mage with them."

"When are they trying him for cowardice?"

"That's the thing," he said, "I am thoroughly ashamed of the Mage establishment. They claim that the Guard Captain didn't send enough Guards in some sort of attempt to get rid of Salvador. They tried him for negligence and blocked him from the Source."

"What!?"

"They didn't even use the truth seer for the trial," Randy said, "What the hell is going on?"

Rage was building in me again, "The bastard is trying to weaken the Guard. No matter how much power he has, the Guard is the power base for all of it. If he controls the Guard he controls all of it. I can't see him controlling someone like Riordan. We need to keep a close eye out for other plots. Try to see if we can locate the Guard Captain who was blocked and get him here. I may be able to help him some."

"You can't save everyone, Boss."

"We can damn well try."

"You can't unblock him," Randy said quickly, "They'll look for that and say you defied a decree from the Council. They'll block you."

"They'll try," I smiled and Randy almost stepped back a step. Rage was trying to break out.

"Sir, you have to think of the bigger picture," he said, "If you're declared rogue or blocked, there's nothing you can do that won't be done facing almost every Mage in the Guard. Some of us will back you. But it will be a civil war amongst the Mages and right now we can't afford that."

"Just find him and bring him here," I said, "I won't violate the laws but I want him protected until the time when the Archmage is confronted for his crimes. And they are crimes. One day he'll face the consequences of his actions just like everyone does. When that day comes, I'll be right there waiting."

"Yes sir."

I turned and strode out of the room toward my office and as I entered, the phone began ringing.

"Colin Jaegher," I answered.

"Hey, Son," Kharl's voice returned.

"What can I do for you, Old Geezer?"

"I think we have a problem here, Son," He said and I could hear the worry in his voice.

"Is it about the Sacramento thing?"

"That's part of it," he said, "Price seems to be more erratic lately and the deal with Franco is just part of it."

He continued, "Yesterday, Lyrica was running on the trail when she saw Price and four other Mages up in the trees. She turned and headed back down the trail instead of going on. Anything sound familiar to you?"

"I'm on the next plane back," I snarled, rage boiling inside of me, "If he hurts one hair on that girl, I'll kill him and I'll melt the fucking Academy to slag."

"Calm down, Son," he said quickly, "If you do that, they make you a criminal and turn the whole Guard against you. Some would still follow you and we'd have a civil war. There's no way that wouldn't bleed over into the public eye. We've got a much easier solution, a temporary solution but a lot easier."

"What is it?" I said shortly.

"Lennox Flynn is going to take Lyrica to the Scotland Academy for a few years. We want to send at least two personal Guards for her and I thought you would have a suggestion or two as to who they should be."

I didn't even hesitate, "Trent and Mattie. I hate to lose Trent here but I want someone like him there and Mattie is one of the best Guards I know. You just make damn sure she's safe, Dad."

"You know I will, Son," He said, "I love that kid and she has Guards with her all the time now. He can't touch her where there are witnesses and we have people around her all the time."

"As a matter of fact," he said, "I think we may just send her to Knoxville until Flynn heads back to Scotland."

"Do that," I said, "No one will dare attack her here."

"Hell, son," Kharl chuckled, "The first thing she said when she told us was that she wished she had went on up and kicked their asses."

I took a deep breath and beat some of the rage down, "She probably could have, to be honest. But they would have been trying to kill her, not block her. They know she can stop a block. I'll wait, for now, but there's swiftly coming a day of reckoning. I shit you not. If I have to break my oath and every law in the country, I will. He'll step across a line that he really doesn't want to cross."

"And when it comes, we'll be at your back, Boy."

Chapter 52

I sat in my office, reading over the list of recruits heading to Knoxville. Surprising enough, there were three Mages coming in and fifteen new Guards. Over the last few years, almost all of the new recruit guards cycled through Knoxville. Partially, so I could check the shields and I think Jack wanted them to meet me and see that all Mages aren't like the ones at the Academy.

More and more, the Academy was filled with the kind of Mages that would do anything the Archmage asked. Whether it was out of fear or just trying to gain his favor. The whole situation was enough to make me want to puke.

The incident in Sacramento was an indicator that Price was preparing to move his agenda up a notch. Steve Franco was on his way to Knoxville, I wanted to make sure nothing happened to the man. He did not deserve the shit storm that fell on him and I wanted him safe until I could do something about his situation.

My thoughts were interrupted by the ringing of the phone.

"Jaegher," I answered.

"Hey, Colin," Gregor Kherkov said, "Thought I'd call and give you a heads up. They're sending a few Mages to you. We had a choice of Salvador or another Mage named Graves to go to Knoxville. I took the advice of Miss Jayne and sent you Graves. She had one message for me to give you. She just said 'Fix him, she's not scary enough'."

"That's a little cryptic, don't you think?"

"That's just what the young lady said and I have no idea what she means," he said.

"Has she left to come here, yet?"

"She and her two watchdogs are with your new recruits. I have to say, I think you couldn't have picked a better pair to go with her. Trent is as easy going as they come and Mattie won't hesitate to kill anything that comes for her. Both are intensely loyal to you, and therefore to her."

"I'd trust those two with my life." I answered, "But I'd trust any of the Knoxville Guards with my life, I have many times."

"Hmm, there was one more thing Lyrica said for me to tell you about Graves." He said, "She said he held as much fear in him as you do rage and you'd know what had to be done."

"Oh Lord, I have an idea what she means for me to do. And she's probably right, she's not scary enough for it," I let out a long, drawn out sigh.

"What is it?"

"It'll make him or it'll break him and I'm not sure which it'll be until I see him."

"His father is the highest ranking Mage on the Council, if that tells you what you may be dealing with."

I tapped my finger on my desk for a moment, "If it was like Salvador, she wouldn't have said fix him. There has to be something good about the man or she wouldn't have said that."

"Oh he's a much better person than Salvador," Gregor said, "He's just, how can I put this gently? Very cautious."

"If Lyrica is right, he's scared shitless. I know how much rage is in me and if his fear is anywhere close to that, I don't know how he walks out of his house each day. But I'll deal with it and I'll let you know what happens when it's done. You don't need to know any details until then."

"That sounds decidedly unpleasant. Please call with good news, when you do."

"I'll do the best I can."

"Heh, you always do, Colin. Be careful."

"Always," I said and heard his laughter as I hung up the phone.

***

"Welcome to Knoxville," I said to the gathered recruits as they stood before me in the Dome. Around the edge of the Dome, several of the Guards stood watching. Jacobs and Prada were both near the door watching. I could also see Lyrica's Soul, she was staying back in the hallway until I was through.

"You Guards will be going with Lewis." I motioned to the huge man to my left, "He will show you your quarters and give you the dime tour of the facility."

I turned to the three Mages, "I don't know what you three have heard about me, and I really don't care. I am a Soullord. This means I can see into your very Soul and I know what lurks inside. I can see what you feel and I can see what your intentions are before you even take action."

All three were looking at me with fear rolling through their auras. I glanced toward Prada and Jacobs, who both had confusion rolling through theirs. This is not how I usually act toward people and they were a bit nervous.

"In California, politics lead to the end of a good man's career and the death of a good Guard. I will tolerate none of that shit here."

I looked dead at Kevin Graves and did the hardest thing I'd ever done.

"You are consumed by fear and today you will learn how to use that fear. Up until now, the fear has used you."

His eyes were wide and I could almost see him trembling.

"Step forward and join me in the practice ring," I demanded harshly.

"Jacobs, get us a set of practice blades."

The fear was growing, more and more in Graves and I hated every minute that this went on, but it was necessary. If I waited, his fear of the infamous "Soullord" would fade some and I needed all of his fear for what he would have to do.

I looked into his eyes, "Strong emotions bring a focus you cannot even imagine, when you embrace them. Your fear is as strong of an emotion as anything you will ever feel and you *will* embrace it. Use the power of that fear and become more than you ever thought possible."

Jacobs returned with the practice swords and handed Graves two of them and me the other two. He looked at me with worry in his aura. He could see the rage building inside me. Most of the

Guards can tell when I start raging and Jacobs was definitely worried.

"Feel the power of your fear," I said as I began letting the rage come forth.

I could see his fear rocket as my eyes began to smolder. I was seeing him through heat waves and he was trembling.

"Now reach out, grab it by the throat, and make it yours!" I roared and started for him.

Fear will force fight or flight. He had spent his whole life with flight as the answer. Today he would learn fight, one way or the other.

He turned and shot away from me and I roared in fury as I shot after him.

"You can't run from me!" I snarled and hit him across the lower back with my left blade.

He screeched and shot forward with me on his heels

"I'm faster than you," I whispered in his ear and slammed him across the shoulder with my right blade.

As I followed hot on his heels around the Dome, I projected a memory of three Soulguard Elites dancing around me. They kept hitting me until the rage jumped and I attained the focus from it.

"That's where you find it," He jumped as he heard me whisper in his right ear. I was right on top of him and I struck him with my practice sword again.

Around the Dome we went and he got faster and faster, but I was right on his heels and every time he slowed I hit him again. I could see the terror peaking and knew that the moment of truth was almost there.

Soulguard | Christopher Woods

Suddenly Graves turned and faced me, I could see the very point when the focus came. His eyes cleared and the panic was gone. There was a thinking brain behind his moves and I deliberately held back so that he could attack and not feel totally outclassed. I do have nearly twenty years of training.

We began sparring and I blocked every attack but I could see the dawning realization of what he had done.

"That is the focus I'm talking about," I said softly where only he could hear. "Use the fear to grab that focus and you are better than you could have ever imagined. You think faster, you act faster and you *never* have to run again."

I turned and walked from the Dome, leaving the twins to show our new Mages around the facility. They looked at me with pity rolling across their auras. They knew how much it hurt me to torment that boy into action.

As I stepped out of sight I leaned against the wall with my face in my hands. I let out a drawn out sigh. The kid would always have fear but he knew how to use it now. Whether he does use it or not, we would have to see.

I heard voices from the Dome.

"He wouldn't have chased me around the room like that, I'd have fireballed his ass."

I heard a snort and Randy Quincy said, "He'd have fed it to you. Did you not see what just happened when that young man harnessed his fear? He almost blurred, he was moving so fast. The Boss was just playing with him. He could have beaten that boy down at any time. He learned to harness his emotions a long time ago and you'd be amazed if you ever saw him fight Demons."

"Wait till I tell Kevin's dad," the man said, "He'll be in some back room supporting Mages after this."

Randy laughed, "You think they can touch him? They tried to tie him from the Source, and four Mages died. He removed a permanent block from a Mage's stream. Even the Demons have sent a creature no one has even heard of to try to kill him and he cut its head off. Good luck, if you intend on making him your enemy. The best thing you can do is follow orders and watch that man to learn what a Mage is supposed to be."

"Oh, no," he mocked, "Be good or the Soullord will come get you."

I stood and started to walk away, I really didn't want to hear the rest of that conversation. The way Randy had talked made me sound like some sort of hero or something and I know I'm not a hero. Too many people have died for me to make me believe something like that. I just do what I owe them. My best.

I stopped as another voice joined the conversation, "That's right, the Soullord will come get you. When you are a six year old girl, alone and frightened, facing a Wraith and a hundred Demons who want to kill and eat you. He will come and get you, and he will stand alone between this little girl and that horde of Demons. Then he will kill them all and take you somewhere safe. And because this little girl has lost her whole family to the Demons, he will give her his own family. He will make sure you are trained to fight and always be there if you need him."

She paused a moment, "I know he will do this because he did that for me eight years ago and not a day goes by that I'm not thankful because it's another day I have that would have been taken away from me. I can look around at the Souls of the men and women here and I see memories of similar things that he has done for all of them."

"What have you done, Will Sanders? What have you accomplished that would make you able to say anything about him? Until you have faced what he has faced and made the decisions he has had to make, I would suggest you keep your damn mouth shut."

I stood there with my mouth ajar as I heard the words Lyrica spoke. I also heard the deadliness in the last sentence. She had come a long way from that tiny little girl I had found in an old farmhouse. She was fourteen and as deadly as any Guard or Mage I'd ever seen. She had always been a cheerful and sweet girl, but, as Sanders was seeing, she was not someone to trifle with.

I headed down the hall before anyone saw me. I don't think that was something I was supposed to hear, even though I felt a lump in my throat as I had heard their words.

Chapter 53

I awoke from a dead sleep when the portal opened and the Demons started crossing over. They were to the north and not all that distant. I jumped from the bed and got dressed. The rage was trying to surface and I beat it down.

When I reached the Dome, I found the RRT. Some were playing poker, some played dice. The ready Mage was Kevin Graves and his fear soared as I entered the Dome.

"Boss?" Rictor looked at me, "Got something for us?"

"Yeh, head north," I answered and after a second, "Take the kid."

Graves' fear spiked again but he nodded shakily.

"Take the whole team," I said quietly to Rictor, "but if it's a very big nest, call me. The kid needs to go in and see it for himself. But I don't want to send him alone on a large group yet."

"Got it, Boss."

I hated staying behind with a passion, but Graves really needed to be put to the test and what I felt wasn't a large nest of Demons.

I watched as my Guards left without me. I kept my expression as iron as I could even though I wanted to go with them so bad. I guess that is the hardest part of being in command. Sending out men and women to face the enemy while you are not there with them.

I had the feeling this would become more and more commonplace since the Council had finally decided that leaving me here as the only Battle Mage wasn't going to force me to screw up. Now they had given me many more ways to screw up than I had before.

Will Sanders was arrogant and very self-centered, but there was courage and a strong sense of duty down deep in his Soul. I knew that, with the right situation, he could become a great Battle Mage.

Olliver Garret, was steady. He was the type of person who, when given a task, approached it as a craftsman would approach a job. He would use what it took to get the job done, no more and no less. He always got the job done though.

Then there was Graves, who, I believed would become one of the greatest Battle Mages any-one had ever seen. If he goes one direction instead of the other. If he continues to run he will be useless to the Soulguard. The focus I had seen in the young man, if used, would be remarkable, to say the least.

There was no way I was going back to sleep, so I retrieved two of the short swords and returned to the Dome. Then I began to Dance the Blades, cy-cling through the stances at random. The true art of the Dance is to be able to switch from any stance to any other in an effortless fluid movement.

It was nearly three hours later when I felt the Demon presence disappear. Regardless of how Kevin Graves had done, the nest was gone. I would find out, soon enough how the kid had fared.

I wished that Lyrica was here to see his re-sults as well. She was the reason he was here in the first place. But she was in Scotland by then. I would just have to call her and tell her the news after I heard how he fared.

Several hours later I sat in my office and waited for Rictor to report. He sat down slowly.

"That was the damnedest thing I've ever seen, Boss," He shook his head in wonder, "We entered a cavern, and Demons flooded into the other side. I heard a shriek and I just knew the kid had run. But, he shot right through us and when he was in front, I swear, I've never seen anything quite like it."

He ran his hand across his buzzed hair, "He just looked like he exploded. Those disk things you shoot went everywhere. Fireballs flew all over the place and that Soullance thing you do was plowing across the room. All at the same time."

"He just kept screaming and killing anything that moved until every Demon in that nest was dead. I just knew he'd burn out but he just kept firing everything until all of them were dead. The rest of us, combined, killed fourteen Demons. Do you believe that shit?"

I had a huge smile on my face.

"You knew he would do that?"

"I had a feeling about the kid after I saw the focus he achieved when I chased him around the Dome. I felt he could have gone in one of two directions, but I never dreamed he would be this good. I watched the memory as you reported and I am very impressed. It makes what I did to him worthwhile."

I leaned back in my chair with relief filling me. I had been really worried that the kid would have gone the other way.

"Just what the hell did you do to him?"

"I showed him how to use all that fear as a weapon like I do with the rage," I said, "and I'm happy to see he learned the lesson."

***

"How do you use so much power and not have any build up inside you?" I asked, "Even when I reach that focus point my rage gives me, I can't do that."

"When I hit my focus point, it's like the world almost stops. I have all the time in the world, it seems like to aim and fire everything. I've always had a knack for feeling the power flows, and this focus lets me actively regulate what is let into my stream. No more than was there before but no less either."

"I'll be damned," I muttered, "I can actually see the flows and the power slips by me. Even with the world moving slow I can't seem to get the time to do all that."

"My focus point must be deeper in than yours," he said, "The world is slower or I'm faster, whichever you want to call it. I just have more time to act in."

"Goes to show, no matter how good you are, there's always someone better." I smiled and put my hand on his shoulder, "As for now, you're the only one I've ever seen that can reach that much focus."

***

"I swear its Déjà vu," Prada complained, "I mean, really? The same frigging cave and the same situation?"

We stood looking into the cave where I had done my first patrol. And down under the earth I could see human souls, just like before.

"We brought a lot more people this time," I said with a laugh. "Olliver, when we get down there, we'll cut our way to the prisoners and you shield them. We'll take care of the rest."

Olliver nodded. He's steady and does what he's told. I've noticed this in him since he'd arrived in Knoxville. He may not be the most innovative or destructive of Mages, but he does what you tell him to do. You don't have to wonder if he will or not.

"Let's get it done," I said and the world slowed down. I charged into the cave mouth with my swords flaming. Twenty-one Guards and a Mage charged in after me.

Moments after we hit the central cavern, we were standing near the same alcove full of people and Olliver raised a shield across the front of it.

I turned back toward the horde of Demons packed in the Cavern and let the beast burst free. With a scream of rage I was amongst the Demons and the Dance began. To my left, as always was Rictor and to my right, Prada. And they moved in synch with me. I think Sam was right, I believe I do project my movements into the Guards around me. When we fight together, we are one great big killing machine. If Janacek had been correct in his beliefs and we do pave the road to the afterlife with the Souls of our fallen enemies, then our road is gonna be one big son of a bitch.

When the deed was finished and I could detect no more of the ugly Souls around us, we returned to the shielded people that Olliver had calmed a great deal.

"I think I got a frigging piece of Demon down my damn shirt," Prada mumbled and squirmed a little.

"Want me to get it out for you?" Jacobs asked and ducked as she flung something squishy at him.

"Just offering to help, no need to get ill about it."

"How many damn nests have we already found this year?" I heard Ramirez asking.

"This makes seven, so far," answered Ric. "But the year's only half through."

"That's kind of weird, right?" Ramirez said, "One or two is normal, but seven? Friggin weird, no doubt."

As we neared Olliver and the people I could see a respect in Olliver's aura that wasn't there before. It was accompanied by a bit of fear of me, but there was less fear of me now and a bit more respect. Perhaps if I spent some time with each of them, we could get past all the stories they'd been told at the Academy. We are on the same side, I'm not some ogre or something.

"I bet they don't reuse that mine in West Virginia," Lewis said from the back of our group.

Prada chuckled, "No frigging doubt. Hey maybe you should kick a crapload of bombs back in here as we leave so they don't try to use this one a third time."

"Nah, I think we got this one memorized by now," Jacobs said, "If we keep drawing this cave, we know where everything is."

"Not like that place in New York," Holsey returned, "You know, that one with the big hole in the middle. Didn't someone fall in that hole full of shit? You remember that place, Jacobs?"

Everyone laughed as Jacobs looked around sadly.

"I hate you all."

***

A flaming disk shot over our heads and slammed into the packed Demons charging across the cavern toward us. Sanders sent another soon after. He was behind us but had his disk launchers raised high enough to clear our heads by five feet.

"Lewis!" my voice boomed as I amplified it, "Take Chambers and Rooney and rearguard Sanders!"

The three of them broke formation on the left side and turned to head back behind Sanders. That's when I felt it coming up from the rear.

The world slowed and I spun in place to open fire with four launchers at the same time.

Sanders aura pulsed with anger and fear until he saw I wasn't shooting at him but over his head. He dived to the right and the shredded body of a Wraith collapsed right where he had been standing.

Our eyes met for a split second and I could see the gratitude rolling through his aura. I turned back to the front and joined the rest of the Guard once more.

"You through playing around back there, Boss?" Rictor laughed.

My sword severed a soldier's head, "Maybe, maybe not. Let's get this over with."

I opened up my improved Soullance and Pulled hard. I raked it across the packed Demons and pieces fell everywhere. It left a scorch mark on the other wall of the cavern. Not many of the Demons in that part of the cave system survived.

"Maybe you should've started with that and then just clean up the mess after," Jenna said from the left flank.

"Takes all the fun out of it if I do it that way," I answered as more Demons piled into the Cavern to be met with Sanders' disks.

After the Wraith is already gone, I don't have to conserve the power for them. So once it's dead the Mages can actually open up. We're not like the Kid, he's a frigging machine when he's in the thick of it, power builds up in us as we use the Source.

I can use more than an average Mage can due to my tolerance for the Source in my body. I think it's a trait of the Soullord. With two Mages down here I had let Sanders open up from the beginning while I saved the power for the Wraith. It's nice to have two Mages at a time on a run.

As we made our way back out of the caves, Sanders walked up beside me, "Thanks, that thing would have got me for sure. I thought they stayed behind all their forces. That's what they say at the Academy, anyway."

I felt the rage claw and try to come out and Sanders paled a bit, "Are they trying to get everyone killed? Don't they read the frigging reports? I send em in every time we do one of these. Damnit! The frigging Demons aren't stupid, they're adapting to our successes and changing their tactics."

"We never heard anything about this in our tactics classes."

"I never got to go to a tactics class at the Academy," I said a bit more calmly, "Who teaches that?"

"Lucius Salvador," he answered, "He's been teaching that class for the last ten years."

"I wasn't there long enough to get to that. They had to send me out after the incident with Gavin."

He looked at me a moment, "What really happened with Price?"

"He tried to block me from the Source after he already blocked Paige Turner as a practice run. He failed, he died."

"They say you killed him on purpose and got away with it."

"I would have if he hadn't screwed up and killed himself. Think about it, if he tied us from the Source and it was discovered, he'd face abuse of power charges. He had to dispose of us if he'd have succeeded. He couldn't let either of us live after that. They had planned this from the start, I have no pity for him or the ones who helped him. I have no pity for the one responsible for the idiot's actions and we both know who was behind it."

"He couldn't be the one..."

"He damn sure is the one who put the whole thing in motion. Because I stood up to him once. He trained Gavin to do the block and threw his son under the bus. He figured either he succeeds and I am gone or he fails and I am disgraced and tried for killing him. Either way I'm gone and he gets what he wants."

"But..."

"His followers are doing the same thing, Salvador sent his son to California knowing the boy was a coward. Either he causes the problem that he did or he dies. Either way a good Guard Captain is removed."

"And don't think for a minute that Graves didn't have the same thing in mind with his son. He was sadly mistaken in the potential of that kid and we have a powerhouse to throw at the Demons now. The politics are getting harsh now," I pointed to the Guards around us, "and we're stuck in the middle of it all."

"It boils down to one simple fact," I said, "Whoever controls the Guards, controls the Soulguard as a whole. I don't know if it's power or money or both that drives the man, but Archmage Price wants all of the people who defy him in any way removed."

"But, to send his son out to die for his vanity seems a bit much," Sanders said.

"I've seen into that man's Soul, Will," I stared at him, "He's more than capable of doing just that."

***

As we entered the Guard base the secretary looked up and smiled our way.

"Janet, get Sandy and Randy on the phone, please. I need to see them in my office, and tell them I need a list of contacts at each base if they can do it. We need to get some information out to the other bases and I think we're being ignored."

"Yes sir."

I turned to find Sanders and Rictor both standing behind me, "You really think they've been ignoring your reports?" Sanders asked.

"The odds are the other bases are getting the same type of reaction from the Demons, but if they aren't yet, I want them fully aware of what's been happening here. It could save some lives. They've figured out that if they take out the Mage, the Guard is much easier to take down without his support."

Chapter 54

"I'm really worried about how frequently we keep finding the bastards," Ric said. We were sitting at a booth at Puello's Grill.

I nodded as I took another bite of the gumbo. It was really good and I had just gotten lucky to find it as the soup of the day.

"Yeah, something feels off about things and I can't seem to wrap my head around what it is. We need to do something and I'm not sure how to do it."

"What's that?"

"I want to capture a Wraith."

"Are you crazy?" he stopped with his hand outstretched toward a piece of bread, "Capture? A Wraith?"

"I'm afraid a soldier won't have enough information. I need a Wraith. It's time we found out what the Hell is really going on."

"What makes you think you can find anything out from it? We don't even know if they can talk our language."

"They can."

He looked at me for a moment, "And when did you have this conversation with a Demon?"

"A long time ago, one of them talked to my real father. I saw it in Kharl's memory. It laughed at them and said, 'You're too late man-things.' It was while they were on a mission and the Demons massacred the New Mexico Guard post. It was the day I was born."

311

"Ok then," he said, "Then all we got to do is work out the details. First we take more Guards, you'll be busy catching a Wraith so we'll clean the nest out. Don't look at me like that. Do you see any other crazy Soullords around? Nope. So you're on your own with that one. We'll keep the rest of em off you, though. When the nest is clean you can figure out how to make one of those big bastards talk, cause I got no idea."

"I really hate that they transferred our Mages back out of Knoxville. I was getting to like Sanders and the Kid was hell on wheels in a fight. This whole prospect would be easier if any of them were still here."

I guess the Council had figured out that the Kid wasn't another Salvador and gave up on that plan. It was a great feeling when Kevin had come and thanked me for scaring the shit out of him. He said it showed him that he wasn't a coward like he had always thought he was.

"Yeah except the Kid probably would kill it before we could capture it anyway. I guess we'll find out how to make it talk after we catch one of the big bastards."

"All right, from now on keep a forty man RRT on standby at all times. With the frequency of the incursions, it shouldn't be too long before we get a nest. Hopefully it will have a Wraith in it."

"You got it, Boss."

"I just have a very bad feeling about how they've stepped up their game. We have to get some information."

***

I eased into the cave a bit behind the forty Guards, well actually thirty eight. I kept Jacobs, Lewis, and Holsey back with me as rear guard.

"Do I even want to know why you're bald and he has pink hair?" I asked Jacobs while pointing at Holsey. The two of them had been playing practical jokes on each other for nearly two years now.

"Probably not," He answered through clinched teeth.

I chuckled, "All right, I won't ask."

I was scanning the area in front of us and I could feel a good sized piece of that evil darkness off to the right behind the other guards.

"To the right," I said, "it's a Wraith and some soldiers or its one of those damn Mages. You guys take the soldiers I'll handle the Wraith."

Suddenly the Demons sprang from the alcove they were hiding in to ambush the group ahead of us. I opened my portal a tiny bit on the Wraith trap and moved it in front of the thing. It ran into the target area and I opened the portal all the way.

The Wraith slammed into the inside of my shield and halted. There were ten soldiers with it and they turned immediately toward us and my three Guards went to meet them.

I had left a hole where the Demon's stream led to the portal so I wouldn't kill it. I wasn't sure whether a shield would sever its Soulstream or not, but we needed it alive.

I looked forward and every Demon in the whole cavern seemed to be looking at me. They tried

313

to charge toward me but there were two stacks of Guards in our formation and they couldn't get through.

Were they telepathic? It's possible, that would explain how every Demon in Little Rock had known the moment I killed the Demonmage.

The Wraith kept pounding on my shield and I shrank it tight around it, immobilizing it.

"You be still."

It stared at me with hate and rage rolling through its aura.

"You," It hissed as it seemed to realize who I was, "You are the reason we are here."

Its voice was a mix of hiss and growl, but the words could be made out.

I looked into its hate filled eyes, "And you are the reason I'm here."

It just stared at me as my Guards killed the rest of the Demons in the cavern.

"I want some answers, and I think you'll give them to me," I said standing inches from the thing.

It began laughing, or I think it was laughing. It sounded much like a growl and a cough.

"Not Kresh. Not to do your bidding."

"What's Kresh?"

It looked and motioned with it's head toward a corpse of a lesser demon. It nodded toward a soldier, "Kresh'far."

"I Kresh'sor'an, I Master. No fear of you, Man-thing."

I Pulled and sent Soulfire coursing through the shield that was tight against the Demon. It screamed.

When I stopped it looked back at me and bared its teeth, maybe it was smiling, "Like pain. Do it again."

There was no fear in its aura and I didn't see a lie there either. Maybe the bastard really likes pain. The way it had said Kresh gave me an idea. It had said it with disgust or something like it anyway. I'm working with best guess as to what they feel. It looked like disgust would have in a human.

The lesser Demons have a Soulstream of about three inches, a soldier has a five or six inch stream and this Wraith had close to a ten inch stream. Where the Stream passed through the hole in my shield, I began pressing closed. Its Stream was shrinking on the inside of the shield and I was watching the intelligence fade from its eyes.

It screamed in pure fury but it couldn't budge. As I expanded the hole back up I could see fear in its aura, now.

I pointed at its chest, "Talk or you remain Kresh."

I actually saw the resignation pass across its aura. If there was one thing it was afraid of, it was being reduced to that.

"I talk if you kill me. No Kresh, death."

"That I can do," I said.

"You kill Kresh'ma'nar four cycles ago. Whole world in uproar. Only one hundred fifty-seven Kresh'ma'nar in whole world. Now five hundred clans, as you Man-things say, come here to destroy all Man-things and start over. Each Kresh'ma'nar have five hundred clans. Now one has one thousand, he come here with five hundred."

My stomach felt ill. There had been thousands of Demons in the clan my father had destroyed so long ago and now five hundred of those clans were coming here.

"When?"

"Two of your days from now first wave come."

"Dear God," Ramirez mumbled from behind me.

"Where?"

"Only seven gates can take many at same time. Coming in place Man-things call Kansas, first. Only one gate can be open at time."

"Why do you come and kill us?"

"Always done, Makers create, we slaves. Makers defeated and we eat. Never be slaves again to Makers, now Makers slaves to us. Now time for you to do what promised. Kill me."

I looked at it for a moment and my sword flamed. My shield trap left its head uncovered and my blade severed its head cleanly.

"We have to go," I turned to see all three Guards behind me with pale faces. They had heard exactly what I had, "Now."

"Damn right we do, we gotta warn everyone," Jacobs answered.

"Friggin Kansas," Holsey muttered, "Right in the middle of the US. How the hell do we stop five hundred thousand Demons?"

"We kill em all," I answered, "There are close to a thousand Guards in the US and nearly a hundred Mages. We all go to Kansas and we kill every Demon that sets foot on our planet. It's the only thing we can do."

***

"I know you don't have any use for me, Price," I said into the phone, "But this goes way beyond us. We didn't have time to send this up the chain of command. In two days time there is going to be a massive invasion. The Demons have decided that we've hurt them too much and they're going to clean house."

"Just how would you know this?" He asked without emotion in his voice.

"We just captured and interrogated a Wraith. They plan to destroy the human race and start again with a select few humans as breeding stock. We're just cattle to them."

"And you believed this Wraith?"

"I was very persuasive in getting it to talk. We need to mobilize everyone, I'm getting the Knoxville post geared and ready for transport to Kansas."

"They're invading Kansas?"

"It said there are only seven of their gateways big enough for armies. It said the first wave was hitting Kansas in two days. We're talking hundreds of thousands of Demons."

"I'll place the calls and get everything moving," Archmage Price said and hung up the phone.

I turned to Rictor, "Looks like things are underway, let's get our boys geared up and ready for action."

We spent the next few hours getting our armor and swords set and calling in all the off duty Guards who were scattered across Knoxville.

I tried to call in to Greg and see how things were going but the lines must have been busy, I didn't get any answer. The switchboard must have been swamped, as the Guard began a full mobilization. I'd get Greg later.

Chapter 55

"Hello, Greg." I answered the phone.

"What's the deal with this nest in Kansas?" he asked, "The Arch mage said you were the one to report it."

"Nest?!" I felt a pit open in my stomach, "It's a full on invasion, Greg."

"What?" he asked, "We're already on the plane and headed that way."

"Who is on the plane?"

"The Elite Guards, me, Nora and a few more Mages."

"Didn't he mobilize the Guard?" I asked, "He was supposed to mobilize everyone. We're talking hundreds of thousands of frigging Demons."

"Dear God, you can't be serious."

"As serious as it gets Greg."

"We're bound for Wichita. You know if they're already here we'll have to go after them. We can't just let people die."

"I'll call in and see if we can't get help. I'll call back in a few."

As I hung up I had a sinking feeling. Price had finally played his cards. He was targeting my parents and the Elite Guards at the same time. I just knew this was the retribution I'd been waiting for over the last eight years. Maybe I was wrong, but I didn't feel like I was wrong. But what sort of end-game was he after? This could destroy the world, it couldn't just be vengeance on me. There had to be something else.

I dialed in to the Academy. No one answered. I tried again and still no answer. I tried another number and got a response.

"Colin?" Daphne Cavanaugh answered, "What the hell is going on? The Mages say the whole Knoxville base has gone rogue. What are you doing out there?"

"Daph, we're in some serious shit here," I said, "We captured a Wraith and interrogated it. The Demons have decided we're too dangerous to live and are massing a full out invasion. Their first force will hit Kansas in less than twelve hours."

"Why are they saying you're rogue then?"

"It's Price, he sent the Elites alone to face hundreds of thousands of Demons. He plans to cull the Guard down by getting rid of the ones who defy him. I think he has more than that in mind but I may be seeing more than there is. He is also targeting me because of his son I think."

"What do you need me to do?"

"How many Guards can you muster to send to Kansas?"

"I have a hundred Guards but some of them are out of communication at the moment. I can bring probably seventy or so. I can't guarantee it. We are defying orders to do it but I think my Guards will follow my lead. But we don't have transport."

"I'll get transport and call you back."

"You got it, I'll get the troops ready. Good luck Colin."

I hung up the phone and called another number.

"Hello," a familiar voice answered, "What the hell have you done this time?"

"Sam, I know you don't know me all that well but we're in some deep shit."

I told Sam Keller the whole story and he was silent for a whole minute.

"That sorry rat bastard!" He cursed, "He's using this to weaken the Guard, but if that many Demons run loose in Kansas, we'll never be able to hunt em all down. He's signing the death warrant for half of the US. I can't guarantee the Mage support but the Guard will follow me in this for you."

"For me?"

"You still don't understand the support the Guard is willing to give you, boy. What's the plan?"

"I'll call back in a moment. Start getting the troops ready and I'll see about transport."

"You got it."

I hung up and called one more number.

"Hello Colin, what can I do for you, Young Man?"

"Senator Deacons, we have a serious situation and I need your help..."

***

"I need you to get to Kirtland Air Force Base, you'll meet a C-130 there for the flight to Wichita. We'll meet you there and I got us some more help from Pittsburgh."

"Great, but we don't have the vehicles for that."

"There won't be any secrecy after today, Daph."

"I guess not," She sighed, "We'll be there."

"Thanks," I said.

"We're Soulguard, Colin, it's what we do."

I hung up the phone and dialed Sam, "I need you at the Pittsburgh international airport in an hour and a half. They're flying a C-17 in from Stewart Air National Guard Base in Newburgh, New York. We're meeting in Wichita and I hope they aren't already here."

"We'll be there," Keller answered, "If we survive this, you know we'll have to do something about Price, don't you?"

"Yeah, Price has gone too far, He'll have to be dealt with. Lord knows how we'll do it," I said, "Good luck Sam and we'll see you in Wichita."

I put the phone away and turned to the Guards gathered in the parking lot.

"Men, you all know what's happening in Kansas and we've been preparing to move the whole contingent out to join the battle. Some things have changed. The Archmage has chosen to send only fifty Guards and a few Mages to face this and everyone has been ordered to pay no attention to me. Word has gone out that we've gone rogue."

There were exclamations and the whole group seemed to erupt in fury. I saw the red of rage rolling across the crowd.

"I think you all know as well as I do why he targets us with these accusations. But I am going to Kansas anyway. I kill Demons and that's where the Demons are. Damn the Archmage and his Council of boot lickers. Hundreds of thousands of lives will be lost if we can't stop what's coming there. I won't order anyone to join me but you all are welcome. There will be no repercussions or hard feelings if you choose to follow orders and stay out of it."

"I think I speak for all of us, Sir," Jacobs stepped forward, "We'll follow wherever you lead and if you want to go to Kansas then by God, we go to Kansas!"

A hundred voices roared approval and I felt an overwhelming sense of pride in my Guards. Not one chose to stay behind.

"Then get your gear, we're heading for the airport. A National Guard C-130 will meet us in less than an hour."

"Sir, we don't have enough vehicles to take everyone," Ramirez said.

"We'll take it at a run. There's not gonna be any more secrecy after this. Hundreds of thousands of frigging Demons are gonna be hard to hide. Today we go public."

It only took a few minutes to ready everyone. I turned to find Sandy and Randy Quincy standing behind me. Body armor looked completely wrong on the two.

"I need you here guys," I said, "I need you to contact anyone you can and get more reinforcements down there if it's possible. You both look ridiculous in all that body armor anyway."

"We're ready to fight, Sir." Randy answered. I could see the fear in his aura, he was terrified, as was his sister. But they would both join me if I let them. I felt a large lump in my throat as I looked at them. Why do they have so much loyalty to me? I'll never understand how people can be so dedicated to me, and I know it was dedication to me. I'm a frigging Soullord, I can see it inside them.

"You two are amazing. Now go find me some more reinforcements."

"Yes Sir," They both headed back inside.

"You bring out the crazy in everyone, boss," Rictor said from right behind me.

"It seems so, Ric," I said softly. Then I turned to the Guards.

"All right!" I yelled, "Fall in! We're heading straight to the interstate and to the Airport at high speed! Let's go!"

I leaped forward as the world slowed, my Guards right on my tail. We sprang over cars and anything else that got in our way. In moments we were on I-40 and we picked up speed. I'm not sure how many wrecks we caused. It's not every day you see a hundred men and women running down the interstate at ninety miles per hour. Luckily it was rush hour and the cars weren't moving very fast. We leaped over the lines of cars entering from the side ramps and in minutes we were turning down Alcoa highway.

Several minutes later, I enhanced my vision as the Airport came into view. I picked out the Military craft and pointed. We slowed a bit, veered to the right and off of the road and shot straight for the aircraft. There were several National Guardsmen at the rear of the plane. Two were completely surprised by our arrival at seventy miles per hour. One, a young man wasn't surprised but awe rolled through his aura.

I stopped in front of him, "You must be the General's kid. Tell him we really appreciate his help. A lot of lives are depending on us."

I saw a little bit of frustration from the comment and a memory of several people calling him the General's kid and laughed.

"Big shoes to fill, eh?," I turned and Ric was already loading everyone up, "Try being the son of Kelvin Demonkiller. And tell your father that there'll be more groups needing transport if things go right."

"Yes Sir," he said, "My father told me what you're doing and good luck."

"Thanks, we'll need all the luck we can get."

As I stepped on the ramp I heard the small blonde woman's voice, "Is that a freaking sword on his back, Brisco?"

"I believe it was," the other National Guardsman answered, "Did you see their eyes? Those guys have been in some serious shit."

The ramp closed and I didn't hear any more from them. I headed forward toward the cockpit. As I passed the guy at the controls for the door I saw he was nervous and confused. Our equipment probably looks strange to guys who use guns as primary weapons.

"They told us you would give a destination when you got here," the pilot said as I entered the cockpit.

"Wichita, Kansas. How long a flight will that be you think?"

"About five hours, man."

"Thanks," I said and headed back to where Ric was sitting.

"Five hours or so," I said, "Daphne should be there by then but Keller will be a bit later. He's a couple of hundred miles or so farther away than we are. He's got a faster plane though, I may be wrong."

"That will give us some time to go over your open ground tactics with Daph. You sure you can make a shield that big?"

"I won't be carrying it by myself," I said, "I'm pretty sure it'll work, I just don't know how far we'll actually get into em with it. We'll just have to see."

"I just love your experiments, Boss."

"Don't we all," I heard Prada's voice.

Then Jacobs started singing Rocketman and I shook my head, "I'll never live that down."

I sat down and leaned my head back. As my eyes closed I heard Ramirez, "At least we don't have to listen to that racket all the way there."

"You'd rather listen to this loud assed plane?" Jacobs asked.

"As a matter of fact, yeah."

Chapter 56

"Holy shit," Jacobs said, "You guys feel that?"

"It's still an hour away from us," I said as I opened my Inner eye to look for it.

"That thing must be huge," Holsey said.

"I can't believe you kept the pink hair," Lewis said to Holsey.

"Why not? He's still bald," Holsey said, pointing at Jacobs.

I started feeling the rage building inside of me.

"Starting to get that look in his eyes again," Prada said, "The killing starts soon after."

The Demon portal was so strong, I was having a hard time beating down the rage. I jerked as Ric squeezed my shoulder but it helped. They know what I deal with every time we fight Demons and they help when they can. It really means a great deal to me that they care as much as they do.

I spent the next hour struggling with the Demon inside me. I was ready to get off the plane as soon as it stopped.

"They're both here, Boss," Ric said, "but I don't see the Elites."

I had a sneaky suspicion where they were. One of the first priorities would have been to get the attention of the Demon army so the innocents could run.

I met Daphne and Sam as I got off the plane, "We don't have time for practice so I'll tell you what I have in mind."

I looked at Keller with a question on my lips.

"It's your show, kid," he said, "just tell me where you want me."

"Daphne, I want you on the right flank and Rictor on the left. I want twenty Guards on each side and stack the others in a chevron formation right behind them. When I raise the shield we'll all be pushing it."

"What shield?"

"You'll know it when you see it. When I raise it, pull your ranks up against it and get as many in on the push as you can."

She nodded even though she wasn't clear on what the shield was yet.

"Sam, I need you in the center doing Mage things. You see anything bigger than a soldier you burn it down."

I turned to the two hundred and fifty six Guards forming up.

"I can't thank you enough," My amplified voice boomed across the airstrip, "my brothers and sisters."

I pointed to the horde of news helicopters heading north, "The world will be watching and the whole Guard will be judged by the actions we take today. We'll do the Guard proud. And if we walk the road to Paradise today, it will be paved with *thousands* of Demon Souls!"

The Guard roared. One of the pilots from our plane stepped off the plane, "Who the hell are you guys?"

"Who are we?" my voice boomed.

"Soulguard!" two hundred and fifty nine voices replied in unison.

"North at a run!"

I surged forward as the world slowed and the Guard fell in behind me. We were at a small airport to the north of Wichita and we headed straight north. The area was flat and we didn't bother with a road. We ripped across the plain at close to eighty miles per hour.

The evil feeling of Demons grew closer and closer and there was a huge darkness ahead of us. We had covered ten miles when I felt a Pull like I'd never felt before. It was huge and the horizon lit up in the distance.

"What the hell was that?" I heard a Guard ask. I was afraid I knew what the answer to that question was and I felt a sinking feeling.

Minutes later we were near enough to see the horde of Demons on the other side of a small township. People were fleeing south and we angled to the side and charged straight through the town, toward the Demons.

I could see a white glow out in the center of that horde. There were a lot of Demons trying to get to them but there was a massive wave of them heading for the town.

All the way here I had been weaving a shield and it stretched across the front of our formation. It was shaped like a razor sharp arrow head and it rested against the shields of the Guards in our chevron formation.

"Shields up!"

Every Guard turned on their personal shield. I opened the portal on the arrowhead and it flared to life. Every Guard who could get to it moved into the shield to push.

I looked at the horde in front of us and the rage was boiling out of me. In the center was a huge Demon with an ugly purplish black glow around it.

"See that big bitch in the middle?!" my voice boomed.

"Hell yeah!"

"That's the target! And I want it's head! Full speed!"

With another roar the Guards poured on the speed.

The arrowhead slammed into the horde of Demons with an explosive crash and Demon parts and Demon blood exploded in every direction. We didn't even slow down for several moments. We plowed through nearly half the distance from the outer edge to the Demonmage before our formation was bogging down.

"Diamond formation!" my voice boomed.

The Guard fell into a formation with twenty guards per side of a diamond. The rest formed a second diamond inside and a third inside of that one. Sam Keller was in the middle looking for Wraiths. I dropped the arrowhead and drew my swords which flamed to life.

"Let's dance!"

My Guards had formed the outer diamond and most of them had been practicing the Dance of Blades with me. The world slowed and the Dance began. My swords blurred and Demons died. To my left Rictor's swords took life after life and his soul was filled with glee.

I love Marines.

To my right, Andrea Prada danced and Demons died.

"Wraith inbound! Three o'clock!"

I heard Sam cut loose with his fireballer. The Wraith exploded before reaching the Guards. We cut our way ever further toward the Demonmage.

"Switch!" my voice boomed and the Rednecks stepped smoothly back while the next rank of Guards stepped up. Daphne Cavanaugh stepped into the point position as I stepped back.

"Wraith 3 o'clock!"

"Wraith 9 o'clock!"

"Wraith 1 o'clock!"

Just as those voices rang out, the Demonmage erupted with ugly purplish black fireballs. I quickly formed a flat shield and placed it in front of the first fireball. It slammed into the shield and drove me backward ten feet. The next one I angled the shield so it just deflected the fireball right into a tightly packed group of Demons.

They were incinerated. The fireballs kept coming and each was on a different trajectory so I had to concentrate on deflecting them all.

As this was going on, Sam unloaded into the first Wraith at 1 o'clock. It exploded after three fireballs slammed into it. He turned and opened fire into the Wraith at 3 o'clock. The other one slammed through the lines and aimed straight at Sam's back.

It was mere feet from Sam when out of nowhere, Jacobs hit the thing high on the back, wrapping an arm around its throat. He hit it so fast it drove the Wraith toward the left and it missed Sam by inches. It roared and reached back to rake its claws up Jacobs' back ripping long gashes into the man. His shield blunted a bit of the force and kept the claws from killing him outright. He reached to his belt and drew a dagger which lit with Soulfire. Then he raked it across the Wraiths right eye.

It roared and began spinning, trying to get ahold of Jacobs. Finally it grabbed his left leg and snatched Jacobs from behind it. It raised the Guard to look at who had been on its back and opened its mouth to mangle him with its huge teeth.

Jacobs armed plunged into its mouth and he slammed the flaming dagger through the roof of its mouth, right into its brain. It slammed its jaws closed, severing Jacobs' arm, just below the elbow and it spasmed, ripping his left leg off below the knee.

Jacobs cartwheeled outward toward the Demon horde to fall limply to the ground. Soldier Demons charged the downed Guard, but Holsey, of all people stepped across him and began holding the horde back. In seconds, Ramirez joined him, while several guards I hadn't met pulled Jacobs inside the formation.

All of this I saw afterwards through the memories of several Guards. It took all my concentration to block the fireballs flying toward us. If they had been aimed at me, it would have been easier, but the fireballs were flying toward all different points in our formation. Then we reached the point where I was in range of the bastard.

I opened the portals on six disk launchers and pushed the shields up high above the heads of my Guards. Then I Pulled hard and all six launchers sent fiery disks flashing toward one point. Straight at the chest of the Demonmage.

Each of my launchers fires two disks per second and there were six. The disks began slamming into the thing's shield and it stepped backward with each strike. It took five seconds before the first disk penetrated the shield and slammed into its chest. It screamed as disk after disk ripped it to shreds.

Then I slammed my triple shield out to cover the rest of my men and opened the portals. The few Demons inside the shield were dealt with quite quickly.

There was a massive roar from every Demon on the field and they all turned toward us.

"That got their attention, Boss!" Prada yelled.

"Damn straight!" another Guard yelled as the Demons charged and slammed into my shield.

That's when I turned to find Sam Keller bent over Jacobs pushing life-force into the man.

"That crazy son of a bitch killed a Wraith!" Holsey was hovering behind Sam. I watched the memories flashing across auras and shook my head in wonder.

"You know, if he lives through this he'll be insufferable," Prada said beside me.

"It'll be worth it," I said, "Get some people to help him, we need to close ranks with the Elites. They've been hammered for over an hour."

Chapter 57

I opened a hole up high in my shield dome and began lobbing Soulbombs out into the horde of demons. Sam had stabilized Jacobs as best he could and began doing the same.

"When the shield goes down, diamond formation. The Elites are the target. We join forces, now that I think they're definitely focused on us," My voice boomed, "Rednecks to the front rank! I'm on point!"

I looked at Sam Keller with a savage grin, "Fire in the hole!"

I cut the tethers on thirty Soulbombs, He had made twenty-seven more and he cut the tethers to them.

The explosion was deafening. Demons and parts of Demons exploded in every direction. I dropped the shield and shot forward with the Guard in perfect formation. My eyes stayed focused on the Elites as they began closing the distance toward us as well.

I could see the individual Souls now and relief flooded through my as I saw both Kharl and Kyra were still alive. I could also see Paige's aura and Darrel's. But I didn't see Nora's and I knew what that explosion must have been, earlier. Gregor was still there so it had to be Nora.

As we hit the horde of Demons again I Danced once more and the rage was fed Demon blood. I saw the Wraith coming head on at me and I opened up with the disks again. It made short work of the beast and I kept dancing. I glanced left to see Ric with a smile of pure happiness on his face. He's never happier than when he is fighting.

I love frigging Marines.

I kept my eyes on the other group. Kharl's soul was burning like a furnace over to the left side of the group and Kyra was moving so fast her soul looked like a firefly off to the right. They were each leading a group of Guards on the flanks.

Suddenly, the firefly stopped and her Soul flickered. A great pit opened in my chest, I heard a horrible wail and I realized it was me. I saw the vision of my birth mother in the midst of the bloody massacre where she'd died. I saw my friends ripped apart in a cavern. I saw all the dead at Morndel and all the losses we had already taken here, but the one person I knew I couldn't bear to lose was my mom.

The rage wasn't just peaking through the surface any more, it flowed like a tidal wave across my consciousness and I embraced that flood.

I went berserk.

I screamed in fury and began Pulling with all my might. My disk launchers spewed fiery death and my swords launched arcs of power into the horde between me and my mom. I surged forward across heaps of dead Demons, slamming arc after arc into the masses in front of me. My disk launchers spewed fire through Demon after Demon. My swords melted and I dropped them to sling arcs from my fists instead.

I saw another Wraith and leaped to its back, before it knew what was happening. I reached down and ripped its head off with my bare hands. Then I jumped from its back into another packed group of

Soldiers. I never slowed down, screaming in fury, I ripped them apart with my bare hands.

Suddenly, I was in an open area and there were no Demons around me. I was still screaming in rage and looking for more. Then my eyes connected with those of Paige Turner and I realized I was there. I looked back to see my Guard was right behind me and I slammed my shields back up around us all.

The fire was dangerously high in me but my first act was to leap to Kyra's side. Kharl closed in from the left flank and when he saw Kyra laying in front of me he ripped the soldier he was fighting in half with a roar and went airborne. He landed right beside us to fall to his knees and pull Kyra to his chest. He cradled her head in his arm and tears were flowing freely down his face. Kyra was barely alive and I did the only thing I could think of.

I reached down into her Soulstream and Pulled gently. I didn't know whether it would work or not but I had to try. The Source flowed up her stream and the horrible gash in her side stopped bleeding. Her soul began to stabilize itself and I noticed that the fire that had built up in me was noticeably less.

"Told you he'd get here," She mumbled to Kharl.

He looked at her with love flowing across his aura. They'd been together for close to thirty years and he had finally realized he loved the woman.

I knelt beside her and kissed her forehead, "You'll be ok now, Mom, I love you."

Kharl looked at me, "Thank you, Son."

Soulguard | Christopher Woods

I nodded at him and stood up, turning to find Rictor and Daphne waiting patiently for me.

Sam Keller stood behind them with awe flowing across his aura.

"You take us to the greatest places, Boss," Rictor said with a grin. The sad part is he meant it.

"What are our losses?" I asked with dread.

"Thirty two dead, seven critically injured and forty three wounded."

"God, I'm sorry. I lost it back there."

"Lost it?" Ric snorted, "Most of those losses were from before you did that, I'm on fire and I'm gonna kill everything move."

Daphne chuckled, "Accurate description but it needs to be shortened a bit. I'd hate to try to remember all that every time I wanted to order it done."

"We were right behind you on the way in," Ric said.

I sighed and turned to look for the wounded. I saw the small group that Paige was tending and headed that way. As I passed the critically injured I stopped and Pulled through their streams as I had done with Kyra. By the time I reached Jacobs I was Pulling from the Source to power myself as I Pulled through his stream. His Soul stabilized and his eyes opened.

"Did I get the bastard?" he groaned.

"Hell yeah you did," I answered, "Only Guard dumb enough to tackle a Wraith by himself. They'll sing songs about it."

"God I hope it's a better song than Rocketman," He muttered as his eyes closed again.

I turned to find Paige standing behind me with a haunted look in her eyes. I stepped forward and placed my hands on her shoulders.

"Are you ok?" I asked softly.

"I was ten feet from her when it came through," she said and I watched her memory as she saw it in her mind.

Wraith warnings sounded from everywhere and Nora had opened fire with disk launchers. She killed three of them but the fourth came in from behind. Nora didn't have an Ivan Jacobs and she managed to turn, half facing the beast as its claws ripped through her side. Incredibly fast, she'd latched onto the creatures arm. You could tell that her spine was severed as she dragged herself around to latch onto the Wraith.

It had happened so fast, Paige hadn't even gotten her fireballer charged all the way before it was already too late.

It surged through the Guards and out into the horde outside the perimeter. It began trying to dislodge Nora but she held tight. Paige was looking straight into her eyes when Nora Kestril Pulled the world inside out.

Gregor barely got the shield up before the blast wave rolled over them. And the last look on Nora's face was burned into Paige's memory. She had a sad look of acceptance just before she screamed as the Source consumed her and Left a crater where the Wraith and close to four hundred demons had been.

"Damn," I said softly, "I'm sorry Paige. I have to go, just stay strong."

She nodded with a sadness filling her Soul. She and Nora had become very good friends over the last ten years.

I made my way over to Gregor who gave me a strange look, "What the Hell did you just do? Those Guards Pulled from the Source."

"It must be one of those Soullord skills," I answered, "I've never done that before but I couldn't just watch her die."

"Amazing."

I looked out at the horde of screaming Demons pounding on my shield and an idea began to form. Something else caught my eye and I poured power into my eyesight to see a group of helicopters on their way toward us.

"I think we have reinforcements incoming," I said with my voice amplified, "Clear a spot in the center of the shield."

I opened the top of the shield and pushed the edges high enough that the Demons couldn't get in and with a little push I made the whole thing glow brightly so the choppers could avoid it.

I looked again at the horde outside, "Mages," My voice boomed again, "Soulbombs out the top of the shield all the way around us. Let's clear out the perimeter so I can expand the shield."

We began forming the Soulbombs and lobbing them outside.

"Fire in the hole!"

We cut the tethers on a hundred and thirty Soulbombs and there was a tremendous roar outside of the shield as the blast wave destroyed everything within a hundred feet around the shield.

Immediately, I pushed the shield out to that point and began crafting two twelve inch tendrils, One was at the end of the weave I'd used for my shield and the other was ten feet out along the tendril I used to feed it.

I stopped, inches above the ground with my tendrils and motioned to Gregor. I lit up an arch at the north end of the shield and one at the south.

"I need a shield about six inches inside of those spots but don't let them touch my shield."

"What the hell are you doing?" he asked.

"We need this shield to stand without a Mage, I'm tying it to the Source."

"God Damn it, Colin," he exclaimed, "It took twenty five Mages to make the Dome. You're gonna do this by yourself?"

"You gotta point," I said, "Sam, Darrel, Paige, I may need support. Be ready if I do."

"You got it," Darrel said and Sam nodded. Paige walked over and stood at my right shoulder, prepared.

"Thank you," I turned to Gregor, who just shook his head and placed the shields where I had asked. I opened the areas in my shield on the other side of his shields.

"It's a matter of timing, you see..."

I slammed the end tendril into the Source. Power surged up the shield and quickly flowed toward me. Just before it reached me I slammed the second tendril in and severed my link. I was a tiny bit slow and the power recoil slammed into me, throwing me backwards twenty feet. But the power had not entered me, so I was fine.

The shield flowed with power from a twelve inch stream. Nothing was piercing that.

"Crazy bastard," Sam was muttering as he picked himself up. Apparently he had been right behind me.

The helicopters got closer and I could see the Souls of Guards and one Soul I recognized the moment I saw it.

I was smiling when Rictor walked up, "You blew yourself up again?"

I shrugged, "Hadn't done it in a while, thought it was time."

He chuckled, "So who you think is in the choppers?"

I grinned, "You'll see."

The choppers began hovering and Guards started dropping from them, down into the shielded area. Rictor's eyes widened and surprise rolled across his aura as he heard a familiar scream as one of the forms jumped from the helicopter.

"I'd know that screech anywhere!" I heard Jacobs yelling, "Somebody help me sit up, Damnit!"

Paige headed back over and tried to get the man to calm down.

"You don't understand, darlin, that's the Kid!" he kept trying to sit up, "If the Boss is turning the Kid loose out there, I gotta see it! Lean me on Lewis, there, he's big enough to prop against!"

As the small man landed, his scream stopped and he stepped forward with a sheepish look. He was still the wiry little guy we knew and loved. But there was a sadness in him as well.

He looked at me and gave a little smile, "Boss."

"Hey Kid, glad you could come to the party," I said with a grin, "Where'd you get all these Guards?"

"Denver and Sacramento. Olliver and Sanders are both on the last chopper, there."

"Good," I nodded to him, "The more, the merrier."

All told, they brought a hundred and fifty more Guards with the three Mages.

I heard Paige still talking to Jacobs, "That's just Kevin, what are you talking about?"

"That's a good question," Gregor said to me, "You said Kevin had improved a lot but everyone seems to be jumping for joy here."

"Just give it a few minutes and you'll see why," I said with a laugh.

Chapter 58

"This is what I want," I said with my voice amped, "Kid, you'll have the Denver guys and I need a Mage for backup."

Sanders stepped forward, "I'll back him."

"Ok take twenty five of the Sacramento guys as well. I want about twenty or so around the backup Mage and the rest in diamond formation on the Kid."

"I want to send out three waves of us, You guys get the first run. Then I go with the Rednecks. Sam, you want to do support on this one?"

"You got it."

"Bring ten of your Guards to finish out my numbers, Ramirez!" I yelled, turning to him, "Get fifteen guys for the backup group's defense."

"Got it Boss."

"Third wave is Gregor and the Elites with Daphne's troops as well. Olliver, you ready for the Backup spot there?"

"Yes Sir."

"Darrel, you and Paige are the Gatekeepers. Darrel on the north and Paige on the South."

They both nodded.

"Everyone get set, work out your positions, first wave goes in two minutes."

I nodded to the Kid and pointed with both arms, "This area, all the way out and back. Anything in that area is crispy. How're you feeling?"

"Scared shitless."

"Good. What do you see out there?"

"A target rich environment, Sir," he answered with grin.

"Ready?"

He nodded and I pointed to the north gate, "On my mark, open the gate!"

The Kid stepped to the middle of his group. I could see the fear spike.

"Mark!"

The gate dropped and the Guards poured out, slaughtering anything in the immediate area. Then the Kid screamed in terror and shot forward. As soon as he passed the lead Guard, I felt him Pull so hard it made my teeth hurt. He exploded with power and everything within a fifty foot area in front of him was incinerated. He never even slowed down as he shot forward, and his Pull never decreased.

When I fight, there are times when I'm Pulling hard and others when I'm not. It fluctuates some but the Kid doesn't.

"Dear God," Gregor muttered beside me, "I could do that for maybe three minutes. Won't he burn out?"

"He's a frigging machine, Greg," I answered, "He goes till he does what he sets out to do."

He shook his head sadly, "Nora told me this would happen."

"What's that?"

"She said, after you left the Academy, that we'd be support Mages before this was done. I laughed at her because I've bought into my own reputation of being the second most powerful Mage in the US. I wish she was here to say I told you so."

"Me too, Greg," I said softly.

The Kid reached the outer edge of the horde and the whole formation turned and swept back toward us. Sanders burned a Wraith that was coming from the side.

"Looks like it's our turn," I said, "After the Kid calms down a minute, tell him he did great for me, I'm gonna be a bit busy."

I headed to the front of the Rednecks. Ric stood to my left and Prada to the right.

I drew two swords I had gotten from Lewis. He was wounded and he knew I'd melted mine. I looked out at the horde of Demons and let the Rage wash over me.

"Friggin growling..." I heard from off toward the Guards I hadn't worked with before.

"That's a good sign," I heard Daphne chuckling.

Then the Kid and his group were inside and I let the beast out of its cage. With a howl of fury I shot out the opening with a hundred Guards and Sam Keller right behind me. We ripped into the Demons and I reveled in the slaughter.

This is what I'm made for. This is what I'm good at and I could actually let the rage out completely. We ripped through the horde of Demons, straight toward the outer limits of the horde. I saw a Wraith but Sam burned it down, so I continued forward.

As soon as we broke through, we turned left and headed back in. We were about halfway back when a Wraith hit our line right beside me. Prada and Ramirez both were grabbed and thrown out into the horde about fifty feet ahead of us. My rage spiked and I hit the focus point the Kid had told me about.

The world slowed to a crawl, and my blade removed the Wraith's head. I leapt to where Prada and Ramirez landed. The soldiers around them were inches from the downed Guards. I grasped the back of their armor and hurled them both back into our Guards' ranks.

It seemed like I had infinite time as I leapt out of the group of Demons. I surveyed the field around us to see a wedge of ten Wraiths heading straight for us. Before I even landed, I opened up with all six launchers at six different targets. My Soullance slammed into a seventh. And two fireballers hammered two more.

They were right in front of the shield and I charged the last Wraith with my fists glowing with Soulfire.

I passed on the right side of the beast and my left arm ripped through the bastard's midsection, tearing the Wraith almost in half.

Then we were inside and I was standing there with my chest heaving as I beat the rage down.

"Keeping that?" Kharl asked as he went by me, toward the door. I looked down and found the spine of the last Wraith dangling from my left hand.

"Hmm," I shook my head, trying to clear some of the rage and turned to find all of my Guards with rage slowly subsiding from their auras. They had bloodshot eyes and veins standing out on them. Apparently, I'd projected much more than just my movements to them this time.

"Damn, Boss," Ric muttered as he got his rampaging emotions under control.

"Thought I was a goner," Prada said as she walked up. She looked at me for a second and kissed me, "Thanks."

There were several whistles and jeers as she walked back to her previous spot.

"Thanks, Boss," Ramirez said, "I'll kiss you if you want but I'd rather not."

"Nah, that's ok, Luis," I said with raised hands.

I turned around to see the third wave head out the opening. I heard Gregor mumbling as he went out.

"I'm retiring, I swear it. I'm a frigging dinosaur."

"I think we all are, Greg," Kharl answered.

Kharl was at the point position and he charged into the horde of Demons to do what he's always been a master of. The others followed him flawlessly and Greg burned several Wraiths as they made their pass.

There was a bit of power built up inside me so I headed for the wounded to heal them and get rid of any excess power. If there is one group I'm not worried about it's the Elites and Greg. They've been fighting Demons for over a hundred years.

The thing that bothered me the most about them was the fact that Jack Riordan and Tien Yueh weren't present and I dreaded asking the questions I would have to later.

As I neared them I heard Jacobs talking to Paige, "That's what I was talking bout. I couldn't miss that, now, could I?"

As I finished stabilizing the new wounded Guards, Rictor approached.

"How many did we lose?"

"Three dead, seven wounded." He said, "Would have been more if you hadn't projected that rage. I mentioned it to the others and it was like it gave us more speed and focus. Definitely a new way to do things."

I turned to the door as the Elites re-entered our shield.

"All right, Kid, South door this time," My voice boomed and the Kid's group hit the south door to do much the same as they'd done to the north.

We each made three trips out into that horde and their numbers just seemed endless. More and more were flooding from the giant gateway.

"They'll bleed us dry," I said to Kharl and Gregor, "We can't keep doing this as long as that gate is spewing Demons."

"We don't have many choices, here, Son."

"I know," I answered, "I have to get a look at that Gate. If we can shut that thing down we can work on killing the rest of em then."

"Next runs will be west then," Kharl said, "That'll give you a chance to look it over."

"Kid!" I yelled and Kevin headed our way.

"Boss?"

"I'm shadowing your next run, I want a look at that gate over there. When we get there I need a shield and we'll pause long enough for me to look at it. Have Sanders do the shield."

"Yes Sir," He turned and started giving orders. A large swell of pride surged through me as I watched him.

I turned back to Kharl and Greg, "Hold down the fort till we get back and we'll see what's what then."

"Ric! I need ten with me. We're shadowing the Kid to look at this gate."

"Gotcha, Boss," He turned and barked out names. There was no point in asking for volunteers, we were all volunteers already.

In a few moments we were all ready, "Hit it, Kid!"

The Guards shot out the north door and turned west. The kid screamed and shot forward, exploding with firepower.

I beat down my rage and held to the back of the group. I poured disks into a Wraith that tried to hit us from the side and it stumbled and fell in a flaming heap.

After a bit, we were right up beside the Gate and it was huge when you're standing right beside it.

"Shield!"

Sanders pushed a shield out and opened his portal to solidify it. The Guards made short work of the Demons inside of the perimeter.

My eyes were on the giant portal. There were twenty huge cable-like tendrils that seemed to flow from inside of it and join the outer ring of the portal. Maybe if I could cut those the portal would collapse. I opened up my Soullance and fired into one of the tendrils. A small fray showed where I shot but that was all, so I Pulled hard and poured the power to the lance. The fray grew a tiny bit but there was no way I had enough power to cut it.

I felt that cutting the cables would be the only way of shutting the thing down. I'm not sure all the Mages we had here could combine and cut the things.

"Ok, men, we can fall back to the shield."

The Kid nodded and Sanders dropped the shield. The Kid screamed once more and exploded out to the front again.

"I can't help it, I love to see that boy work," Rictor said, running beside me.

"It's like a work of art," I returned.

Chapter 59

"The power cables are tough on that thing. I can't get enough power into my lance to cut it. That's the strongest thing I have."

"Is it the design or just not enough power?" asked Greg.

"Definitely power, the design will work with whatever power I can pour through it."

The Kid was out in the horde again with his Guards. I was standing with Kharl, Ric, Daphne, Caprida, Sam and Greg. We were close to the injured and Kyra motioned for me to come to her.

"Mom?"

"You just pulled power through our streams to heal us, Son," she said, "Can you Pull it and use it instead?"

My mouth dropped open. It hadn't even occurred to me to try something like that. Two hundred Guards would channel a hell of a lot of power.

I hugged her, "You're a genius, Mom."

"I know," she said, "Now go clear up this mess. My side hurts and I want to go home and retire. I'm too old for this shit."

I returned to the group and Rictor said, "He's got that let's experiment look on his face."

"Oh dear," Daphne muttered, "Now it begins."

"Ric, I need a volunteer for some craziness," I said as I rejoined them.

"Let's do it, Boss."

I love freaking Marines.

"When I Pull, all I want you to do is focus on not letting power from it enter you. I want you to focus on a point twenty feet above my head and when you feel it come up your stream, steer it there."

He had a huge grin on his face.

"Ready?"

"Hell yeah. Light the fire."

I reached into his stream with my mind and Pulled much harder than I had done for the wounded. I watched as it rose and veered out of Ric's stream to a point above my head where it rolled out of the tendril he had formed with it.

"You all right, Ric?"

"This is what it feels like to Pull?" He asked with awe rolling across his aura, "It's amazing, Boss."

I stopped my Pull and made my decision, "New game plan, boys and girls!"

I turned to where the Kid had just entered the shield again with his troops, "I need a hundred guys here with the Kid. Sanders as support and Olliver to hold the gates. Everyone else, except the wounded, is invited to be a part of the biggest Pull ever attempted. Volunteers only! This could be the most incredibly insane plan in the world."

"I'm going to Pull power through everyone to power a way to destroy that gate. I don't need to tell you what's happening if the gate stays open. There are over a half a million Demons on the other side, intent on coming here and killing everyone."

"In five minutes, I'm going out that door," I pointed toward the north opening, "What say we end this before more of our brothers and sisters have to die in this damn place?"

The Guards roared as I turned to the Kid, "I want you to cause as much of a ruckus as you can stand over here. Come back here in between runs to rest, but I want crispy Demons everywhere. If we succeed there won't be any more than what's already here, so the numbers will actually dwindle. I need as many as you can get over here and pissed off."

"Yes, Sir," He said and turned to his men, "You heard the man! Let's go make some damn Demons irate!"

"Sam," I said as I headed for the door, "When we get there, you're the shield bearer. All of the Mages will be support and all the Guards will be the battery. I'm the gun. Let's get it done."

"Yes, Sir," he said and smiled. I think he found it amusing to say that to someone seventy years his junior.

I headed for the door. Gregor was waiting there with every Mage except the three I had designated to stay here.

"Frigging support Mage," he was mumbling as I walked up, "She was frigging right."

I laughed and turned to find that every single Guard who wasn't under the Kid's command was forming up with us.

I'd never been so proud of my Guard. And they are *mine*, my family, my friends, my brothers, my sisters, my Guards.

"Open the gate!"

As the shield dropped I let the rage out and shot out the door like a rocket, my new set of swords alight with Soulfire and ripping through anything that got close enough for me to reach. We headed straight toward the gateway.

We reached the area directly in front of the gate where I could plainly see every inch of it.

"Here!" my voice boomed and Sam opened his shield portal a small amount and placed it where he wanted. Then he opened it wide and the shield solidified. We slaughtered the Demons inside of the area and I turned to the gateway.

The amount of power I figured would be used wouldn't work with my Soullance. I had to craft a new one, the feeder tube was close to four feet in diameter and I used power to adjust the lenses to reduce all the way down to three inches. It worked with my projected power, I just hoped it would work with the amount I'd be pouring into it.

I turned to the Guards, "It's very important that you don't let the power into your body. Focus on the area twenty feet above my head. I'll take it from there. Focus. The Source is an unforgiving bitch and it *will* burn you down."

"We're ready, Boss," Rictor looked around at them and back to me, then nodded.

I turned to the Mages, "Every one of you will need to be in this, I had to Pull when I just did one at a time."

"We're ready," Greg said, "You know this is crazy, right?"

"We specialize in crazy, Greg," I answered.

I turned to the Gate and reached out with my mind to find all of those Soul streams and when I had felt them all, two hundred and forty-one streams, I Pulled.

I went to my knees and the three Mages placed their hands on my arms. Strength flooded back into me as the Source wasn't Pushed from them into me but Pulled through them in a huge torrent. My body soaked it up as I Pulled from the Guards, and Power exploded everywhere.

I reached up and steered that power into the Soullance and a blindingly brilliant beam blasted out the other end. I hit the first cable and the beam started cutting it!

But it was slow, I Pulled harder and the beam brightened. The first cable snapped and I started the second. Around the gateway the beam cut. It was close to halfway done when Darrel suddenly went slack and fell behind me. I looked back to see he was still breathing. His body had just shut down.

I saw power ripping up the other two's streams and turned back to the cutter.

I made it through three other cables when I felt Greg fall.

Paige began screaming and I knew we weren't going to make it but I had to keep going. Four more cables!

Suddenly I fell to me knees and had to stop. Paige had fallen.

"Damn it! Just fucking once, let things work!" I turned to check and both Greg and Paige were alive.

"Use me," Sam said and stepped forward.

"No, if the shield comes down," I pointed to the horde of Demons pounding on the shield, "they get in and if I'm Pulling from the Guards, they can't fight. I'm *not* letting my Guards die like that!"

I snarled as I turned back to the Gate, "I know what to do but I don't know if I can survive it. I guess I'll find out!"

I could stop here and search for some other solution, but every solution I could think of involved more of my Guards dying. I can't stop because I'm afraid for my life, knowing it will cost more of theirs. It's just not in me to, because if there's one thing I know beyond a shadow of a doubt it's that Soulguards *never* quit. Not one of my brothers and sisters would hesitate to give their life to end this and I could do no less.

"No, wait just a sec..." I heard Kharl start.

I let the rage come and with it power and focus. My Soul erupted and four huge tendrils formed. Not from my stream, but directly from my Soul. I reached out to all of the Streams inside of the shield, except Sam's and Pulled with every ounce of my being.

As the power exploded across the sky I slammed all four massive tendrils down into the Source and strength flooded into me. The lance surged back to life and the beam sliced another cable and another.

More power was flooding into me than I needed and I poured it into the Lance with the huge stream of power slicing the last cable.

The portal began to lose its pattern and suddenly it seemed like it imploded. I heard a massive roar as every single Demon on the field had its Soulstream severed.

Now the part I dreaded was upon me, as soon as I stopped Pulling from the Guards, those tendrils would be pouring into me.

"Tell them I did my best," I said to Sam, who was staring straight at me with a look of horror at what I had done.

Then I formed a shield around me and held it poised above the four streams. When I stopped Pulling from the Guards, I slammed it down through those Tendrils, severing the connection with me and the shield took all of that power instead.

Fire roared through me as the excess power flooded my body and I screamed as I released every-thing into the sky as I had done one time, long ago at Morndel Academy. There had been so much power pouring into me, I smelled burning flesh and knew I was done. But we had won, and if I had to go, my road to the afterlife would be paved with a hundred thousand Demon Souls.

Blackness descended and my vision faded.

Chapter 60

Rictor Hughes paced from one end of the room to the other. Each time he turned back toward the door, he would stare at the man laying in the infirmary bed.

"Damnit man!" Ivan Jacobs said from the second bed inside of the room, "Pacing back and forth ain't gonna help him!"

"There's gotta be something we can do," Rictor snapped, "He's fighting for his life."

"It's a Source Coma, Mr. Hughes," said the small woman in a nurse uniform who had just walked into the room. "No one has ever survived a Source Coma. He's already broken all of the records. He's lasted twenty four hours and the longest was six hours."

"It's not just a coma," Rictor glared at the nurse, "Don't you feel how the Pull keeps changing? That's what it feels like to fight right beside this man. He's fighting. He's fighting Death itself."

The nurse stepped back at the fierceness in Rictor's voice.

"There's nothing we can do Mr. Hughes," the girl said, trying to calm him down. But she cringed as he stared into her eyes. She could see something burning in his eyes and she backed out of the room quickly.

"By God, there is too." He said savagely, "Prada! Ramirez!"

Andrea Prada and Luis Ramirez stepped into the room, both looked to the man in the bed as they came in.

The man's Pull was weakening as they spoke, "He needs help and Lyrica won't be here for another ten hours, I'm going to be Support."

"They say you can't support a Source Coma victim, they say it will kill you," Prada said softly.

"Then I die with my Captain."

Prada stood straighter, "But not alone. Luis call in the Rednecks I want volunteers for some craziness."

"Get my damn chair!" Jacobs yelled, "Not much use for a Guard with one leg and one arm, but I can do this!"

***

Kharl Jaegher snapped out of a sound sleep. He felt a massive Pull from the Academy.

"What the Hell?"

"That, my love, would be his Guards doing something incredibly dangerous. They're supporting him," Kyra said.

"Courageous fools," Kharl mumbled, "Let's go join em."

Kyra smiled, "Let's do that."

***

Lyrica Jayne strode into the infirmary, there were Guards surrounding Colin. The Source was pouring through them. She stepped to his side and looked deep into his Soul. She was sure that the Guards pouring power into him were the only reason he was still alive. She'd felt them Pulling for the last hour on the plane. She could see how drained their Souls were and shook her head in amazement.

"I'll take it from here," she said softly in Rictor Hughes' ear, "Now it's time for me to work."

Rictor withdrew and with a pleading look said, "You gotta save him, he did this for us."

In that instant she saw the memory of the final moments inside that shield flash across Rictor's aura. She felt the tears that she wanted to shed as she watched her Angel connect directly to the Source to power the cutter.

"I will," she said, "now go rest before you fall over."

As the Guards pulled back, Lyrica sat and placed her hands on his chest where there was a large patch of scar tissue from the burns inflicted by the Source.

She reached down deep into the Source and Pulled as she delved into his Soul with her mind.

***

"You stand before the Council, Sam Keller," boomed the voice of Archmage Price, "We understand that with your actions, you prevented a catastrophe, but you defied a direct order from the Council."

Sam Keller smiled and shook his head.

"Due to lack of information, it is true that an inadequate force was sent to deal with the situation in Kansas. And therefore, no one under your command will be held accountable for the disobedience. But in any organization, the orders of your superiors have to be upheld. To defy them has it's own consequences."

Sam started laughing.

"Do you find these charges amusing, Keller?" snapped Luciuos Salvador.

"As a matter of fact, I do. You really have no idea what's coming. It's sad, in its own way. But you'll see when he wakes up. That's all that they're waiting for. When he awakens you all are done."

"No one wakes from Source Coma," Roman Graves said harshly.

"No one has tied directly to the Source to support themselves as they Pulled from the Streams of over two hundred Guards either," he shrugged and with a surprised look said, "Oh yeah, I guess someone *did* do that."

"That's impossible!" Allen Denton exclaimed.

"Really?" Sam returned and started laughing again, "Whatever. When you get through patting yourselves on the back you can let me know what you have in mind for me. I don't have time for this stupidity."

He stood and turned to leave the Council chambers.

"You will respect the authority of this Council, Mage!" boomed the Archmage.

"Do you feel that?" Sam turned and they could see the savage joy in the man, "They could feel that in New York! That's two Soullords, Pulling the world apart! And when they're done you'll face the consequences of your treasonous actions!"

As he said this, he pointed straight at the chest of Archmage Price.

Then he turned away and walked out of the Council chambers.

***

"Daphne Cavanaugh, you are standing before Council to face the charges of disobeying a direct order from your superior as pertaining to the..."

"That's not exactly why I'm here," Daphne interrupted, "I'm here to give you warning. The only warning you will receive. Run. Hide."

"Has everyone gone insane?" Salvador exclaimed.

"Maybe," she said, "When the Soullord awakens, I would suggest you be gone."

She turned to leave and Roman Graves stepped in front of her.

"You are not dismissed," he paused and sneered, "Guard."

"Step aside," Daphne said with fire in her gaze as she dropped her privacy shield, "or I'll cut your heart out."

His face turned pale and his eyes widened in fear. Daphne Cavanaugh's Soulstream had swollen as Colin had Pulled the power through it. It had swollen to five times its original size of four inches. She was the most powerful Mage in the whole Council room aside from Price.

He moved and she strode out.

"What the hell happened out there?" Allen Denton asked softly.

Suddenly, the Pulling that everyone had been feeling for the last three days ended.

Price smiled and said, "Finally. Luciuos, Roman, burn the body."

"With pleasure," Salvador answered.

"Roman, has your son been dealt with?"

"Yes, Sir, it's done," He answered.

"Good."

Chapter 61

Lyrica stood up shakily and Trent reached out to steady her. The Pulling had stopped and he could see that Colin was still breathing. Relief flooded through him as he saw his friend's chest rise and fall.

Lyrica bent back down and kissed him, she whispered something Trent couldn't make out and stood back up.

"He'll be fine, now. He can rest for a while. He was fighting for three days straight."

She turned and started for the door when she saw the ugly Souls of Five Mages approaching. She stepped out in the hall with rage coursing through her, a leftover from her trip into the Soul of Colin Rourke.

"We've come for the body," Roman Graves said with satisfaction rolling across his aura.

"If you touch him," Lyrica replied savagely as she reached out with her mind, grasped all five of their Souls, and pulled them halfway out of their bodies, then slammed them back in, "I'll rip your Souls apart."

Denton screeched and fled, Graves and Salvador both fell to the floor with spasms wracking them. Regina Worthington and Russell Fisher both fell unconscious to the floor.

When the spasms ended, Lyrica looked down at both of the Senior Mages, "Pick up your trash and leave, Now."

After they staggered down the hall with the others dragging behind them, Lyrica turned to Trent and Mattie.

"Put Guards on him until he wakes. When he does, he will do what he does best, his duty. Don't let him go alone to face those jackals. Wake me, I'll stand with him when he does."

"We all will," Trent returned.

As Lyrica walked off to find a place to sleep Mattie turned to Trent, "I wonder if he even knows how that girl feels about him?"

"I doubt it, for someone so perceptive, sometimes he's blind as a bat."

***

"I'll bring all of the evidence before the Council, today," Gregor Kherkov said to the man who sat in the chair across the desk from him.

"Are ye sure ye should go in there alone?" Lennox Flynn asked.

"I don't want it to be a show of force. The Council cannot deny the truth when Guilefort and I present it to them. If we truly need a big hammer, I'll call in the rest of them."

"Tis true, we have an unholy big hammer if we need it," Flynn said. "The bloody Council canna deny the truth when Guilefort is there. It should be enough to prove the guilt of the Archmage. Then the Council will be forced to act."

"That is my hope," Gregor returned, "We could wait for Colin to be present but I think it would mean more to the Council if the evidence was brought forward by someone, *not* at odds with Price already."

"True enough, old friend. If ye need us we will be near."

"Thanks, Len."

Flynn stood and left Gregor's office. He headed directly to the infirmary. As he stepped into the infirmary he couldn't help but see the Guards stationed in the hallway before Colin's room.

The man pulls a dedication from 'is men unlike many people can, Flynn thought.

There were ten Guards outside of the room, or more accurately, ten very powerful Mages. No one would enter who wasn't welcome.

They all knew Flynn and he nodded as he passed one of the women he'd met earlier, Cavanaugh was her name. She had been the one who had dropped her privacy shield to show him what the Soullord had caused with that insane Pull.

He shook his head in wonder as he remembered coming completely awake from a dead sleep in Edinburgh. He'd felt that Pull from halfway around the bloody world.

As he stepped into the room, he saw Lyrica. She sat in a chair beside the Soullord reading a book. She looked up as he entered and smiled.

"Len," She greeted him warmly, then she looked to Colin for a moment, "He should be waking up in the next few days. I don't even want to get into what I saw inside of his Soul, I'll just say it was a fight to end all fights in there. He fought for three days straight."

She looked toward the door with that look Flynn would see in her eyes as she looked right through things, at Souls. "Because of them," she nodded toward the door, "he didn't have to fight alone."

***

"What we are here for, is to ask," Gregor's voice boomed across the chambers, "no, to demand answers from a man who has committed treason against the Soulguard and against Humanity itself."

***

"Gregor is going to the Council, today," Lennox said, after a moment in silence, "E's takin te truthseer with 'im. Tis a confrontation e is after. E was meanin to wait for young Colin, 'ere, but 'is honor will not allow it to wait any longer."

"There was something really off about those Councilors yesterday, I think we should go and back him up," Lyrica stood up with one last look at her Soullord.

Tis a great big lot o trouble that boy is in when she gets a little older, he thought with a smile.

"Then by all means, let's go talk to the Council, Lass."

The two of them walked out together, Lyrica had spent a great deal of time with Lennox Flynn while she was in Edinburgh. He was like the kind

Uncle that always looked out for her. Mattie and Trent both fell in behind them. Every step she made, one or both of them was always there.

Lyrica didn't mind, Trent was Colin's oldest friend and Mattie was one of the greatest fighters that Lyrica had ever come across. Her father must have been something else to have trained her as well as he had. Lyrica had met Mattie's father several times but hadn't trained with him any. It was sad to think that she had lost the only family she had left because of the travesty the Archmage had created with his crusade to destroy the Guard.

Right now the job was all Mattie Riordan had to hold on to and Lyrica would never presume to take that from the grieving woman.

The two Guards were unusually silent. There was always a joyful banter going on between them, but the current situation had even put a damper on their conversations.

Lyrica could see the pain in Mattie and she could also see the pain in Trent as he watched her. Neither of them would ever admit it but they were perfect for each other, and one day they would see it themselves.

***

"It has been brought to my attention, that there was a call made by The Knoxville Mage Captain informing the Archmage personally of the invasion over twenty-four hours ahead of time."
The Councilors looked at Greg in stony silence.

***

They exited the elevator on the floor where the Council chambers were located and Lyrica felt a Pull that jarred her insides.

"Dear God," Flynn mumbled as Lyrica went supernova. She shot forward faster than the eye could follow and slammed through the Council chambers door.

***

"All that is required is for you to answer the question, Price," Gregor said.

Beside him stood Simon Guilefort and Gregor repeated the question, "Did Colin call you with information that there was an imminent invasion by an army of Demons coming?"

Price just stared at Gregor without saying a word.

Gregor turned to the Council, "This is a question that has an answer that will shake the Soulguard to the core. This man has plotted and deceived too many men and women to be left unaccountable. Here is the list of men and women whose lives were lost due to this man's treason. Jacob Andrews, Saundra Adams, Franklin Banks...." the list went on and on, "Nora Kestril, Jeromy Kieser, Floyd

Kramer..." each name seemed to slam into the room like a hammer blow.

He had called out fifty-one of the one hundred and five names when every Mage in the room turned and focused on him and Guilefort. He stopped and raised a stream shield around Guilefort and himself just in time. There were twenty-three Mages in the room with them, including the Archmage, and every single one of them Pulled.

"Oh shit," he mumbled and raised two more shields like Colin had shown him, slamming the other two out against the first.

Fireballs slammed into his shield and they felt like blows to the gut. There were so many, he wasn't sure he could hold. Even with the larger Stream he now had, he was feeling the shields weaken.

Then the door exploded inward and slammed into the wall on the far side of the chambers, it struck endways and embedded three feet into the rock wall with a huge metallic crunch. A form shot into the chamber glowing like the sun and all hell broke loose around Gregor. He'd seen something similar from Kevin Graves in the battle with the Demons. But Kevin has a twelve inch stream. Lyrica Jayne has a twenty inch stream and she was Pulling hard enough to shake the whole Academy.

"PRICE!!" the girl screamed as power exploded from her. Nine Councilors were burnt down instantly, another eight flamed soon after. Then she did something that scared the living shit out of Gregor.

He wasn't sure, exactly what it was, but she reached out with her hands and ripped the Souls completely out of Archmage Price, Luciuos Salvador, Roman Graves, Allen Denton, Russell Fisher, and Regina Worthington. He knew that was what she did because the Souls still looked like the people that they were ripped out of as they screamed in eerie silence and were sucked down into the Source.

***

Lyrica shot toward the doorway to the Council chambers as the world slowed almost to a stop. She had learned after the episode with Kevin Graves to find that focus point deep within her that made her mind work faster than her body. It was almost like running through a world that was stuck in a still frame. She hardly slowed down as she kicked the door completely across the Council room.

The second she entered, she took in the situation. Every single Mage was attacking Gregor and Guilefort. All of them were shooting fireballs and they were slamming into Gregor's shield. He was pouring power into the shield but each hit staggered the man.

What the hell were they all attacking him for? His appeal was supposed to be to them for support in the removal of Price. It wasn't supposed to be an attack. It was obvious that Gregor was totally on defense and Guilefort looked out of Gregor's shield in stunned silence.

She looked to the Mages to find that only six of them had even bothered with shields. The only thing she could see was hate rolling through their auras. There was so much hate in the room she could almost feel it pushing into her mind.

"PRICE!!" she screamed and opened portals on eight disk launchers and her Soullance, simultaneously. She targeted nine Mages with no shields and fired one shot per Mage. Then she fired at the other unshielded Mages.

She was pretty sure that a full out power struggle with the Archmage and the other five Mages would leave her lacking. And it would be a stone bitch to get through the man's shield, much less the shields of three Senior Mages and two medium strength Mages. So she reached out with her mind as she had done in the hallway of the infirmary and ripped the Souls completely out of their bodies. They were screaming silently as their Souls were pulled down into the Source.

Lyrica stood in the middle of the Council chambers with Soulfire burning all around her as Lennox Flynn stepped inside the room.

"Jesus, Mary and Joseph," He gasped, "Ye dinna leave any for us. At seems a wee bit selfish of ye, Lass."

She pointed at Regina Worthington, "For some reason, that one still lives, sort of."

There was a tiny sliver of her Soul still inside of her body. When it wouldn't release from the woman's body, the rest had ripped away. It was ugly and purplish in color, much like a Demon's Soul.

"There's something strange about that woman. Maybe Colin can figure out what it is," Lyrica said. She looked up with that far-away look in her eyes.

"He's waking up," she said with a smile.

Chapter 62

In the blackness, I heard voices. I opened my eyes. As my vision cleared, I saw Rictor standing directly between me and the door to the room where I lay on a bed. His Aura was ablaze and he held two flaming swords at the ready. He was as ready to fight as I'd ever seen him and I wondered what was happening. My eyes closed again and I slipped back into the dark.

After some time I opened my eyes again, slowly, to find Rictor standing at the end of the bed where I lay. He was standing directly between me and the door again with his full battle gear on. He stood with his back straight and his aura was filled with a turbulence that was uncommon for Ric. As I raised my head, I could see why. His Soulstream was swollen to at least twelve inches and the power flowed across his aura much faster.

Just what the hell had happened out on the plains of Kansas? Had all my Guards had the same sort of reaction to my Pulling through them? If so, the population of Mages in the US just increased three hundred percent.

"If I can manage it," I said, "I'd like to not ever do that again."

He spun in place impossibly quick and his aura was flooded with relief and happiness.

"I have to agree with you there, Boss," he said with a slightly crooked grin, "That was crazy, even for you."

He turned back toward the door and yelled, "Prada! Ramirez!"

Both of them walked into the room and the first thing I saw was the much larger Soulstreams on both of them. Prada's was as large as Rictor's and Ramirez's was close to ten inches in diameter.

"It appears I'm not the only Mage in the Rednecks now."

"Not by a longshot, Boss," Prada returned, "Every single Guard who went out there to the gate is much the same. Several are almost insanely powerful. You should get near Gregor and Turner."

"They made it alright? I was worried after they went down," I asked.

"We lost a lot of good men and women out there, Boss," Rictor said, "But all who went to the gate are still alive."

My eyes were feeling incredibly heavy and Prada said, "Rest easy, Boss, your Guard has your back."

I slid back into darkness.

The next time I awoke I felt much stronger and I saw Kharl standing guard between me and the door. I gasped as I saw his Soulstream. It was twenty inches or more.

He turned at the sound and smiled, "Boy, you're gonna give me a heart attack if you keep doing stunts like that."

"I'm in no rush to do it again, Dad."

"I'd say," he said, "Next time we can find something that doesn't involve Source Coma and almost certain death."

"I could really use a cheeseburger."

"Yep," a voice came from the other side of the room, "He's back."

I turned my head to see Jacobs in the other bed in the room.

"Glad to see you made it, Ivan. I was worried about you."

"I'm just taking a break, Boss. Wraith killing is hard work."

"I'm thinking Eye of the Tiger would be a good song for you, Ivan. Maybe I need to speak to Holsey about it."

"You wouldn't."

"Rocket man..." I started singing.

"Man, I hate that damn song," he whined.

***

"...and the mystery continues to baffle the American people. Who were these valiant defenders and where did they go after the battle?" I sat in the infirmary bed with the back raised and watched the screen.

It showed some of the footage of the battle in Kansas. There were some really detailed shots of us as we charged into the horde of Demons and bodies exploded around us. The camera zoomed in to show a close up of the moment when Jacobs attacked the Wraith.

"Look, Boss!" He exclaimed from the other bed, "I'm famous!"

The scene shifted before the part where Jacobs lost his arm and leg, "Parts of this footage had

376

to be cut because of the graphic nature. Whoever this man was, he was severely injured but, as of this moment, there are no reports of anyone fitting his description checked into any hospitals we can find."

"What sort of abilities do these supermen have? This is footage at one point where the man we presume to be the leader appears to explode with energy of some sort."

The scene had changed to the point where I had gone berserk. It was an eerie feeling to actually watch it as it happened from a different perspective. It was hard to believe that it had actually been me in the front of that wave of destruction that rolled across the Demons between us and the Elites.

"The real question, again, is who are these people and where did they come from?"

I looked away from the television as Rictor entered the room. He looked distressed, and I can't really blame him. I'd ordered him to quit stalling and give me the names of our losses. He'd told me that one hundred and five of us had perished on the plains and another eighty six had been wounded.

I turned the TV off and turned to face him. I had dreaded this moment from the time I woke.

"Do you want the list, Boss?"

I nodded and Rictor handed me a paper. I could see the grief in him as he handed me the list. He looked straight ahead and began.

"Andrews, Jacob. Adams, Saundra. Banks, Franklin," the names hit me like hammer blows. These were my brothers and sisters, my friends. "Grayden, James," The names went on and on. "Kestril, Nora. Davies, Lawrence," I closed my eyes and leaned my head back as tears slid down my face.

377

"Rostov, Nikoli. Riordan, Jackson," I felt a hole in my soul as he said, "Shoffner, Patrick. Seymore, Jenna," And the list went on and on. The final name was another hammer blow. It was one I expected but it hurt just as much as if I hadn't known it was coming, "Yueh, Tien."

As I opened my eyes I saw that mine weren't the only tears flowing. Rictor's face was wet as well and I heard a sniffle from the other bed in the room. I made myself not look. There are some things that should not be interfered with and a man should be able to grieve as he will without any judgments.

After some time in silence I leaned forward and said, "Now, someone had better tell me what happened after, because I can't seem to get any answers from anyone about it."

"All I know is that Gregor went to the Council with Guilefort. He demanded answers of the Archmage right in front of the Council and the truth seer. But the Council attacked him outright. All twenty-two of them and the Archmage. Then Lyrica hit the scene and destroyed them all. Gregor won't go into much detail and Lyrica is quite upset. She is with your mom and dad right now and Gregor is waiting for the chance to talk to you about it, I think. Even I can see that, whatever happened, shook him to the core."

***

378

"Colin, what I've seen in the last week has terrified my beyond anything I have ever experienced," Gregor said. He was sitting in his office across his desk from me. There was fear and uncertainty rolling through his aura. "I've never been scared of anyone or anything until now. What you Soullord's can do is beyond anything I've ever contemplated. She ripped the Souls completely out of their bodies with her mind."

I watched the scene play out in his mind. I could feel the fear that overwhelmed him as he remembered what had happened.

"She made the destruction of ten Senior Mages, twelve middle range Mages and the Archmage, himself look easy. Like she hadn't even broken a sweat," he said.

I watched his memory of it and saw the door explode inward to fly across the room. Lyrica shot into the room, a teenage girl with worn jeans and a pink t-shirt with the words 'I R SMART' printed on it. Her hair was flying straight behind her and there was power exploding in every direction. What Gregor saw as a terrifying sight I saw as, quite possibly, the most beautiful thing I had ever witnessed.

"But that's only part of it. What you did in Kansas was something unprecedented. You not only Pulled from another person's stream, you actually created two hundred and thirty-seven new Mages. A great deal of them would be called Senior Mages because of the power level they are at."

"The things you two can do are terrifying. Everything is in an uproar about the deaths of the Council. But they attacked us. I don't understand why they all attacked us. I find myself at a loss as to how to proceed. All of my preconceptions are shattered and I have no answers anymore. What are we going to do now?"

"We're going to appoint a new Archmage and then we're going to go prepare for the biggest war this planet has ever seen."

"You know who will have to be appointed, don't you?"

I nodded.

***

I stood in front of the Memorial wall. There were a hundred and five new name placards attached to the wall and I reached up to touch one.

"Did you know him?" Lyrica asked from behind me.

"Yes, Jacob was the reigning poker champ in Knoxville," I answered.

She stepped forward and pointed to one of the Elites, "Peter Samson, He lost his family in 1872 to a Demon attack. For many years, all he had was his hate to drive him. He joined the Guard soon after and spent over a hundred years with the sole purpose of killing Demons. But he still let a little girl into his heart and taught her much about the world around us as well as a great deal about the sword. He always had a smile on his face when he saw me."

I put my arm around her shoulders and pointed to another name, "James got this idea that he was gonna get drunk, even if it killed him. He went to Kentucky and bought a whole carload of Moonshine. He got pulled over on the way back and the arrested him for running Moonshine. It took some serious finagling to get him out of trouble with the law. They just wouldn't believe that it was all for his personal use."

She smiled as I relived the memory in my head so she could watch it. She pointed to another name, "Johannes Calibri. He caught me trying to fly after your fiasco in Little Rock. Afterwards, he didn't tell on me, but joined me in trying to devise a shield to use for it."

She smiled as she relived that memory so I could watch it.

We stood there for hours, pointing out the different names of our friends and family. Nora Kestril, friend and Mentor to both of us. I told her about Lawrence Davies, the gentle giant. How he'd looked so awkward as he started to learn the Dance of Blades because he was nearly seven feet tall and as broad as a barn.

We talked about Tien Yueh and Jack Riordan. I told her about Patrick Shoffner, the local guy from Knoxville who had talked so much about the people around that area.

I told her that I knew that my Guards had lied about his death. They said that no one died from the massive Pull out by the gate. They had tried to protect me from the guilt I would feel after finding that Pat had let his focus slip too much and the Source had consumed him. There were three more that died the same way out there and it was a miracle that there weren't more.

"They tried to soften the blow and I thank them for trying," I said, "It's very hard to lie to a Soullord."

She hugged me and I talked about Jenna Seymore, friend and lover. It hurt to talk about my friends yet it helped so much to be able to talk with someone who doesn't look at me in fear after the things I have done.

And I'm sure it's much the same for her. After the incident with the Council, no one can look at her without the fear being present. I can see her guilt at the fact that she had killed people, not Demons, people. She can see the guilt I feel when I think about the fact that I should have taken action years earlier and none of this would have happened as it had. But we can at least find solace together as we stand and remember the friends who have fallen.

Everyone in the Soulguard may fear her but there is one who doesn't, me. We are two of a kind. Soullords. And we will do what we must to protect our world from the enemies that are massing to destroy us from without, and the enemies who would doom the world that operate from within.

Around us the Soulguard celebrates a great victory and rightly so. We had defeated over a hundred thousand Demons on the plains of Kansas. We had stopped, at least for the moment, a great invasion. Saved hundreds of thousands of lives. They had a right to celebrate.

But this is just the beginning. If they were ready to destroy the world because of the loss of one of their Kresh'ma'nar, Demonmages, what would they do after losing another and a hundred thousand Demons as well. I think we'll find out soon enough.

Chapter 63

The Council chambers were crowded with Mages as the argument continued. They had been arguing for five hours straight.

"We must change the way things have been done! Our following of the traditional ways led us to the situation we are in right now," Paolo Ferdinand said once again. He was one of the Senior Mages from South America.

"We face a massive Demon invasion! We can't begin changing things at this stage! It stands to reason, the next most powerful Mage will take control immediately and we can begin the preparations for war!" Luis De'Laroche returned. He just happened to be the second most powerful Mage in the world under Archmage Price.

None of the Mages were aware of the fact that Gregor's stream was now as large as Price's had been.

"If ye plan ta give the Medallion of Office ta the most powerful Mage, it should go ta Colin Rourke or Lyrica Jayne. Miss Jayne is only sixteen so it would rightly fall ta Colin to take the Office," Lennox Flynn interjected.

I shook my head, "The one problem with that is the Archmage needs to be a Mage. Lyrica and I are Soullords. Follow tradition or don't follow tradition. It makes no difference, I will not be the Archmage because I am no Mage."

Gregor spoke for the first time since the meeting had started, "I would suggest that we give the Office to the most powerful Mage in the world as a temporary duty until we can get the rest of the matter settled. We can then set up a vote to place the person who the Guard wants to represent them and lead them. In the meantime, we have issues that have to be settled."

Gregor paced across the room so that everyone could see him, "One pressing issue is the ceremony of Last Rights for our fallen comrades. We won a great victory but our fallen need to be laid to rest."

There were many nods and I could see the respect of the Guards who were present, as well as a good number of Mages, grow as they heard someone finally address an issue that had been hanging over the Academy since the battle.

"Can we all agree on that, at least?"

There were nods from the majority of the Mages present and I could see the satisfaction roll across De'Laroche's aura. His aura looked much like Price's had. He was arrogant, self-serving, and there were large ugly spots in his aura.

"Since we are in agreement, finally," Gregor said, "Colin, would you be so kind as to give the Medallion to the Mage with the largest Soulstream? Then we can get down to the business we need to be discussing."

I nodded and with a small smile I picked up the gold medallion that had hung from Price's neck for ninety years. De'Laroche waited, expectantly and looked confused as I walked past him toward the most powerful Mage in the world. That Mage backed up a step as I approached and sighed in resignation as I placed the medallion around her neck.

"You must be joking!" De'Laroche yelled in fury.

"You have to do it," I said, "*You* are what this office needs. You can do this."

Paige Turner dropped her privacy shield and there was a wave of power rolling from her that made my teeth hurt. What had happened after Gregor had fallen in Kansas had ripped her stream wide. Now instead of a stream that came from the Source to circle her and enter like most of our streams do, hers came directly up from the earth to encase her. It was nearly three feet in diameter and the power flow from her passive stream almost made a thrumming noise until she raised her shield once more.

"I take it there are no objections?" Gregor asked as he looked around the chambers at the pale faces of a hundred and forty Mages.

"Christ!" a British voice mumbled, "What *happened* in bloody Kansas?"

"That's not the half of it," Gregor answered, "We have two hundred and thirty-seven new Mage trainees and quite a few of them are more powerful than some of the Senior Mages present. They are well versed in all of the focusing techniques already so I think we can accelerate their training a good bit."

Paige stepped forward, "We need to divide them up and send them to the various Academies for training. As they finish training we can decide where they will serve."

She walked out in front of the Mages filling the room. I could see the uncertainty in her aura but she hid it well from someone without my particular gifts.

"As Gregor said, our first duty will be to see to the Last Rights of our friends. I would like to hear any suggestion as to how we can accomplish this while the US Military is camped on the plains of Kansas."

"I can call on Senator Deacons and see what he can do for us," I said.

"Do that," she said with a nod, "While Colin is finding out about that, I need to appoint a group of Councilors. I would like to begin with some of the Mages I know. Since I am unfamiliar with a lot of you, I can only start with the few I do know and I will begin adding more as I meet the rest of you."

She turned to Gregor, "I would like to begin with Gregor Kherkov, Lennox Flynn, Darrel Barnes, Samuel Keller, William Sanders, Kharl Jaegher and Daphne Cavanaugh."

"Excuse me," Paolo Ferdinand looked confused, "Aren't the final two Guards?"

"Not any more. They are two of the new trainees I spoke of. And the first thing that will become apparent to all of you is that I am not a traditionalist. Don't be surprised when there are Soulguards as well as Soulmages on my Council of advisors."

She looked at the silent Mages, "My first act will be to appoint Colin Rourke as the Warmaster of the Soulguard. It will be his duty to fight this war that is about to begin and it will be him you must answer to if you fail in the duties laid before you. Until the Demons are stopped, he is officially my second in command and his word is my word."

"There are many more experienced people…" I began.

"Am I your Archmage?"

"Yes you are," I answered with pride. I could see the doubt in her but I could also see that iron core that I knew was there too.

"Then do your duty."

I nodded in acceptance.

"Now go see to your Senator."

"Yes Ma'am," I said with a small smile. I turned and strode out of the Council chambers.

Lyrica stood outside waiting for me. She had stayed out of the room for the time being so that the Mages could deliberate without her reputation looming over them. She would have to face this from now on. She was the one who had destroyed the entire Council and the Archmage in a single fight. It would take some time for the Soulguard in general to begin to accept this and see her as something more than a weapon again.

At this moment there was a great fear of her and a great fear of me in almost every Mage. It was present in a great deal of the Guards, as well. But the Guard knows that we have always been a part of them, regardless of how powerful we become. So their fear is tempered with respect and loyalty.

"It went well?"

"Yep, Paige is the Archmage and we are free to go prepare to fight our war. She's quite capable of doing the job. She just needs to learn it for herself."

"What's our next move?" she asked.

"We need to perform the Last Rights for our fallen. Then we have to go meet the US military on a formal basis and start the preparations for the Demon's return."

"How do you think the military is gonna react to us?"

"They need us," I said, "Even though they don't realize it yet. Perhaps Senator Deacons can arrange something in the meantime."

***

The plains of Kansas looked like some alien landscape in a movie. There had been a great deal of activity over the last seven days, since the battle had occurred here. The stench was awful from the decaying bodies of what I had heard from the Senator was one hundred and thirty eight thousand bodies. They were scattered all across the plains.

Deacons had also told me that they had found at least fifty different human bodies as well. Some of them were just parts of bodies. I asked if he could have them returned to the battlefield. The Guard handles its own dead.

He said he would try and he had succeeded. After he had met with the President and given him the whole story.

So we stood looking at a large area, marked off so that no one would be inside the perimeter when the fires began. I had told Deacons that the scientists could have some of the Demon bodies. We would have to study them in more detail.

The Archmage stood before four hundred Mages and close to a thousand Guards. There were cameras watching and this had been discussed for some time.

"Today we mourn the loss of many of our friends," her voice carried across the whole crowd, "Our family, our teachers, our comrades."

There was no nervousness showing through, even though I could see it in her aura, "Not one of them tried to avoid the duty they were called for. They all came to this place to protect Humanity. That is our mandate, to protect Humanity from the creatures that lie in this field of battle. We will not hesitate to face our enemies, just as these noble Souls did not hesitate. If not for them and those who survived, this victory would not have been possible."

She turned toward the battlefield and drew two swords from the harnesses she had strapped to her back, "We salute you!"

The swords lit with Soulfire as every Mage and every Guard drew twin blades to join her. We all held them over our heads, crossed and glowing brightly. As we pulled the crossed swords apart, the sound sent a chill down my spine. Every Mage Pulled and a massive bolt of fire shot into the sky.

Paige turned back to us, "Warmaster, please send our friends on their journey."

I had spent several hours in the Dome figuring out how I was going to do this and I had found that, if I don't do the actual Pull through someone else's stream, I can handle the power without having to do crazy crap like tying straight to the Source. My Soulstream is strong enough for what I would need.

I stepped forward and stood beside Paige, facing the battlefield.

"Pull!"

Fifty Mages Pulled and sent the power up into the sky. I raised my arms and reached out with my mind. I began spinning all of that power in a huge Maelstrom high in the sky above the field. My Soulstream surged with power as my body soaked it up.

There really wasn't as much power circling around in the sky as it looked like. We had decided to make the whole thing as visual as we could and there really isn't a great deal of power needed to set the dead afire. When the Demons are living, it takes a great deal more.

"May the road to Paradise be paved with the Souls of your fallen enemies," My voice boomed across the plain.

"Prepare a place for us there, my friends," My voice cracked a bit, "We will join you soon enough, but not today."

With that I brought my arms down and the whole maelstrom of power slammed down onto the plain and a wave of flame surged across the battle-field. The wave stopped at the marked boundary and Smoke poured into the sky as all of the bodies burned.

"Farewell, my friends," I said softly and Paige put her hand on my shoulder and squeezed gently.

Epilogue

Kevin Graves sat on his bed, his mind focused. He felt the flows of Power around him. He could almost feel the flows as they knotted around his Soulstream. He couldn't believe his own father had blocked him from the Source. He was a bastard but he was still his father. Even worse the group of Mages hadn't stopped there. They formed a shield around him and tied it to the Source. His own father had left him here to die slowly without food or water and his Soulstream barely large enough to live at all. The Soullord had better live through this or he was screwed.

He let his mind wander along the flows of power that he could feel around him.